VOYAGE TO THE CITY OF THE DEAD

Above the town the Aurang split into a series of gentle cataracts where dim figures worked with long fishing sweeps. Terraces heavy with fruit bushes stepped toward heaven.

Neat narrow streets ran down to the Aurang and continued on the far shore, and water wheels turned steadily in the swift current. The buildings had flowerlike domes and elegant arches; graceful, winding walls connected the main structures; small towers bloomed amid the larger structures.

Bells and wind chimes were everywhere, dangled from windows and rafters and projecting beams. The tinkling and clanging and bonging were audible even above the rush of the Aurang.

"Isn't it magnificent?" Lyra was enraptured. Behind her the alien .... an impolite noise.

About the Author

Born in New York City in 1946, Alan Dean
Foster was raised in Los Angeles, California.
After receiving a bachelor's degree in
political science and a Master of Fine Arts in
motion pictures from UCLA in 1968–69, he
worked for two years as a public relations
copywriter in a small Studio City, California,
firm.

His writing career began in 1968 when
August Derleth bought a long letter of
Foster's and published it as a short story in
his biannual *Arkham Collector Magazine.*
Sales of short fiction to other magazines
followed. His first try at a novel, *The
Tar-Aiym Krang*, was published by Ballantine
Books in 1972.

Foster has toured extensively through Asia
and the isles of the Pacific. Besides travelling,
he enjoys classical and rock music, old films,
basketball, body surfing, and karate. He has
taught screenwriting, literature, and film
history at UCLA and Los Angeles City College.

Currently, he resides in Arizona with his
wife JoAnn (who is reputed to have the only
extant recipe for Barbarian Cream Pie).

Voyage to the
City of the Dead

Alan Dean Foster

NEW ENGLISH LIBRARY
Hodder and Stoughton

Copyright © 1984 by Alan Dean Foster

First published in the USA in 1984 by
Ballantine Books

This edition published by arrangement
with Ballantine Books, a Division of
Random House, Inc.

First NEL Paperback Edition 1986
Third impression 1987

British Library C.I.P.

Foster, Alan Dean
   Voyage to the city of the dead.
   I. Title
   813'.54[F]   PS3556.0756

ISBN 0 450 39874 9

Printed and bound in Great Britain
for Hodder and Stoughton
Paperbacks, a division of Hodder and
Stoughton Ltd., Mill Road,
Dunton Green, Sevenoaks, Kent
TN13 2YA.
(Editorial Office: 47 Bedford Square,
London WC1B 3DP) by
Cox & Wyman Ltd., Reading

For Daniel, with love,
for when he gets older and starts traveling. . . .

TSLAMAINA (HORSEYE) WESTERN HEMISPHERE

NORTH POLE (TRUE)

LIMIT OF POLAR GLACIATION

GUNTALI PLATEAU
(Average 3000 M. Altitude)

GUNTALI PLATEAU

KAHAENG RIVER

TARANAKI R.

JAKAIE
STOPAPASIRUT

MADAUK RIVER

AJJANG RIVER

CHOTIEK RIVER

HOCHAC

KIRRIT

SKSHALDING

BARSHAJAGAD CANYON

VALIATI RIVER

TULA

CHENBA

LOSAKU STEAMER STATION

KO PAIS?

SUMQM

GROALAMASAN OCEAN

N
W — E
S
SOUTH POLE ⊗

OVERHEAD VIEW OF
BARSHAJAGAD CANYON
AT THE
TOPAPASIRUT

KHADING R.

FEAR RIVER

TOPAPASIRUT

SCALE
0 500 1000 2000 4000

EQUATOR —— · ——

UPPER LIMIT OF IMPACT CRATER · · · · · ·

GUNTALI PLATEAU ☐ CANYON or RIVER VALLEY

TEMPERATURE ──────────── METERS

20° (GUNTALI PLATEAU) ── 8000

40° ── 6900

AURANG
RIVER
VALLEY

60° ── 5000

TURPUT

80° ── 3300

SKAR RIVER

100° ── 1800

120° ── SEA LEVEL

Cross-section of Barshajagad Canyon at latitude of Turput
city, approximately 3000 km. upcanyon
from delta port of Losithi.

PROMPAJ MASSIF (14,200m) ──────── METERS

13800

MT. ARACUNGA (11,000m)

11800

9800

JAKAIE

8000

6800

JAKAIE
VALLEY

5000

SKAR RIVER ──────── SEA LEVEL

Cross-section of Barshajagad Canyon at Topapasirut.

[I]

They didn't call in the Guard because the intruder was already half dead. Still, they were upset.

Muttering angrily among themselves over the outrageous breach of protocol, the members of the Zanur looked to their leader for direction, but Najoke de-me-Halmur held his peace. It was up to the intruder to explain himself, and fast. Hands still hovered close to sheathed knives, although it was becoming apparent this was no assassination attempt—the intruder was too enfeebled to present a threat to anyone but himself. So Najoke stayed his hand as well as his lips. Seeing this, the other members of the Zanur calmed themselves.

Two unkempt servants attended the intruder, and they had their hands full keeping him on his feet. He was completely bald, as befitted his age, but more than age had been at work on that body recently. Pain was evident even in the movement of the eyes, and their owner was breathing as if he'd run a long ways, for all that two younger Mai supported him.

Several of the more impatient members of the Zanur started toward the stranger. De-me-Halmur stayed them with a wave of one slim, six-fingered hand. "Patience, my friends. Let us hear what this despoiler of etiquette has to say. Retribution can come later. We are no judges here."

The leader's words sparked the withered visitor's attention. He shrugged off the helping hands of his servants, much as he continued to push away the clutching hand of death. Though unsteady and shaking, he stood straight and by himself. "Good members of the Zanur, I beg forgiveness for this intrusion on the affairs of state. When one has little time left, one has no time at all for protocol. I have much to tell you."

De-Yarawut rose and pointed, hairless brows drawing together. "I know you. You reside in my district."

The elderly speaker tried to bow to the side, as etiquette required, and the effort nearly sent him sprawling. His servants rushed to help but he gestured them back.

"I am flattered by your remembrance, Zanural de-Yarawut. I am Bril de-Panltatol. A humble trader who works Upriver." The drama of the oldster's intrusion, his unforgivable breach of tradition, was beginning to fade. And he was known. No surprises were here.

Legends sing of the wrongness of such thoughts.

"No excuse can be made for your interruption, de-Panltatol," de-me-Halmur said. "You know the penalties."

"Your most excessive indulgence, Moyt, but as I said and as you can see, little time is left to me."

De-me-Halmur had not become ruler of a great city-state without the occasional ostentatious display of compassion. "You must have bribed efficiently to obtain this entrance, oldster. You are to be admired for that. Say what you have come to say."

"Good members of the Zanur, I have for most of my life been a trader of fine woods and metals between our great city of Po Rabi and the Upriver. Hai, even as far as Kekkalong." Kekkalong was a very long way Upriver, and many of the Zanurals had never journeyed beyond the boundaries of the city. They listened to the rover with a little more respect.

"I am a good citizen and work hard for my city. So I listen well to any tale or rumor that suggests the opportunity to increase my wealth."

[2]

"As do we all," Zanural de-Parinti commented. "Get on with it."

"Among the many tales of the Upriver are those which speak of a dead place, home to spirits and ghosts and demons beyond counting, who guard such wealth as could not be counted in a thousand lifetimes by all the accountants of all the city-states that ring the Groalamasan itself."

"A wonderful story, I'm sure," another Zanural called from his council seat. "I too have heard such stories."

"It is well known," de-Panltatol continued, "that the nearer one travels to the source of such tales, the more vivid and impressive they become—or else they fade away entirely.

"This particular tale is told over and over again in a hundred towns and villages of the North. I have listened to it for more than fifty years. I resolved finally to pursue it to the last storyteller. Instead it drew me onward, pulling me ever farther north. Sometimes the tale smelled of truth, more often of village embroidery, but never did I lose track of it entirely.

"I went beyond maps and merchant trails, always up the Barshajagad, following the current of the Skar and in places abandoning it completely. I walked—I, Bril de-Panltatol— upon the surface of the frozen Guntali itself!"

Now the whispers of interest were submerged by ill-concealed laughter. The Guntali Plateau, from which arose all the great rivers of the world that drained into the single ocean that was the Groalamasan, was so high and cold and thin of air that no Mai could travel upon it. Yet the wrinkled old trader was laying claim to such a feat.

Like his fellow merchants and Zanural, de-me-Halmur refused to countenance the possibility, but neither did he laugh. He had not become Moyt of Po Rabi by dismissing the most elaborate absurdities without careful dissection. "Let this one continue proving himself the fool, but let him not be convicted until he has finished his story."

"Up past even far Hochac I went," de-Panltatol was breathing harder now, "and my journey was but beginning. I lost servants and companions until I was obliged to travel on my own, because none would go farther in my company. All believed me mad, you see. I nearly perished many times. The rumors and the river led me ever onward."

"Onward to what?" another of the Zanural snorted derisively.

The oldster glanced sideways and seemed to draw strength from his scoffers. "To the source of all the tales and songs. To the land of the dead. To the part of the world where demons and monsters make their home. To the top of the world, good Zanural."

This time the laughter could not be contained. It did not appear to discourage the old trader.

"I found the City of the Dead. I, Bril de-Panltatol! And I came away with a piece of it." He frowned then, and wheezed painfully. "I don't remember that time very well. My mind was numbed by all I had endured. How I stayed alive I don't know, but I drove myself to make another boat. I made many boats, I think. It's hard to remember. I disguised what I had brought away beneath a bale of Salp skins and brought it all the way Downriver, all the way back to my home, to Po Rabi."

De-me-Halmur's wide black eyes flickered. "A most interesting and entertaining story, de-Panltatol, but all such tales of demon cities are entertaining. I hope you are a better trader than you are a storyteller." Polite laughter rose from the other members of the Zanur.

"Is that what you broke into our conference to tell us?" snapped another Zanural angrily. "If you can do no better than that, I promise you your age will not save you."

"There is only one thing I can add to what I have told you," the exhausted trader admitted. "For it I have ruined my mind and my self, so there is little for you to threaten me with. My triumph will be short-lived and I will not buy the seat on the Zanur that I longed for." A few insulted murmurs arose among the Zanural, loudest from those whose fortunes were smallest.

"So I will leave my tale to you, together with that one other thing, and let you judge, Zanural of the city, if I might have been thought equal in wealth to sit among you." He turned and blew on a small bone whistle that hung from a cord around his neck.

A dozen laborers entered in two columns of six. Between them they held ropes attached to a low dolly. Laughter gave way to curiosity and confusion among the members of the

[4]

Zanur. The dolly had six axles and fat rubbery wheels made from the treated sap of the arer tree.

From his place at the head of the long council table de-me-Halmur saw the pile of fine gray Salp pelts piled high on the dolly. They were valuable but not exceptionally so. Certainly they weren't heavy enough to require the use of a six-axle and twelve strong Mai to pull the load. He could see the way muscles strained against something massive but concealed. He stood slightly, unconscious of the movement, to have a better view.

The laborers halted and moved aside. With the aid of his servants Panltatol staggered to the dolly. Disdaining help, he reached out and shakily pulled the skins onto the floor. They'd been sewn together and came off as one.

There *was* something else on the dolly, as de-me-Halmur suspected, but the sight of it struck him speechless—a single metal bar reposed on the wooden platform. It was twisted and bent by some unknown force and was as thick as a large Mai's body. But that observation passed quickly. The Zan-ural were interested in its composition far more than its shape.

It had not been polished and it displayed long gashes and much pitting, evidence of exposure to powerful chemicals or energies. Its color was familiar.

"I did not actually enter the place of the dead." Panltatol's voice was weakening. "I was near, very near, when weather so terrible it cannot be imagined except in dreams finally forced me to retreat. This relic I found on the banks of the Skar, where the river had carried it. This alone I was able to bring back with me. Zanural of Po Rabi, this is my legacy."

Forgetting their dignity, abjuring protocol, they left their seats to examine the massive metal bar. Sensitive six-fingered hands caressed the smooth gray substance. The dull silvery sheen was a property of the metal itself.

It *looked* like sunit. It had the color of sunit. It felt like sunit. When three of the Zanural from northern Po Rabi tried to lift it and could not, they were positive it was sunit.

De-Changrit, who on the Zanur was second in power only to de-me-Halmur himself, removed a small ingot from the money belt that circled his waist. It was a *serl*, the largest denomination coined by any of the great city-states that lined the shores of the Groalamasan Ocean, newly minted in powerful Chienba. He placed it in one of the gouges cut in the flank of the bar and tried to calculate the worth of the twisted mass in his head. He was a superb businessmai and his estimate was very near the mark.

"Several million," he announced aloud. "At least." Having already made their own calculations, several of his associates nodded by way of confirmation.

De-Panltatol abruptly sat down on the edge of the dolly, leaning back against the bar for support. He ran one hand gently across the cold metal, lovingly, as if it were a woman reclining in his hammock. There was not a Mai among the Zanur who did not feel the same love for that bar. It represented a great and compact fortune.

When the murmurs and excited conversations began to die down it was Changrit who asked the question uppermost in all minds. "Is there more?"

His tone was respectful now, no longer sarcastic or accusing. Thus vindicated, Panltatol seemed to draw strength from some unknown source. They were no longer laughing at him.

"Honored sirs, I do not know. I found only this one piece, washed up on a rocky and wild shore. But the rumors that drove me to the top of the world always spoke of more in the City of the Dead."

Many signs were made by the Zanural, for they were as intensely superstitious as the common folk. Daily their lives were punctuated by the performance of rituals designed to ward off unfriendly deities and spirits, which all Mai knew ruled the affairs of each individual from birth to death. At the rear of the chamber a wide-eyed servant hastily dumped more incense in the ritual burner, in case the spirits in attendance that day were possessed of particularly large noses. The air of the chamber was immediately suffused with sweet fragrance.

"No actual City of the Dead exists," one of the Zanural ventured hesitantly. "It is not a real place."

De-me-Halmur used his hands eloquently. "No such solid piece of sunit as this exists, yet it sits there before us."

"More," Panltatol mumbled. "More in the City of the Dead."

"How much more?" asked Changrit with becoming avariciousness.

"They say . . . the rumors say . . . that the city itself is built of sunit." Dead silence greeted his declaration, appropriately. "I am sorry I did not go farther." A thin smile appeared on his withered face. His right arm lay like brown cloth against the cold metal. "I am so tired, honored ones. I must rest a while."

"Wait!" Changrit rushed forward. With his own arms he supported the oldster, a sign of the esteem in which Panltatol was suddenly held. "How do we find the City of the Dead? How could one retrace your travels?"

"Why, don't you know?" Panltatol whispered. "There is no City of the Dead. The journey cannot be made. But I made it. I, Bril de-Panltatol, went where it is impossible to go. But you can't follow, none of you." He said it with vehemence as he unexpectedly sat up without aid. "You can't follow because only an insane one could make such a journey. I am mad, you see, and you are not." A sudden thought made him blink with confusion.

"Very tired." He leaned back against Changrit again and closed his eyes. They would not open again.

Changrit gently lowered the thin body. "A true Mai. He sacrificed everything in hopes of improving his fortune. I honor him."

"We all honor him," de-me-Halmur said, "as we will honor his memory."

"What of the sunit?" Lust was apparent in the voice of the Zanural who voiced the common thought. All eyes were on the bar.

"You know the law," de-me-Halmur said sternly, if a trifle reluctantly. "I covet it as much as any of you, but it goes to his family and employees." He made a protective sign in case certain spirits were listening. "The law is clear."

Zanural de-Peyetmy was almost in tears. "Couldn't we bend the law just a little?"

"I am sworn to uphold it, and I will do so. Those who would bend the law ultimately find themselves strangled by it." Murmurs of assent sounded from around the table.

"Of course," de-me-Halmur went on, "there is the matter of a death tax." A few smiles appeared. "Also the fact that de-Panltatol undertook this journey without proper authorization, and we still must deal with the matter of his rude intrusion into the Zanur Chamber." He studied the bar. "I would say that perhaps half should go into the city treasury."

"That still leaves a nice fortune." Changrit had retaken his seat on de-me-Halmur's left. "No family could be disappointed to receive such an inheritance. Now that the law has been dealt with, how are we to deal with this remarkable story?"

"A great journey," one of the other Zanural announced portentously. "One to be enshrined in memory and song. I myself will commission a song cycle to commemorate it."

"A thoughtful gesture," de-me-Halmur agreed, thankful for the Zanural's support. His proposal meant that de-me-Halmur would not have to pay for the requisite memorial. Other Zanural cursed themselves for not thinking to make the clever political move.

"Now who shall volunteer to help equip a new expedition to journey to the top of the world in search of this rumored City of the Dead?"

Suddenly every member of the council sought to shrink in his seat. One, bolder than the rest, said sharply, "I would not venture more than a thousand legats Upriver for all the sunit on Tslamaina."

"Nor would I," de-me-Halmur agreed. "De-Panltatol was quite right. None of us is mad. The very idea of setting foot on the Guntali Plateau is a concept only a disturbed mind could conceive. To attempt to retrace his wild path would be impossible." He gestured toward the bar and the body lying next to it. "We must be satisfied with this."

"Not necessarily." All eyes turned in surprise to Changrit. De-me-Halmur waited warily for any suggestion his rival might make. Each had much respect for the other, so much so that they never employed assassins. Such methods they left to cruder Mai while they dueled with words and gestures.

"It is true that any journey far up the Skar is daunting, let alone one to the top of the world. One might undertake such an expedition only to perish within sight of one's goal. It is more likely any travelers would end up staring at the inside of a Na's belly instead of the City of the Dead." Zanurals executed signs indicating anxiety.

"Or else they would find themselves deceived by the Tsla. We do not have the means for accomplishing such a journey, but there are those who do."

"I don't see them here," another Zanural called. Laughter punctuated his observation.

Changrit gave him a withering look until the laughter had subsided. "A good merchant knows his responsibility to the Zanur, to his city-state. He knows also his own limitations. I am quite aware of mine as you must be of yours.

"But there is something new come recently to Tslamaina. I speak of the visitors from the sky."

Uncertain mutterings were silenced by de-me-Halmur. "I've heard much of them. What is it you propose, Changrit?"

"I can propose nothing unless recent information I have received from my agents can be confirmed. Call for the ambassador to Losithi."

There followed a long delay, made palatable by a regal midday meal, while Ror de-Kelwhoang, ambassador to Losithi, was summoned from his offices in the Ministry. He arrived in due course, breathless and puzzled.

"For what reason have I been summoned in such haste, honored Zanural?"

There was much respect among the members for the skills of the elderly Kelwhoang, just as there was in the Zanur of Losithi. Po Rabi's main rival in trade and commerce, it lay several hundred legats to the southwest and controlled the western end of the Skatandah Delta, the great marshland formed by the emptying of the Skar River into the Groalamasan.

Midway between the two city-states but slightly nearer Losithi lay the station established by the strange visitors from the sky. Their science was much advanced and gain was to be made there for those who knew how to ferret it out. The visitors were carefully courted by diplomats from Losithi as well as Po Rabi.

"Tell the Zanur," Changrit instructed the ambassador, "what you told me several weeks ago concerning the visitors from the sky. The *new* visitors."

"New visitors?" De-me-Halmur frowned, as did several

[9]

other Zanural. "You mean that more of the large bug-creatures have arrived on Tslamaina?"

Kelwhoang looked toward his sponsor Changrit uncertainly, but received a gesture of openness by way of reply.

"All are friends here today, Kelwhoang. Speak freely."

The ambassador nodded. "There came upon us a day rainy and cold, which forced me to—"

De-me-Halmur interrupted him. "Our time is valuable, Kelwhoang. Spare us the poetry."

"Forgive me, Moyt. I was taken aback by this sight." He indicated the monstrous bar of sunit.

"Understandable. Your attention to potential profit marks you well in our sight. Still, make your tale concise."

Kelwhoang gestured in agreement. "Members of the Zanur. As you know, I make it my business during the long journey between our city and Losithi to take note of all of interest that transpires within the Delta. The visitors from the sky keep to their building-that-walks-the-water, but I have cultivated my acquaintance with them.

"Thus did I learn that five weeks ago allies from the sky arrived among them. I was astonished to learn that these newcomers look not like those who built the sky-station, but much like us." That bit of news prompted gasps of astonishment from the Zanurals.

"You mean," Guptinak asked, "that they are not as horrible to look upon as the large bug-things?"

"No," said Kelwhoang, gratified by the reaction his revelation had produced. "They are much like Mai, only taller, taller even than a Tsla but not so large as a Na. They have more body hair and their features are sharper and more pronounced, rougher and not as beautiful. They suffer from our climate much as does a Tsla, unlike their bug-thing friends who are quite comfortable in the Delta. One male and one female, similar enough to us that at a distance one could almost think them Mai.

"I did not meet them myself, only saw them conversing with the Moyt of the station, the one called," and he struggled with the difficult alien name, "Porlezmozmith. Later I was able to talk with her and she remarked on the similarity between us and the new visitors. Truly the resemblance is striking between us. These newcomers' faces have smaller eyes, larger ears that are great curved winged things visible even at a distance. Oh yes, they have but five digits on their hands and feet instead of the normal six, even as the bug-things have but four, though they have that extra pair of arms and legs. It may be that these new visitors are more akin to us than the Tsla or the Na, with whom we share our world."

"All fascinating," de-me-Halmur said, "but how does this profit us?"

"Tell them what the bug-thing told you his new guests have planned," Changrit prompted.

"Ah. I was told they brought with them a wondrous magical boat which walks upon the water more freely than the station the visitors first built. It does not depend on wind or muscle for power but carries its own energy inside it. I was told that it can travel at great speed *Up*river, against the current of the Skar."

More mutters of astonishment rose from the assembled members. "We've heard much of the wonders brought by the visitors from the sky," de-me-Halmur said. "I sense your thought, Changrit, but surely they would not sell us this amazing craft?"

"Never," the ambassador admitted. "I have been told many times by the Moyt Porlezmozmith that they can have only the briefest of contacts with us and that they are forbidden by their own laws to sell us any of the advanced tools and instruments they have brought with them."

"No profit in that," one of the Zanural grumbled. "Truly these visitors are alien."

"These newcomers who are like us," the ambassador continued, "are scholars, not merchants. They intend to make a study of the Barshajagad, the canyon which cradles our river Skar."

"Now that makes sense," de-me-Halmur commented. "There is always profit in good scholarship." He made a sign to invoke the spirit of knowledge and insight, but finally had to ask, "What is in your mind, Changrit?"

"These visitors from the sky still know little of our world. Beyond the Delta they are ignorant, for all their knowledge. They know nothing of the ways of the Skar, or of the Hotiek or the Aurang or any of the lesser tributaries. They know nothing of the peoples who inhabit the canyon. They will need guides."

"Ah!" De-me-Halmur's expression was fed by enlightenment. "Friendly locals to show them the way."

"Yes, to show them the way."

"And good friends that we are, it behooves us as the rulers of Po Rabi to find volunteers to assist them?"

"Every chance we can find," Changrit agreed firmly.

"How do we know that these strange creatures have any interest in traveling up the Skar farther than the town of Ibe?" a Zanural wondered aloud.

"We do not," Changrit admitted. "How does one divine the intentions of aliens? Yet if they are as similar in appearance to us as Ambassador de-Kelwhoang says, who is to say that their motivations are different?" He looked away from the table. "You've no idea how far they intend to go Upriver, Kelwhoang?"

"No. The bug-Moyt was not too clear. He did say a long journey. Certainly farther than Ibe."

"Then our course is clear, Zanural." De-me-Halmur leaned forward the better to emphasize his words and gestures. "We must do our utmost to ensure that these visitors make use of our good intentions and accept the aid that the people of Po Rabi will freely extend to them."

"Assuming they accept," said another member. "What if they do not travel to the region of our hopes? What if they reach Kekkalong and decide they have journeyed far enough?"

"Then perhaps," Changrit murmured quietly, "they might at that time be persuaded to loan us the use of their wondrous craft. I'm certain that the loquacious Ror de-Kelwhoang will employ all his admirable verbal talents to ensure that the immediate requirements of the Zanur are met."

"I shall do my best, of course." The ambassador performed an elaborate gesture designed to invoke the spirits of all the great diplomats of the past. He glanced sideways at the huge, gleaming mass of solid sunit.

"However, if I am to do my best, honored ones, it would help if you could explain to me the reasons behind my mission. Would I be remiss in assuming it has something to do with the astonishing wealth that lies next to a dead Mai in the center of this chamber?"

"You would not," de-me-Halmur said. "Seat yourself."

Gesturing his thanks at the honor, de-Kelwhoang joined the table as Changrit related the events of the morning.

The subsequent discussion and laying out of plans lasted well into the evening. The heat of day was followed by the heat of night and still the Zanur sat in extended session. Bureaucrats and guards gossiped and wondered, but still the rulers of Po Rabi remained sequestered in their chamber.

It was only when they finally adjourned in the early hours of the morning that someone thoughtfully directed attendants to remove the stiffened corpse of that soon to be memorialized merchant–explorer Bril de-Panltatol. Great care had already been taken to ensure that a proper share of his legacy was safely transported to the city treasury.

Greater care and craft might make possible the seemingly impossible task of securing for the Zanur of Po Rabi the rest of his legacy.

[II]

Etienne Redowl was sick of measuring current flow. He was sick of taking samples from the river bottom. Recording the ebb and flow of sandbars and mudbanks no longer interested him, nor did watching the analyzer spit out graphs listing gravel composition mineral by mineral.

But there was nothing else for him to do at Steamer Station.

It seemed as if they'd been waiting for permission from the native authorities to begin their Upriver expedition since the beginning of time. Anyone who thought the bureaucracy of Commonwealth Science and Exploration difficult to penetrate should have to cope once in his life with the byzantine machinations of the Mai of Tslamaina. The station's location between the rival city-states of Po Rabi and Losithi only made it tougher to obtain the necessary clearances.

There was no pushing the matter, however. Where a Class Four-B world was involved, Commonwealth policy was strict. Porlezmozmith, the officer in charge of Steamer Station, was sympathetic to the Redowls' plight, but not to the point of challenging regulations. So the husband-wife team sat and sweated and waited.

Etienne paused on the ladder long enough to adjust the thermo-sense on his fishnet shirt and shorts. Minuscule cooling units woven into the material struggled to cool his skin. He checked his wrist telltale. A fairly mild afternoon, with the temperatures hovering around a hundred and twenty degrees and the humidity a mere ninety percent. He longed for the coolness of their quarters on the station platform above.

The thranx found the temperature a mite hot, but the humidity suited them just fine. That was why they'd been chosen to staff the only Commonwealth outpost. For them it was almost like home. For humans it was pure misery.

Survey should have named it misery, Etienne thought. Instead it had been named for its geology. That geology and the unique civilization it had produced were the reasons why Etienne and his wife Lyra had braved endless application forms and sweltering weather in order to be the first humanx scientists allowed to work beyond the boundaries of the outpost. Or such would be the case if the native authorities ever gave them the okay to travel Upriver. Until that happened they were stuck at the station. Months of waiting for permission to arrive, endless days spent battling the terrible heat and humidity had sapped his initial enthusiasm. Lyra was bearing up better beneath the day-to-day disappointment, but even she was starting to wilt.

He forced himself to see Tslamaina as it looked from high orbit. The refreshing, cooler image reminded him again why they'd come to the world its discoverers had named Horseye. Lyra had no room for flippancy in science and preferred Tslamaina, the native name, but the image certainly fitted.

Eons ago the planet had collided with a meteor of truly impressive dimensions. In addition to creating the vast circular basin that was now filled by the Groalamasan Ocean, the concussion had badly cracked the planet's surface. That surface, high above the single world-ocean, comprised the Guntali Plateau.

Water running off the Guntali for hundreds of millions of years patiently enlarged those surface cracks, eventually resulting in the most spectacular river canyons ever encountered. The combination of geological and climatological factors necessary to produce such awesome scenery had not been duplicated on any other of the explored worlds.

Of all the river canyons by far the greatest was the Barshajagad, which in the Mai language meant "Tongue-of-the-World." More than two thousand kilometers wide at the point where it finally emptied into the ocean, it reached northward from its delta some thirteen thousand kilometers to vanish in the cloud-shrouded north polar wastes. From the edge of the Guntali, a few hundred kilometers Upriver, to the surface of the slowly moving river Skar, the Barshajagad dropped approximately eight thousand meters in elevation. Where mountains rose from the plateau, the disparity was even greater.

So wide was the Barshajagad at its mouth, however, that a traveler on the surface of the river could not see where the gradually ascending slopes finally reached the plateau to east and west.

The result was an astonishing variety of life forms organized into ecological regions not by latitude but by elevation, as nature made use of the different temperature and moisture zones that climbed the canyon walls.

Three different intelligent mammalian races had appeared on Tslamaina, each confined to its own portion of the river canyons. The intensively competitive and primitively capitalistic Mai ruled the ocean and the river valleys. Above them in the more temperate zone between three thousand and fifty-five hundred meters were the Tsla. Clinging to the frozen rims of the canyons and freely roaming the Guntali were the carnivorous Na. Or so the locals claimed. None of them had ever seen a Na, and since Mai society was infused with a healthy respect for and belief in thousands of spirits, demons, and ghosts, Lyra Redowl, circumspect xenologist that she was, was reluctant to give instant recognition to the existence of this legendary third intelligent race.

Temperature and pressure and not national or tribal boundaries kept the races of Tslamaina separated. That made for a sociocultural situation every bit as unique as the local geology, as Lyra was fond of pointing out to her husband.

Their hope, the dream that had brought them across many

light-years, was to take a hydrofoil all the way up the Skar to its source, making a thorough study of the geology and the people of the planet as they advanced. But Tslamaina was a Class Four-B world. That meant they could only proceed with the natives' permission, and that permission still was not forthcoming, despite repeated anxious requests.

So Etienne had been confined to examination of the delta soils and the geology around the station which was, in a word, flat. Lyra was better off, able to visit with those fisherfolk who sometimes stopped at the station to chat and to attempt to steal anything not bolted down. Station personnel never ventured reprisals for the attempts. For one thing the attempts were always unsuccessful. For another, it was part of the local culture.

Six months had passed since the shuttle had deposited the Redowls at Steamer Station and Etienne was close to calling off the expedition. Only the knowledge that they would be the first to make an Upriver journey kept him from booking passage out on the next supply run.

It would help if Lyra would learn to keep her frustration to herself, but no, not her. She'd declaim long and loud to anyone within earshot. The thranx were too polite to tell her to shut up, and Etienne had tried many times and failed. After the first month he simply gave up and tuned her out. It wasn't hard. He had been doing it for twenty years. Eight or nine years ago the conflict might have ended in divorce, but now they had too much invested in each other. Convenience and familiarity balanced out a lot of bickering, though sometimes he wondered.

Something was itching sharply on the back of his neck. Holding onto the ladder with his right hand he reached up and back with his left, coming away with something soft and flexible. He eyed it with intense distaste.

It was as long as his hand and thick as his thumb, completely transparent except for the dark maroon color spreading slowly backward from the head. As he held it firmly it wiggled and twisted in search of the blood so recently discovered and quickly vanished.

The *dangui* was an elegant local bloodsucker related to the annelid worms but possessed of a cartilaginous backbone which when flexed allowed it to jump at its intended host.

[17]

It turned red as it filled up with blood. It looked like a glass leech and seemed to find human plasma perfectly palatable, much to Etienne's enduring disgust.

Forcing down the gorge rising in his throat he flung it as far away as he could, heard the faint *plop* when it hit the murky green water. He felt the back of his neck and his hand came away bloody. First stop inside the station would be for antibiotic spray.

The metal stilts on which Steamer Station rested carried a mild electric charge to discourage infestation by such local pests though they rarely troubled the thranx because of their tough exoskeletons. Etienne dealt in smooth, hard surfaces and clean stone and didn't care much for biology, particularly when it chose to get personal.

High thin clouds blocked out some of the ultraviolet, but Etienne was still grateful for his naturally dark coloring, a legacy of ancient Amerindians. A lighter-skinned human would quickly fry under Tslamaina's relentless sun. Though he'd been outside less than ten minutes, the sweat was pouring off him. The cooling meshwork shirt and shorts were all that kept him halfway comfortable.

Even the climate might be bearable if only they'd receive permission from the native authorities. The frustration of waiting was worse than any heat, he mused as he made his careful way up the ladder.

Behind him tall fat pseudopalms thrust enormous green fronds over the lazy water. Table tree roots exploded sideways from their trunks before dipping down into the mud. Nappers, tiny crustaceans with multihued shells, filled the air with their doglike barking.

Little relief beyond the shade it offered was available inside the station since the internal temperature was set to accommodate thranx and not humans. A hundred was certainly cooler than one-twenty, but the humidity was unchanged. Only when he entered the rooms reserved for less tolerant visitors did the humidity begin to drop. By the time he reached their quarters, station machinery had lowered the temperature forty-five degrees and sucked out more than half the humidity.

Lyra Redowl barely glanced up at him. She sprawled in a chair studying her clipboard viewer.

"Anything interesting?"

"Glass leech bit me."

"Bad?"

"I doubt it." He moved to a cabinet and removed a tiny spray can, dosed the back of his neck. "The Skar flows into the Groalamasan, the Groalamasan goes round and round and it comes out here." He gestured toward the lavatory.

She put her viewer aside, spoke coolly. "I don't blame you for being upset, Etienne. I'm as pissed off as you are. But thére's nothing we can do except wait. Make an effort not to take it out on me, okay?"

"I'm not taking anything out on you," he said exasperatedly. "Why do you take everything I say so personally? Can I help it if this damn delay's got me running around like a monkey chewing his tail?"

"You have to work on your self-control. You'll end up with an ulcer."

"I keep control of myself!" He struggled to match his tone to his assertion. "I haven't got time to argue with you, Lyra."

"I agree." Her eyes moved back to the viewer.

He sighed, counted quietly to eight, then plopped down in one of the thin chairs. "What are you buried in now?"

"Varofski on multiple societal interactions."

"Haven't you read that already?"

"Twice. This is my third time around. What do you suggest I do? Squat here and watch thranx shadowplays on the tridee?"

"It would be a change, but I don't want to argue about it."

"You never do. That's why I'm always amazed how regularly you end up doing so." Suddenly she looked up at him and smiled. It was a little forced, but welcome nonetheless.

"Listen to us, fighting like a couple of idiot children. Etienne, I'm just as frustrated as you are. What the hell is keeping those Moyts from giving us travel clearance?"

"Who knows." Rising from the chair, Etienne crossed to the kitchen area and thumbed the switch on the left side of the refrigeration unit. It dispensed fruit juice, heavily salted and sugared. The cooking facilities were nearby but rarely utilized. The Redowls preferred to take most of their meals cold; Tslamaina didn't encourage consumption of piping hot food.

Glass in hand he walked over to stand behind his wife's chair, rested a hand on her shoulder as he sipped at the icy liquid.

"Truce, Lyra?"

She reached up to pat his hand. "Truce. Can't we do something, Etienne?"

"Not a damn thing. You know the law. We're wholly dependent on the whims of the locals." She nodded, returned to her reading.

He never tired of looking at her. After twenty years he still found her physically alluring. Lately she looked even better than usual, having lost weight since their arrival. Tslamaina would sweat you down to skeleton size if you weren't careful.

"I don't understand the delay," she said. "I've talked to the local fisherfolk and traders and they just give me the local variations of a bemused shrug. From everything I've been able to learn both these city-states are hotbeds of new ideas and rapid development. You'd think one or the other would be eager to grant us permission to travel Upriver."

"I'm sure they would," Etienne agreed, "if we could promise them something solid in return. Unfortunately, the regulations protecting Class Four-B worlds prohibit any commerce with natives. No introduction of advanced technology allowed from external sources, and that's what they want to buy from us. The usual nasty cycle. The Moyts would like to grant us clearance for Upriver travel but they want payment in return. We can't pay them what they want because regulations forbid it. So here we sit, and sweat."

"Too true. How's your neck?"

He felt at the shallow bite. "Filthy little monsters. I don't mind dealing with something big and toothy, but I hate parasites."

"Let me give you another shot of antibio." She put down her viewer and reached for the spray. A cool dampness caressed his neck a second time.

"There," she said with satisfaction. "This is no place to pick up an infection, no matter how interesting. We've been lucky so far. Not that we've spent all that much time outside." She hesitated. "Etienne, I'm ready to start chewing the furniture again. We've got to get out of here—Tell you what. Why don't we check out the boat?"

He made a face. "We're going to wear it out before we get started, checking the systems so often."

"No, I mean *really* check it out." There was suppressed excitement in her voice. "Let's take it out for a run on the open sea. It's always cooler on the Groalamasan."

"Porlezmozmith will be miffed. She'll call us down for undue exposure of advanced technology to a presteam society."

"Crap. The local fisherfolk have seen us testing it lots of times."

Etienne grinned down at her. "Woman, you have a devilish sense of humor."

"It helps, when you spend your life trying to make sense of other people's cultures. Come on. It'll be fun. And a change."

Etienne was feeling better by the time they left their quarters. They threw together a cold lunch of native edibles. The consistency of the flat, crackerlike bread was unusual but the taste was delightful.

From their quarters it was a short walk down to Level Three, the lowest of the station, where the hydrofoil hung silent in its bay, a sleek delta-shape built of ultralight metals. A compact electric jet protruded from beneath the stern, looking like the mouthparts of a dragonfly nymph. The hydrofoil was an exquisite bit of engineering and despite its fragile appearance, could take a considerable pounding. Inside, the craft was spacious and efficient.

Ignoring the occasional stare of passing thranx maintenance workers, Etienne operated the bay controls. With a soft whirr the double doors parted, revealing the turgid mix of fresh and salt water that lay twenty meters below.

Bow and stern couplers lowered the hydrofoil toward the water. Lyra was already on board, stowing their lunch and running the autoprogram through diagnostic functions. Disdaining the ladders, Etienne wrapped arms and legs around one of the coupler cables and slid down to the boat. A touch on one switch sent the couplers upward, leaving the boat floating free on the water of the delta.

[21]

A plexalloy dome enclosed the cockpit where Lyra waited in the pilot's chair. The engine came to loud life as the photovoltaic coating of the boat worked to ensure that the fuel cells which supplied power were fully charged. The air conditioning greeted him with a blast of deliciously cold air.

Lyra nudged the accelerator and turned the wheel. They slid from the shade of the station and headed south. Soon they were clear of the last platform trees and high marsh grasses and out on the open ocean.

〚 III 〛

The steady trade breeze caught them, and the humidity on deck dropped quickly to a tolerable eighty percent while the temperature plunged to one-oh-five. Etienne took advantage of the much cooler weather to move out on deck. Occasionally he turned to smile and wave to Lyra, who remained inside the transparent dome handling the instruments.

Intakes mounted on the front of each foil sucked in water and fed it to the electric jet astern. The jet forced the water through twin high-pressure nozzles, sending the boat skimming over the surface at high speed. The hydrofoil had been designed to function as a river runner but could handle open ocean reasonably well as long as the waves didn't crest dangerously high.

Behind them the Skatandah Delta was a long line of green marking the horizon. Lyra sent them flying southwestward, toward the great city-state of Losithi. They were careful to stand well out to sea, clear of the heavy commerce that crowded the waters beyond the harbor.

A thousand kilometers and more to north and south, the

eight-thousand-meter-high cliffs of the Guntali Plateau probed the sky. From the Losithi–Po Rabi area, distance and planetary curvature made them invisible, though there were places where the cliffs dropped sheer to the sea, a sight unequaled on any other inhabited world. Only where rivers like the Skar had cut their way to the ocean were cultivation and urbanization possible.

Lyra's voice sounded through the intercom membrane built into the cockpit dome. "I've got something on the scanner, a few degrees to starboard. Want to run over and check it out?"

"Sure, I want to check it out. What Porlezmozmith doesn't know won't hurt her." He clung to the railing and watched the foils slit the surface of the sea.

Lyra smiled back at him as she angled the boat slightly to starboard. The moving dot on the scanner was soon within sight—a triple-decked trimaran, a big merchant cruiser and a fine example of Mai shipbuilding. Her three hulls rode low in the water, bursting with trade goods gathered from her journey around the circular sea. If she wasn't based in Losithi she would have just arrived from distant Ko Phisi and before that, Suphum. From here she would move on to Po Rabi on the other side of the Skatandah, thence around to Chienba and points east.

She was making good speed with the wind at her back. The trade winds moved eternally clockwise around the circumference of the Groalamasan. Only in the vicinity of the warm southern pole could a native captain test confused winds and sometimes shorten the homeward journey around the great ocean.

Gesturing and chattering, sailors were already lining the upper decks and scrambling into the rigging for a look at the strange alien vessel. More exciting to a Mai seaman than the hydrofoil's silhouette was the fact that it moved at impossible speed and *against* the wind, not to mention without sails. As Lyra raced the hydrofoil around the massive merchantman for a thorough look, Mai sailors and passengers rushed from deck to deck to keep them in view.

After recording the merchantman for their journal, the Redowls passed among a fleet of shallow-hull fishing boats reaping the rich harvest of life that thrived where salt water mixed with fresh.

As they slowed to thread more easily between the first islets and clusters of pseudopalms, one large craft suddenly moved toward them. Its occupants brandished eager expressions together with long gaffs, axes, and pikes. The Mai would gladly have slit the throats of the two humans in order to gain possession of the invaluable hydrofoil. Etienne experienced unscientific thoughts as Lyra nudged the accelerator and left the would-be pirates in their wake.

"Nasty little bastards," he muttered as he stared astern.

"That's not being very understanding of a primitive culture, Etienne," Lyra said disapprovingly.

"All right, so they're primitive nasty little bastards."

"Avaricious, not vicious," she insisted. "You must try to view them in light of their society's laws. A typically primitive plutocratic culture where personal wealth signifies an individual's social standing. You can't let your own viewpoint affect your observations."

"Like hell I can't. Porlezmozmith feels the same way about the Mai."

"She's an administrator, a bureaucrat, a byte-pusher who knows nothing of xenology and cares less."

"All I said was that some of their ingrained habits could stand some modification."

"Environment dictates their actions, not personal choice."

"What environment?" He made a sweeping gesture toward the nearing line of high trees. "This is a warm, lush land. How do you go from that to a highly combative society?"

"They sublimate most of a natural aggressive drive in competition for commerce and trade. Isn't that better than organized war between the city-states?"

"It's healthier, sure, but from the standpoint of what's civilized there's something to be said for slugging it out with your neighbor toe to toe instead of trying to steal him blind."

"Their attempts at thievery are governed by a strict code of rules, Etienne, which is more than you can say for war."

"Leave me to the structure of the planetary crust, not Mai society. It's cleaner."

"You mean simpler, don't you? There are so few variables

in geology. It makes it easy for you, but I don't envy you. There's no personality, no joy in studying the daily activities of a rock."

"Oh no? Let me tell you..."

It went on in that vein for another few minutes before Lyra finally ended it, as she always did. So many of their discussions lately seemed to end that way.

"Well if you're going to act like that then I'm just not going to talk about it anymore." And she turned her gaze resolutely away from him, directing her attention to the scanner.

He fumed silently all the way back to the station.

A services officer was waiting for them in the boat bay. Etienne shinnied up a cable, prepared to send down the couplers. The officer moved to stand next to him.

"Excuse me." Her symbospeech was rough and unpolished, a good sign that Horseye might be her first off-world post. She clung with tru and foothands to a nearby pillar and her four legs were spread wide. Her whole body shied away from the open bay.

That was understandable. Thranx were good floaters but poor swimmers and their breathing spicules were located on the B-thorax below the neck. A standing thranx could drown in shallow water while still being able to see and hear clearly. That was the only reason why Tslamaina was not a popular duty station among the thranx. The climate was perfect but much of the terrain threatening.

So Etienne didn't ask why the officer was clinging to the pillar for dear life, understood why nothing more was said until the hydrofoil had been drawn up into the bay and the double doors closed beneath it.

"What is it?" he finally inquired as Lyra moved to join them. She adjusted her halter top, did not look at him. Her expression was frosty.

"An ambassador from Po Rabi is due to arrive shortly," the officer announced. "Word has come ahead via courier boat. You have been granted permission to travel Upriver through the Delta along those branches of the Skar controlled by the Moyt of Po Rabi."

Etienne let out a whoop and did a back flip, much to the interest of the thranx working in the bay area. Such a gymnastic feat was beyond them. Lyra stood and smiled at the officer. The argument that had accompanied them back to the station was completely forgotten.

"It's about time," she murmured. "Did the courier say anything about the long delay we've suffered, why or for what reason?"

"Nothing additional was mentioned," the officer said, adding a brief gesture of negativity coupled with third-degree empathy.

"I'll bet I know what finally happened," Etienne declared. "Steamer Station's actually situated a little closer to Losithi than it is to Po Rabi. They must have decided that it was time to forget about hard bargaining and grant clearance before we struck some sort of deal with the Losithians."

"I am sorry to dump dirt on your theory," the thranx said apologetically, "but it would appear they still insist on some kind of token payment."

"But we've been through that a hundred times," Lyra pointed out. "They want advanced technology and we're not allowed to give it to them. Don't tell me they've decided to accept our nontech trade goods?"

"No. Commander Porlezmozmith has devised a method of satisfying them without contravening any of the regulations governing commerce with Class Four-B natives.

"Many areas of high ground do not benefit from seasonal floods of the Skar and so do not receive deposits of fresh silt or yield the crops they otherwise might. The commander has reviewed this with representatives of Po Rabi and they understand the implications quite well.

"Salvenkovdew, who is in charge of the station's chemistry section, has agreed to rig equipment to produce high-quality natural fertilizers for such highland fields. Under current regulations this type of fertilizer does not qualify as a high-tech commodity, so it can be traded to the natives, and the Po Rabians have agreed to accept it as payment."

"Good old Porlez!" Etienne exclaimed. "She's been working on our problem all along and never breathed a word of it."

"Probably didn't want to get our hopes up," Lyra said. "I hope the form of payment isn't to be taken as a comment on the value of our expedition."

[27]

"Who cares? We're on our way at last! Thanks," he told the officer. Twin antennae dipped and bobbed by way of gracious reply. "When's this ambassador supposed to get here?"

"The courier could not be certain. Perhaps tomorrow, perhaps several days from tomorrow. I am much gladdened for you both."

"Thanks again. We've been ready to leave for months, though I suppose we can find a few last-minute things to take care of."

"If you will excuse me." The thranx officer released her iron grip on the support pillar and slowly backed clear of the closed bay doors. She looked much happier after she had moved well away from the potential gap.

Deep in conversation, Etienne and Lyra returned to their quarters. Working smoothly they began packing a motile with personal belongings and other last-minute items. They were going to be away from civilization for a long time and there would be no returning for a forgotten chip or bit of clothing.

At least they could consume native foods. That left a lot of room on board for other equipment, extra medical supplies, and tridee cubes.

Stowed in one of the bottom compartments was their cold-weather gear, untouched since its arrival on Tslamaina. They would need the suits when they entered the north polar latitudes. After the relentless heat of the lower Barshajagad, both looked forward to some cheerful freezing.

Two days passed before the ambassador's ship appeared. His retinue was as modest in size and appearance as the vessel which bore them. Ror de-Kelwhoang looked disappointed when he was informed he could not bring any of his escort onto the station, but accepted the determination with diplomatic grace.

In its own modest way the ambassador's official craft was impressive enough. Hired rowers held their double-bladed oars at attention as the ambassador debarked, though they were unable to keep their eyes from wandering toward the strange alien castle that stood high above the water on massive metal legs.

The meeting took place on a deck that encircled the station's lower levels. Etienne and Lyra waited in their briefs and tops. Tslamaina was no place for formal wear.

The ambassador wore little more than the curious humans. His cache du sex was opaque, as was the custom, and his upper garment of silver and copper-colored threads concealed little despite covering him from neck to ankles. It made for a very flashy nonexistent costume. As Lyra had explained, the composition of the material as well as the intricate weave told a knowledgeable onlooker much about the wearer's status, as well as the time of year and what holiday it might be. A good Mai tailor could make much out of little.

Lyra found such details of native life fascinating. Etienne bore her enthusiasm stoically. He was interested in minerals, not millinery.

The Mai ambassador spread his arms wide and turned a slow circle. The movement was fluid but slow, reflective of his advanced age. Porlezmozmith, who had met him before, performed the formal introduction. Her Mai was competent but could not match that of the Redowls; that was due to the thranx larynx, not a lack of linguistic talent.

"Ror de-Kelwhoang, our visitors who would travel your lands, Etienne and Lyra Redowl."

"It is our pleasure to greet you," Lyra added. "We look forward with endless delight to exploring your magnificent country. We are endlessly grateful for the permission to do so granted by your Zanur on behalf of your most powerful and respected city-state."

The ambassador acknowledged the elegant tribute, which Lyra had rehearsed unto boredom, with a slight gesture signifying acceptance. His soft, perceptive eyes seemed fixed on Lyra. That was understandable. She stood eye to eye with the ambassador, which made her tall for a Mai female but not a grotesque scarecrow of a giant like her husband. It was the first time the ambassador had set eyes on the new aliens and he was evidently entranced by the similarities. Etienne had to stifle his amusement at the ambassador's unabashed preoccupation. By Mai standards Lyra's proportions were nothing short of awesome.

"It is with delight that I bring greetings and good wishes from Najoke de-me-Halmur, Moyt of Po Rabi. It has been decided after much careful discussion and agreement on a contract of exchange for certain materials to permit you free passage throughout all the vast territories controlled by our city-state."

"I'm glad everything's worked out," Etienne replied. His Mai was more colloquial than Lyra's, but the ambassador didn't seem to mind the informality of the alien's speech.

"What route will you be taking?"

Etienne smiled disingenuously. He and Lyra had debated the possibility of treachery by the locals and had decided it would be better to appear a little impolite and conceal the exact details of their itinerary.

"We're not certain. Here and there—we travel where our thirst for knowledge draws us."

Experienced diplomat that he was, de-Kelwhoang did not react to the probable evasion. "I envy you your freedom. Alas, my work rarely allows me to vary from a designated course. I have been told of the marvelous devices you possess which enable you to find your way at night and in bad weather as clearly as in cloudless daytime. Nevertheless, we would be remiss in our duty and it would be an offense to our honor if you were come to distress attempting to work your way into the main channel of the great Skar." Etienne was immediately on guard.

"It is also necessary that you carry more than signed documents, which can be forged, to prove that you travel under the protection of all Po Rabi. That way the ignorant bandits and suspicious villagers you may encounter, many of whom have not mastered the art of reading, will allow you to pass freely through their lands."

The ambassador turned and called over the railing toward his boat. A moment later two Mai appeared at the top of the stairs. Their fishnet attire was plain and their attitude deferential.

Etienne's first thought was that they constituted some formal part of the ambassador's entourage, but such was not the case.

"These will be your guides as well as your guarantors of safe passage," de-Kelwhoang announced. He bade each in turn step forward and make gestures of obeisance before the humans.

The male's name was Homat, the female's Irquit. No honorific "de" prefix, Etienne noted. Both wore simple face makeup and had their long hair bound back in single braids in contrast to the ambassador's elegant but thin coiffure. After bending and turning, both extended their hands outward toward the Redowls, palms upward.

After a moment's hesitation Lyra reached out and pressed her own palms to each proffered pair, palm down. The much longer Mai fingers extended well up against her wrist. Each of the six fingers ended in a soft fleshy pad. There were no nails, no residual claws.

Then she stepped back and drew her husband and Porlezmozmith aside, spoke in symbospeech. "What's your opinion, Commander? I don't really want these two along, but I don't want to offend this ambassador either, especially since we're not yet on our way."

"You are the xenologist, Lyra. But it would be bad diplomacy to refuse this offer of aid. They come to you as official representatives of their city. They do not look threatening to me and may indeed prove useful on your journey. Your mastery of Mai customs is far from complete."

"If it was we wouldn't be disappearing Upriver for a few months. Etienne, what's your opinion?"

"If it was up to me I'd rather not have them along, but as Porlez says, this is in the nature of an official presentation and I don't see how we can decline. I'm sure they're being sent along to learn everything they can about us for their Zanur, but I don't see much harm in that. They'll have to stay out on the stern deck anyway, away from any sensitive controls. The air conditioning in the main cabins would kill them in a few hours, or at least make them damn uncomfortable."

"All right then, they can come along. As you point out, Porlez, they may be of real help. If they cause trouble we can hold the Po Rabian Zanur directly responsible. Instruments aside, it'll be nice to have along a couple of locals who are familiar with the territory. Maybe they know how to cook. It would be nice when we enter colder climes to be able to enjoy a real hot meal instead of what the exciter oven throws up at us."

"I guess it's settled then," Etienne said, and couldn't resist adding, "Nice of you to ask for my opinion. Porlez, can you add anything?"

An inflexible thranx face cannot look thoughtful, but the station commander somehow managed to convey that feeling nonetheless.

"Just remember that when you pass above communicator range you're entirely on your own. We have no aircar here and it would be hard for me to muster a rescue party to come out after you under the best of circumstances. We do not care for travel by boat, as you are aware."

"We're aware of the dangers, as we were before we accepted this opportunity," Lyra reminded her. "We're looking forward to our independence and we're quite used to being on our own in difficult country."

"I know, I know," Porlezmozmith said. "I did not mean to sound as if I were chiding you. Once you pass out of communicator range I am no longer responsible for your safety, but I feel concern nonetheless."

Etienne was touched. Such compassion was a widespread thranx attribute and one of those characteristics that had deeply endeared them to humankind, but it still had the power to surprise.

"All the more reason then," he replied, "to have native help with us that we can count on. We'll have ample time to establish the reliability of our guests before we've gone beyond communicator range." He nodded toward the two slightly nervous guides.

"It would seem you are aware of what awaits you," said the commander. "I can think of nothing else to add." They all turned their attention back to the waiting ambassador.

For his part, Ror de-Kelwhoang had listened with interest to the harsh alien babble, which contrasted sharply with the rapid-fire sibilant singsong phrases of his own tongue.

"We thank the Zanur," Lyra said carefully, "for its kind thoughts and accept this offer of assistance with open hearts." Expressions of relief appeared simultaneously on the faces of de-Kelwhoang and the two guides. It would have gone hard on all if the offer had been refused.

Lyra couldn't resist adding to her knowledge of Mai customs. "Etienne and I are mated in the sight of the Ocean and the Oceans of all worlds. What of you?"

[32]

"We are not mated," Irquit replied, instantly establishing herself as senior of the pair. "Neither to each other nor others. The Zanur feels," and she made a deferential gesture toward the ambassador, "that in light of the many dangers that may lie in wait for us Upriver, it would be best if those with no family ties were honored by the opportunity to assist you."

"How encouraging," Etienne said dryly.

"I'm curious," Lyra persisted, "did you two volunteer for this, or were you 'honored' by choice of the Zanur?"

"Both apply." De-Kelwhoang stepped in gracefully. "Not all are qualified to serve as guides on such a momentous journey. Both these two have traveled far past the Skatandah. They have knowledge of its currents and its winds as well as many of the peoples you will encounter. I assure you that we have gone to great lengths to provide the most competent helpers Po Rabi has to offer."

Not wanting to risk impugning the Zanur's motives, much less its methods, Lyra switched to more mundane matters. "Irquit, we have some storage space available on our boat. What will you need to bring with you?"

"Very little. Some simple kitchen utensils and a single change of clothing. We will eat your food or purchase our own along the way. The Zanur has provided us with money. We can also cook for you, if you wish." Etienne looked pleased. "Both Homat and I are accomplished foragers."

Foraging was a word with many meanings in the Mai language, Lyra knew, referring to the ability to bargain sharply, scavenge efficiently, or steal without getting caught.

"We also," Homat said, speaking for the first time, "brought no weapons with us, having been told that should we meet hostile peoples you would manage our defense. We did not wish to bring killing instruments with us."

"Very thoughtful of you." Clearly Irquit is in charge of the little company, Lyra thought. But there was a natural shyness about Homat she found appealing. "That's all settled, then. If you would like to come help us with our loading—"

"No thank you," Irquit said hastily. "If you do not object we would much prefer to remain outside." She was staring with wide Mai eyes at the imposing alien structure. "If we are not to depart until tomorrow we can sleep outside, here, on mats."

"Are you afraid?" Etienne asked thoughtlessly.

Lyra shot him an angry glance, snapped in terranglo, "Don't you have any empathy for alien psychology? Can't you see they're trying to cover their fear gracefully?"

"I only thought that since these two are going to spend the next several months exploring strange country on a strange craft, they ought to start getting used to strangeness as soon as possible."

"They are not afraid," the ambassador said. He was picking his words with unusual care, Lyra thought. "There is something else."

"What something else?" Lyra asked, still upset over her husband's lack of sensitivity.

Ror de-Kelwhoang looked uncomfortable. "I would rather not say."

"Don't worry. We're scientists, here to study and learn about your ways and your world. We're just as interested in what you dislike as in what you like."

De-Kelwhoang did not look in Porlezmozmith's direction. "It is a question of appearances, you see. We place much value on appearance. There is truth in appearances. It is only that we have certain evil spirits cast in the form of..."

"There is no need for apology." Porlezmozmith knew where the ambassador's desperate circumlocutions were heading. "We are used to shape prejudice." She spoke to the two guides. "Remain by yourselves outside, if it is your wish."

Strange, Etienne thought. How could the Mai fear the thranx simply because of their shape? Lyra would have told him to read his history.

"We do not mean to give offense," de-Kelwhoang said quickly.

"None taken," the commander assured him. "This is something we are used to dealing with. I and my assistants will withdraw. It was a delight to meet you, Ambassador. You and your fellows are welcome anytime at Steamer Station. As are those," she couldn't help adding undiplomatically but with ill-concealed enjoyment, "of great Losithi."

The ambassador stiffened at the mention of Po Rabi's rival but, good tactician that he was, retained his composure.

"Thank you."

Porlezmozmith and the rest of the thranx contingent departed, leaving the Redowls alone on the deck with the Mai.

"We wish you much delight and good fortune in your studies," de-Kelwhoang said earnestly. He did not look at the two guides. "We of Po Rabi hold scholarship in high regard, unlike the rulers of certain other city-states. We hope you may see your way clear to sharing your knowledge with us after you return."

"That is our intention," Lyra told him. "This is your world and we are guests upon it, and we are thankful for your assistance." She performed a gesture indicating great appreciation.

Reassured, de-Kelwhoang turned and walked slowly down the stairway ramp. Waiting hands helped him back into the boat. On command the oarsmen dipped their paddles and pushed away from the support pillar where they had tied up. The Redowls watched for a while as the boat turned eastward. Then their attention shifted to their unexpected guests. Homat and Irquit waited patiently, their small bundles of cooking utensils and personal effects looking humble indeed.

"You're sure you want to sleep out here?"

"Please, de-Lyra," said Irquit, "we would feel more comfortable and would be out of everyone's way." She ventured the Mai smile, a thin parting of the lips that barely revealed the small fine teeth beyond. The corners of the mouth did not turn up.

"As you prefer."

"When are we to leave? We have heard so much of your wondrous boat and are most anxious to begin this great adventure with you."

Homat smiled too but said nothing. Not the loquacious type, Etienne decided. Not that it mattered. The two Mai weren't coming along to provide casual conversation.

"Tomorrow morning," he informed them. "We're almost ready and it'll take just a few minutes to put our boat in the water."

Irquit looked puzzled. "It is not in the water now?"

"No. It waits suspended by," he tried to shape his thicker

lips and less bulbous cheeks to form the correct expression, "you'll see tomorrow. Showing is better than talking."

"Yes, better than talking," Irquit agreed. She looked nervously toward the dark building beyond, abode of grotesque bug-things. "We will be left alone out here?"

"Yes." Lyra assured her. "Though our friends are used to a life beneath the ground and have a more flexible work–sleep cycle than we do, they still prefer to sleep during the hours of darkness. No one will disturb you out here and you won't be in the way."

Irquit smiled again. "I am much delighted that we are going with you."

"And we are much delighted to have you along," Lyra replied. "We'll see you again in the morning."

"Come morning." The two females exchanged the palm-to-palm caress a second time, though Lyra was convinced she'd never be able to compensate properly for the lack of a sixth digit.

【 IV 】

The sun was barely aloft as the hydrofoil was lowered
into the calm water beneath the station. The readout that
indicated air temperature clung desperately to the hundred-
degree mark, and there was no chance it would drop any
lower. The Mai stood at the base of the loading ramp which
had been dropped to the boat's stern deck, looking chilled
and uncomfortable.

Afire with excitement that had been lost during months
of waiting, the Redowls ignored them. When the last supplies
had been taken aboard and stowed, they thought to offer
moral assistance to their suddenly reluctant passengers.

Homat and Irquit boarded warily, eyes darting anxiously
about in search of sails and oars. When Etienne tested the
engine, both dashed for the rail and clung tightly to the
unyielding metal.

Lyra wiped morning sweat from beneath her sun visor
and tried to comfort them. "It's all right, it's only our engine.
The device that moves the boat. It's loud, but harmless. The
spirits within are fully contained."

"There are no sails," Irquit observed cautiously.

"Or oarsmen," Homat added.

"No, there aren't. We move by taking water in at the front of our craft and pushing it out the back much faster than we take it in."

"What pushes the water?" Irquit asked, slowly releasing her grasp on the railing; it was undignified. Homat continued to hang on tightly.

"Our engine. It would take a long time to explain. Maybe once we're on our way I'll try." She left Irquit with a re-assuring smile and descended the ladder to the upper cabin.

"De-Lyra, I am fearful!" Irquit gave Homat a disapproving look, but Lyra paused and eyed him pityingly.

"All right then, come on inside. But you won't like it."

Homat followed her, Irquit tagging along because she didn't want to miss anything. Once below, the truth of Lyra's words became immediately apparent. At a cabin temperature of eighty degrees, both Mai found themselves shivering.

Etienne greeted them in the transparent bubble of the cockpit, left explanations to Lyra. Though she used simple terms and kept her science as basic as possible, it soon became clear that such concepts as electricity and light-emitting diodes were beyond the comprehension of their guests.

Before long Homat confessed, "I think I would rather be fearful than frozen," and he led the retreat back toward the stern.

Once outside he hopped around for a few minutes until his system warmed, then busied himself arranging personal effects on the deck. The Mai would sleep where they cooked, away from the terrible arctic climate their hosts appeared to favor.

Reassurances and explanations notwithstanding, it took Lyra another hour of quiet coaxing to convince them that the boat wasn't going to devour them if they let loose of the rail when Etienne raced the engine and sent the hydrofoil leaping forward. She showed them how the boat lifted clear of the surface on its twin metal blades, explained how that enabled them to move Upriver at seventy kilometers an hour.

As time passed and the smoothness and exhilaration of the ride overcame initial fears, both Mai not only relaxed but began to enjoy the journey, though from time to time

Homat made signs designed to keep them from striking a submerged log or drifting helplessly toward the clouds.

Villages crowded the shores of tiny tree-covered islets. Astonished children barely had time to shout before the hydrofoil had raced past their disbelieving elders. The boat's scanner picked out fishing craft ahead, enabling Etienne to steer safely around them long before they came into view.

Larger islands appeared as they moved farther Upriver. There the water had receded from the floods sufficient to permit planting of grains and other foodstuffs. Some villagers were engaged in crude but effective aquaculture, from the raising of crustaceans to the gathering of waterfowl. All looked askance at the spirit boat that roared past their homes and scattered birds and amphibians in its wake.

There seemed no end to the villages. According to the initial satellite surveys, the Skatandah Delta was the most densely populated section of Tslamaina, which was why it had been chosen as the site of the first Commonwealth outpost.

As they traveled toward the equator the temperature intensified, if that was possible, and no occasional sea breeze battled the humidity. Despite months of acclimatization, the Redowls spent the majority of their time sequestered in the air-conditioned interior of their craft. Merely to step out on deck risked a shock to the system. Homat and Irquit were right at home on the stern deck, however, and readily exchanged muted comments about the fragility of the human system.

Homat made a game of trying to outguess the scanner, sitting on the bow and staring at the water in search of submerged rocks or other obstacles. He always lost, but the acuity of his eyesight impressed both Etienne and Lyra.

By analyzing the current and the debris the water carried, the hydrofoil's computer could make a decision on which branch to take, but it was still nice to have Irquit confirm the choice. Without the computer or their guides they could have spent years wandering through the Skatandah in a futile attempt to locate the main course of the Skar.

As the days slid past in superheated study, the Redowls found themselves more and more grateful for the presence of their two passengers. Having completely overcome their fear of the boat, the Mai had revealed themselves as efficient, helpful, and good company. Lyra derived an added benefit from being able to study their reactions to new discoveries, additional information on Mai society which she regularly entered into her scientific log.

They also turned out to be excellent cooks as well as sharp bargainers at the villages where they stopped to purchase supplies, and except for periodic raids on the salt tablet and vitamin stores, the humans' stock of packaged food remained nearly untouched.

Irquit and Homat didn't try to hide their delight. Not only were they enjoying themselves, but Lyra knew they must be anticipating the honors that would come their way after they returned home. Their careers were made. She was pleased for both of them.

It was clear that those Mai fortunate enough to make their homes in the delta were more content than their urbanized relations. Government control so far from Po Rabi was lax, food was abundant, and there was little to inspire conflict. The social setup would change, Lyra suspected, once they left the lush Skatandah region behind and emerged into the main channel of the Skar. Farming above the delta would require more effort and extensive irrigation. Competition would be tough, as it was within the city-state boundaries.

The heat, the friendliness of the villagers, the lazy days passed in discussion and study produced in the Redowls a feeling of inner security. It was left to Homat to remind them that they were traveling on an alien world and not Earth's relatively benign waters.

Etienne had gone over the side and was leaning back against one of the curving support struts that ran from hydrofoil to hull, trailing one leg in the cool water and letting the spray from the foil wash over him. They were traveling fast enough to alleviate concern about glass leeches and he was completely relaxed beneath the refreshing spray.

He gave Homat a curious glance as the Mai started to descend alongside him, carrying a metal prod. Now that he'd overcome his initial fear of the strange vessel, the shy native clambered nimbly over it while displaying an agility Etienne could only envy.

It was the prod that caught his eye. "What's that for?"

Homat gestured with the metal. Etienne wiped spray from his face and looked behind him.

Attached to the foil just beneath the glassy surface of the water and slowly creeping toward Etienne's feet was a thin dark shape, three meters long and as thick as his arm.

"Sandrush," Homat said curtly as he worked his way around the strut until he was holding on behind Etienne.

"Poisonous? Parasite?"

"No. Inhaler."

"What does it inhale? Blood?"

"Inhale you." Etienne watched with interest as the Mai used the prod to pry open the creature's wide round mouth. The teeth were small and curved inward. The jaw dislocated itself and Homat spread the gape wider still. As they watched the sandrush began to fill helplessly with river water until it had swollen to four times its normal size. The dull green membrane was evidently capable of expanding to hold prey larger than itself, and the meaning of Homat's words became ghoulishly clear.

Eventually the pressure of the water proved too much for the powerful suckers that lined the sandrush's ventral side. It relinquished its grip and fell away astern. Etienne was suitably impressed.

"If it gets a hold of you, very bad," Homat explained unnecessarily. "It won't let go unless it dies and sandrush is very hard to kill. Swallow you whole." He turned to climb back up toward the lower deck.

Etienne wondered at the flexibility that would allow an animal to expand so far beyond its normal size even as he thoughtfully removed his legs from the water. He wondered what other charming native fauna lurked just beneath the surface of the river, following the boat hungrily.

Since there was little here for him to study he did most of the piloting, leaving Lyra free to record her impressions of village life and culture within the Skatandah. While the communities there differed little from those clustered around Steamer Station she continued to take her usual copious notes. Even the tiniest change in social structure or clothing or fishing methods was occasion for excitement.

Gradually the marshlands and islands of the delta began to fade behind them. Fewer platform trees and pseudopalms

[41]

were seen, more open water and less land. An unknowing observer might have concluded that the Redowls had taken a wrong turn and were heading once more out into the open ocean.

But the water they skimmed over was now almost entirely fresh. They had entered the main body of the Skar, a river large enough to make the Amazon or Nile òr any of the other known rivers of the Commonwealth look like a meandering creek. From the center of the river it was impossible to tell you weren't traveling on a freshwater sea, because there was no sign of land to starboard or port. Beyond invisible banks the cliffs that marked the edge of the Guntali rose unseen toward a cloud-flecked sky.

Etienne eased the hydrofoil to starboard until the shoreline hove into view. Thereafter they were able to cruise on autopilot, allowing Lyra to concentrate on her note-taking and leaving Etienne free to stare through the telescope mounted atop the observation mast. Numerous villages dotted the bank. Farther inland he saw farming communities and small commercial centers. At the extreme range of the scope's resolving power he could discern the first gentle slopes, evidence that they really were traveling up a river canyon.

While the temperature crept toward the hundred thirty mark in early afternoon, the humidity fell slightly. It required an effort to remain outside the boat's air-conditioned interior for longer than half an hour. Lyra spent much of her time outside chatting with the owners of the small trading boats that pulled alongside whenever they stopped. While she dictated notes, Homat and Irquit bargained for provisions. Irquit did most of the trading while Homat attended to the cooking, having mastered the electric oven the Redowls insisted he use instead of the wood-burning stove he had brought on board.

They were then a thousand kilometers north of Steamer Station and the mouth of the delta, cruising the smooth back of the river Skar at a steady ninety kph. They had barely begun their journey.

Everywhere the Mai citizenry was friendly and open, though more primitive than those of the advanced societies of the city-states that ringed the great world ocean. All was not peaceful and pastoral along the river, however. The presence of village stockades and other fortifications hinted at sporadic conflict, and there were those who were less than overawed by the peculiar visitors' advanced technology.

"Hon, I think you'd better have a look at this." Etienne kept his gaze on the scanner as he took the boat off autopilot.

"What is it?" Lyra's voice sounded over the intercom in the cockpit.

"Ships ahead, lots of 'em. Fishing boats by the computer image."

"What's notable about that? I'm busy, Etienne."

"Lyra, there are at least a hundred boats. That's not usual, is it?"

"No, it's not." The intercom went quiet for a moment and when she spoke again her tone was thoughtful instead of impatient. "Are you sure?"

"I'm quite capable of following the readouts," he said sarcastically. "It isn't normal, is it, for a fishing fleet to attain that size?"

"Not from what we've seen thus far, no, but maybe it's normal up here."

"Why don't you ask Irquit?"

A sigh whispered at him from the grid as she put her beloved work aside. "I suppose I'd better."

Irquit sat on the open rear deck of the hydrofoil, cleaning vegetables for the next meal. Purple and maroon predominated, but that didn't detract from the tastiness, Lyra knew. Homat peeled tubers by hand.

"Irquit, my husband says that there are at least a hundred fishing boats in the river ahead of us." Neither of the Mai expressed surprise at this calm revelation, having already become familiar with much of the hydrofoil's instrumentation. They called the cockpit scanner the iron eye.

Irquit looked uncertain. "That is more than I have ever heard of fishing the river. There are never so many grouped together down by Po Rabi. Is de-Etienne certain they are just fishermen?"

"We can't tell that through the iron eye. What could they be doing except fishing?"

"It could be a war fleet," Homat suggested tentatively.

[43]

"Out to attack one of the villages? This doesn't seem to be a poor area."

"It is sometimes simpler," said Homat with innocent wisdom, "to take rather than to work, no matter how easy the work may be."

She could have argued the point but it was not the time to engage in idle sociological speculation. "Tell that to my husband, Homat."

He made a sign of acknowledgment and worked his way around the boat until he was standing outside the transparent dome of the cockpit. He could see Etienne clearly. Condensation was banished from the clear acrylic by the silent efforts of special air circulators. He leaned toward the speaking membrane.

"De-Etienne, I fear the many vessels you say lie ahead of us."

"Is there any way you can tell what they're up to by looking at them?"

"Yes. If they have their gill nets out I think they're just fishing and not ready for war. Gill nets cost too much to risk in a fight."

Etienne considered. "Better tell Lyra to come forward, then. The iron eye can't distinguish something as wispy as nets. We'll need somebody to make visual confirmation."

"I'm already here, Etienne." The membrane picked up his wife's voice before she stepped into view. Irquit was with her. "You don't have to tell me my job."

"I wasn't telling you your job," he snapped, "I just—never mind. We'll be on top of them in a minute." He examined the crowded screen. "I'll have to slow down or we're liable to run over somebody."

"We've never run into more than four or five boats fishing together before. Too much competition," Lyra murmured. "It doesn't fit the established pattern." Masted wooden shapes were appearing on the horizon ahead.

The roar of the electric jet dropped to a rumble and the hydrofoil's speed dropped radically until the hull once more broke water. As they began to pass among the component vessels, the fishing fleet was even more impressive up close than it had appeared on the scanner.

The craft that plied the warm waters of the Skatandah

Delta rarely required the muscles of more than three or four fishermen. These great bargelike vessels each boasted two dozen crew or more. They lay across the Skar in three rows, blocking a decent part of the river's considerable breadth, and were roped together.

To Etienne's relief they clearly saw the huge gill nets strung between the ships. Since they didn't drift with the current they must utilize heavy anchors to hold them in place. Women and children manned the nets and lines alongside the men.

Every tenth barge was a vast floating platform nearly as big as some of the ocean-going trimarans they'd encountered out in the Groalamasan. The reason for their extraordinary size, as well as for the number of fishing craft, soon became apparent. It had to do with the size of the catch.

Some twenty vessels were swinging close together, bumping sides and full of organized confusion as their crews strained at nets and lines. The water between began to froth and bubble, was finally broken by the emergence of an immense rainbow-hued head. More glowing color breached the surface and the fisherfolk redoubled their efforts to haul in their whale-sized catch.

"Arwawl!" Homat exclaimed excitedly. "I've tasted its dried flesh but never seen one before. They run only in the main river and come nowhere near Po Rabi's shallows."

The chanting of the fishermen was a steady, triumphant chorus now as they hauled in the huge interlocked nets. As they did so ten ships passed to port of the immense barge, ten to starboard. The barge crew lent its muscle to the task and long gaffs, attached to winches, were brought into use. Slowly the arwawl was hauled onto the deck, bending the stern beneath the surface of the river for long moments before the silvery tonnage could be better distributed.

The single catch was enough to feed many villages, Etienne mused, but the fleet apparently wasn't satisfied. Still other nets were out, trailing from the less fortunate boats. He admired the fisherfolk's persistence.

It was left to Irquit, less mesmerized by the efficiency of the fleet, to sound a warning. She moved closer to Lyra, who was intent on recording the fishing with her instruments.

Irquit performed a diminutive half bow. "Forgive me for troubling you, de-Lyra, but I think we are in danger."

"What?" Lyra strained to refocus her attention. "What's that, Irquit?"

The Mai stepped to the railing and pointed over the bow. "I have been watching those four ships." Lyra raised her gaze, saw nothing unusual about the quartet of fishing craft dead ahead.

"What about them? They are fishing, like their companions."

"Not like their companions," Irquit argued. "They are moving toward us. They should be anchored in place, holding their nets against the flow of the Skar. They are drifting downstream."

"Maybe they're trying to reposition themselves in a better spot. Fishermen move all the time."

"I'm sure they are moving to a better spot, but not to catch fish, I think."

Lyra frowned. "What makes you think so?"

"Two drift to our left, two to the right. Their nets lie between. If we continue on this course they will soon ensnare us."

"I'm sure it's not intentional," Lyra replied, but inwardly she wasn't so sure. The boats were very close now and the big gill nets lay concealed by the rolling water. "We'll warn them clear."

"The nets of the Upriver fisherfolk are wondrous strong, de-Lyra," Irquit said anxiously. "I don't know that even your spirit boat could escape from them. There is something more. See how busy the crews are?"

Lyra squinted, peered through her recorder's telephoto for a closer look. "I see. Isn't that normal?"

"I am no fisherwoman, but I have visited this part of the Skar before. To travel downstream is simple. One simply raises the anchors and drifts with the current. Never have I seen so much activity surrounding so easy a task. When one works that hard at something that simple, one usually has something to hide."

Lyra thought a moment, leaned over to call toward the cockpit. "Irquit thinks the four fishing boats coming Downriver toward us might be trying to ensnare us in their nets."

Etienne wished the hydrofoil's scanner could provide more detail. "What's your opinion, Lyra?"

"I don't know what to think, but I don't want to take any unnecessary chances. I'd like to find out so that we'll have a better idea what to expect in case the same situation reoccurs in the future. Let's do our guesswork now."

He nodded. "We'll let them play all their cards, then. Tell Irquit not to worry. I can handle it."

"Handle?" Irquit was trying to divide her attention between the stocky human female and the suspiciously active fishing boats dead ahead. "What does de-Etienne mean 'handle?'" The boats were near enough now for the *otolk* wood floats to stand out clearly against the water.

"He means he's ready to deal with any hostile moves."

"But you must move away, move to avoid them while there is still time! I know that the spirit boat can move quickly to the side, and..."

"Have a calming, Irquit. Etienne knows what he's doing. Everything's under control."

A gentle shudder ran through the hydrofoil's hull as the bow made contact with the heavy nets and two of the oblong floats. As they continued Upriver, pushing the net with their bow, the four fishing boats were drawn toward each other... and the hydrofoil was caught between them.

Explosive roars of triumph sounded from all four Mai vessels and all pretense vanished. It was suddenly clear that they were interested in tougher quarry than fish. Gaffs gave way to long pikes and spears, and the chanting that accompanied the appearance of these weapons was very different from that which had provided a quaint backdrop to the landing of the *arwawl*.

Homat began to moan and rock from side to side. "Doomed we are. These river primitives will show us no mercy!"

Irquit merely looked resigned. "I warned you, de-Lyra."

"And you were right," the xenologist replied calmly as she turned again toward the cockpit bubble. "We've established their real intentions, Etienne. I've made my recordings." She paused as something whizzed past overhead. "Let's not hang around. They have bows."

"Don't you want to observe native weaponry in action?"

She ducked as a wood-and-bone shaft splintered against

the deck. "Don't get funny, honey. If you want to linger, we can switch places first."

"Never mind." He grinned at her as he gunned the engine. The jet nozzle pivoted a hundred and eighty degrees until it was facing toward the bow.

"Hold tight," Lyra warned the two morose Mai. They barely had time to reach for handholds before the hydrofoil shot backward in full reverse. Suddenly nothing kept the four fishing boats apart. The nets fell limp into the river.

The chanting subsided as the would-be pirates watched their quarry vanish astern at sixty kph. Then crews rushed to the oars as all four crews realized there was nothing to stop their momentum. Frantic yells and curses replaced the warlike chanting of a moment earlier.

Etienne slowed and reversed direction once more, watching with interest as the four fishing boats, still linked together by their nets and lines, slewed inexorably toward each other. Loud snapping sounds filled the air as hastily manned oars were splintered against colliding hulls. Curses were drowned by shouts of confusion and conflicting orders as nets became tangled with rudders and broken oars.

Keeping well beyond arrow range, he edged the hydrofoil easily around their would-be captors, toward the center of the river. A few of the unhappy fisherfolk, unable to attack with their short bows, settled for bombarding the spirit boat with ferocious insults. Homat stifled his laughter at their plight long enough to translate those couched in the local dialect or too complex for Lyra to understand. She patiently entered them all into her journal under a subheading drolly labeled MAI INVECTIVE—LOCAL VARIANTS AND DIALECTS. All grist for the xenological mill.

Etienne half-expected some of the other fisherfolk to aid their brethren in the attack, but he was pleasantly disappointed. Instead of joining in, the Mai who'd stood to the side to watch were lining the sides of their own vessels and cheering the spirit boat's escape.

"That's not the reaction I expected," he shouted toward the speaker membrane. "Irquit, what's going on? They don't seem angry at our escape."

"Why should they be? They chose not to participate in the attack on us. So they do not share in its failure. They admire the successful, no matter where they come from. So they applaud our escape." Irquit leaned over the railing to peer astern. The four badly entangled fishing boats continued their steady drift Downriver.

"By the time they get themselves separated, de-Etienne, they will have a long hard row Upriver to return to their homes. That will give them time to think anew about trying to capture a spirit boat. I hope not many were hurt. There is much confusion."

"And I hope half fall overboard and drown." Homat spat over the side. "Let the river eat them. May they stew in their own urine! We meant them no harm and still they would have slain us!"

Lyra paused in her note-taking. "It's difficult for poor people to turn down the chance to acquire great wealth, Homat. I'm not defending their actions, understand, but I can empathize with their feelings." She had to use four connected nouns to make the idea of empathy comprehensible to the Mai guide. "Do you think we'll be subject to more such attacks?"

Irquit made a gesture of uncertainty. "Who can predict? As you say, de-Lyra, your spirit boat represents power and wealth to all who set eyes upon it. Your property will be coveted from the Skatandah to the region of ice." Another thin smile. "Clearly any who try will have much difficulty in taking it."

"We can take care of ourselves," Lyra assured her.

"That is proven. I will not dance with worry next time. None can threaten the spirit boat."

"Oh, we're not omnipotent," Lyra corrected her, "but we're far from defenseless. If necessary we can do more than just dodge gill nets."

"Yes. I have seen the weapons that rest in the holders alongside the round tiller de-Etienne steers the spirit boat with."

"Those are only for use in dire emergency," Lyra said firmly. "We carry them to defend us against dangerous animals, not intelligent peoples. My Zanur would be very upset with us if we used them against your people."

"My people are the people of Po Rabi," Irquit replied, indicating with gentle bloodthirstiness that it wouldn't bother her in the least if it became necessary to shoot a few riverfolk. Lyra sighed inwardly. Once upon a time, back in the tribal days, her ancestors had felt similarly. A few throwbacks still did.

The kilometers slid beneath the hydrofoil's keel by the hundreds, the Skar still running wide and slow, the distant walls of the Barshajagad still rendered invisible by haze and distance. Lyra began to enjoy the bargaining for supplies that took place whenever they pulled in to shore.

"You can learn a lot by watching Homat and Irquit," she told Etienne on more than one occasion.

He would nod politely, but the methodology of native barter didn't intrigue him. Instead, he spent the trading time sequestered atop the observation mast with one eye glued to the telescope, studying the nearing lower slopes of the canyon with their irrigated fields and elaborate terraces.

As a precaution, they spent each night well out in the middle of the Skar. The hydrofoil's autoalarms would alert them to the presence of any potential danger.

Occasionally, Etienne would vary the routine by climbing the mast to turn the telescope skyward, quizzing himself by trying to identify the strange constellations overhead. On this particular early morning there was no rain and few clouds. The humidity was lower than usual and the temperature had plunged into the nineties. He was very surprised to see Homat's wide-eyed hairless face appear outside the transparent scope enclosure. The guide looked nervous, and not from the height.

Etienne unfastened the plastic to admit the edgy Mai.

"Something wrong, Homat?" he inquired solicitously.

"I—I must talk with you, de-Etienne."

"Must be important to bring you up here from beneath a warm blanket."

"It is, very important."

"Just a second." Etienne swung the telescope aside on its gimbaled mount to make more room, thoughtfully shut off the blower that was pouring refrigerated air into the enclosure.

As soon as the temperature had warmed, Homat entered and sealed the entrance behind him. In the cramped space atop the mast Etienne was more conscious than ever of his bulk compared to that of the diminutive native.

"What is it?" Beyond Homat he could see two of Tslamaina's four moons gleaming on the river. The other two would appear within the hour, he knew.

"For a long time I have meant to do this, but I did not know how to do it and have not had a chance to do it."

"Do what?"

"Warn you, de-Etienne. You and de-Lyra are in great danger."

Etienne leaned back in the narrow swivel chair and smiled at the native's concern. He swung one leg idly back and forth.

"We're in constant danger, yes. The fisherfolk we just ran into Downriver demonstrated that."

"No, no!" Homat whispered intently. "Not that. The danger of which I speak is nearer and more insidious."

Etienne studied the guide's face closely. "Homat, what is it you're so frightened of?"

"I am not bold by nature," he explained anxiously. "I have traveled as widely as I have not because I desired to but because I was ordered to do so by those who employed me.

"Now I have found that I cannot go on without telling what I know, de-Etienne. Something within pushes me to make confession. All my life I have been a small person, one who scrapes and nods and follows the orders of others. You and de-Lyra have treated me most fair, better than I have ever been treated by any other employers. I have come to like you very much. For the first time in my life, someone makes me feel important. It is a feeling I want to keep."

"Why shouldn't you?" Etienne found himself taken aback by the unexpectedly emotional confession.

"Because of Irquit."

"Irquit? What can she do to you?"

Homat's wide eyes darted nervously around the plastic enclosure. "Are you sure no one can hear what we say?"

"Of course I'm sure. The intercom's not on and we're high above the rest of the boat. Homat, explain yourself.

Why are you so afraid of Irquit all of a sudden? I hadn't
noticed that she's been treating you badly. She's been very
helpful."

"That is her task. To be helpful until..." he hesitated.
"Mai-with-Hair, remember that what I am about to tell you
is worth my life—Irquit is the direct representative of the
Zanur of Po Rabi."

Etienne was beginning to lose patience with his visitor.
His viewing time was slipping away and he wanted to get in
some sleep before sunrise.

"We already know that, Homat. You are, too."

"No! I am a hired guide. She is responsible only to the
Zanur itself. Tell me, de-Etienne, have you not remarked on
her intense interest in your spirit boat and its functions?"

"Naturally. Do you think we're only attuned to technology? My wife is particularly sensitive to the actions of," he
almost said primitive peoples, but quickly changed it to "other
individuals. Irquit's interest is only natural. Lyra ought to
know. She's studied guests on other worlds beyond this
one."

"I know what that means, de-Etienne," Homat replied
somberly. "Tell me: on those other worlds did she ever encounter any assassins?"

[V]

Etienne's smile vanished and he sat up straighter in his chair. His impatience was replaced by sudden interest.

"Would you mind explaining what you mean, Homat?"

The guide shifted nervously. "Your wonderful craft makes use of many impossible-to-understand spirits, de-Etienne, but it seems to me not so difficult to command them."

"Operation is highly simplified for users not technically oriented, yes."

"Simple enough for Irquit to operate?"

"Maybe, if she were to stick to basic go–stop type directions. What about it?"

Homat gestured forward, past the moonlit bow. "Tomorrow we are to stop at the village of Changrit to restock our larder. Changrit has an alliance with Po Rabi."

"I didn't think Po Rabi's influence extended this far north," Etienne told him.

"Changrit is independent. It is a trade alliance only, but that is enough when much is at stake. Long before Ambassador de-Kelwhoang delivered us to you to serve as your guides, river riders were sent racing north to Changrit. An

[53]

understanding was achieved with the Moyt of Changrit." He brushed absently at the single knot of long hair that trailed from the top of his head.

"The ambush is to take place at night, while you are anchored out in the Skar and less on guard. Your spirit boat is to be taken so that its secrets and treasures may be shared by Changrit and Po Rabi." He hesitated only for a moment. "You and your mate, of course, will not survive."

"I see," Etienne said quietly. "Suppose Irquit proves unable, despite her studies, to operate the boat?"

"All is planned for. In that event it is to be loaded upon a barge and shipped Downriver."

"I don't see any problem, Homat. We just won't stop near Changrit for supplies. Even if they're lying in wait for us out in the river we can simply run past them."

"It may not be so easy, de-Etienne. Even now word is relayed along the riverbank marking our progress. The fighters of Changrit will be ready to challenge you no matter when you try to pass their city."

"I'm curious. How did the Zanur plan to explain our disappearance, in the event our friends back at Steamer Station learned of it?"

"You have been watched and studied. Not all who sought to talk with your mate while you waited to travel were simple fisherfolk. Changrit was chosen because it is the northernmost city with which Po Rabi has an alliance and it was believed to lie beyond range of your talk-through-air spirits."

"That's right enough."

"There is no reason why your friends should connect your disappearance to Po Rabi or any other city. For all they will know you perished when your boat sank in the Skar, as many boats do."

"And what if our friends come looking for us and find our boat in the possession of the Zanur, or the Moyt of Changrit?"

"Then it is to be said that you were swamped by an arwawl, that this was seen from shore, and that your boat was towed to safety but not in time to save its crew. I am not privy to all the details, as Irquit is."

"But they had to tell you this much so that you could help at the critical moment."

"Yes." Homat dropped his gaze, unwilling to meet his benefactor's eyes. "My ancestors are ashamed."

"All right, you've told me about the proposed attack. That doesn't make Irquit an assassin."

"She will become one only if it proves necessary," Homat explained. "She is there to make certain the attack does not fail. When it comes she will pretend surprise and will appear to aid you, but if it looks like the attack may fail, she is to choose a moment when you are not on guard to push you overboard or put a knife in your back. Have you not noticed her skill on things bigger than vegetables." He looked away.

"I just thought she was a deft cook," he muttered.

"Deft indeed, de-Etienne. I have seen her demonstrate her skill on things bigger than vegetables." He looked away. "I was to help in all this, of course."

"Of course," Etienne said dryly. He reached out and pushed a button. A tired moan came from the grid.

"What is it? I was just getting into a really decent dream."

"Would you come up here a minute, hon? I'm observing something I think you'd find intriguing."

"Come on, Etienne. Maybe tomorrow night."

"It may be less visible tomorrow night. I wish you'd come up *now*. Our position tomorrow will be radically different."

"All right, all right," she snapped back at him. "This better be good."

He waited in the enclosure with the nervous Homat until a sleepy-eyed Lyra had ascended the mast to join them. There was very little room to move around with three of them atop the platform.

"What now?" She was still blinking sleep from her eyes, but her expression turned to one of confusion when she noticed Homat.

"Where's Irquit?" Etienne asked her.

"Irquit? What's she got to do with?... On the stern deck, I would imagine, blissful in the arms of the local representative of Morpheus. What the hell's going on up here?"

"Homat has something to tell you."

Lyra listened quietly as the guide repeated the tale he had told Etienne. She considered quietly for several long moments once he'd finished.

"We could turn back. We're scientists, not soldiers-of-fortune and not hard-contact explorers. We're not prepared to deal with large-scale local antagonism. If this town is linked by treaty and duplicity to Po Rabi, we can apply for clearance and protection with the Zanur of Losithi."

Etienne looked doubtful. "Wouldn't work. Word will reach Po Rabi and they'll know we found them out. That could put them into open conflict with Losithi. We don't want to be responsible for starting a major local war. Besides which there's no guarantee we'd fare any better with the Zanur of Losithi than we already have with Po Rabi. Better the devil you know, et cetera."

"They are as envious of your technology as is the Zanur of Po Rabi," Homat agreed.

"Then there's the distance we've already come. Returning and retracing our steps would take at least a month, even if we were lucky enough to obtain immediate permission from Losithi. We've passed the equator and we're above the worst of the climate. Not that this oven has suddenly become comfortable, but it's bound to improve.

"I've no desire to retrace our steps, restudy what we've already thoroughly recorded, and I'm sure you don't either, Lyra. And there's always the chance that Losithi could arrange a similar kind of ambush when we resumed our journey, and they'd be better prepared for us than these Changritites are likely to be. The geology's finally starting to get interesting, Lyra. I don't want to go back to taking mud samples for an additional two months. Despite Homat's fears I don't imagine we'll have any trouble passing through whatever barrier of nets and ropes the locals can erect."

"I know that," Lyra agreed. "It's not that. I just don't want to harm any natives. You know what a resident commissioner would have to say about that."

"There's no resident commissioner on Tslamaina. Not advanced enough yet. No one's going to know anything, and even if we were found out we'd just tell them that we had to defend ourselves, which is likely to be the truth."

Lyra turned her attention to Homat. "What happens once we're safely past Changrit? What about the next town? Could it be in alliance with Po Rabi too?"

Homat spoke with conviction. "No. Changrit is the only far north city allied with Po Rabi. Beyond Changrit much is unknown and all are independent of the city-states that line the Groalamasan. And Changrit was chosen because it alone can muster enough strength for such an attack."

"Everything you've told us makes sense," she murmured. "It's what you haven't told us that worries me."

"I do not understand your words, de-Lyra."

"Why are you so eager to betray your own city?"

"I have told you that I have come to like you, and that you have given me a sense of self-importance and true worth that I have never felt before."

"That's not good enough." For emphasis she added a powerful Mai gesture of disbelief. "You could have kept silent and fulfilled the dictates of your masters. If we had succumbed to this trap you would have enjoyed much honor in Po Rabi, and if we had escaped you would still be safe. Why risk the one by throwing in so openly with us when you'd have been safe both ways by keeping quiet? I'm glad that you 'like' us, but I've studied Mai society for too many months now to believe that you're doing this out of the goodness of your heart."

Homat looked uncertain, turned to Etienne for guidance.

"You'd better tell us the truth, Homat."

"Don't you believe me, de-Etienne?"

"Yes, I do, but my wife's a born skeptic. Unlike intelligent beings, rocks and minerals aren't intentionally deceptive. You're going to have to convince her to convince me."

Homat nodded. When he spoke again much of the nervousness and all of the soft deference had vanished from his voice.

"I told the truth about coming to like you, and about not wishing to be a party to such a vile deception. But de-Lyra suspects me rightly. I have another reason for confessing this now.

"It is true I would risk nothing by keeping my silence, but also would I gain nothing. Po Rabi is my home, but I have traveled widely and have come to think of the world as my home. There are many great city-states where one may make a fine life. In Po Rabi I have little chance to rise above my station. True, if the attack on your spirit boat were to succeed I would return home to a fine reward, but in you off-worlders I see the chance to do much better. With the

[57]

knowledge I can gain from you I can make myself valuable beyond mere 'rewards.' Thus far only Losithi and Po Rabi have dealt with your hard-shelled friends. Suphum would welcome my knowledge and make me a member of their Zanur, as would Tolm and many others. I could not hope to rise so high in Po Rabi on the results of my labors as an assassin.

"I have provided you with information which may save your lives as well as your expedition. In return for this information and for my loyalty, I expect suitable recompense."

Lyra looked satisfied. "*Now* I believe you, Homat." She added to Etienne in terranglo. "Typical power--wealth decision. Very Mai. The fact that we're not of his race doesn't enter into the equation. Business takes precedence over vague feelings of loyalty to home and kind." She switched back to her very fluent Mai.

"You are a more complex person than you've led us to believe, Homat. You're a very effective deceiver." This last was, in Mai, a compliment, and Homat looked quite pleased with himself.

"All of us carry deceptions. They are worth little. Truth is all that can be sold. I am only a simple one seeking to lift himself from the depths in which he was born."

"Having deceived us this long, how can we be certain you won't try to strike your own bargain with some village Moyt?"

"If you do not return safely to your Steamer Station, I gain nothing from helping you now. I do not wish to take the spirit boat. I believe I have more to gain by helping you."

"A straightforward enough commercial decision, Etienne—devoid of sentimentality. I'd rather rely on that than on his fondness for us. Having made his confession and his choice, it's now in his best interests to see to our continued health and safety."

"Delightful so," Homat agreed. "Then you believe me about Irquit and the attack?"

"We'll find out for certain tomorrow," Etienne told him. He turned his attention to the telescope. "Now if you don't mind, Homat, I still have some observations of the sky I want to make and Lyra needs her beauty sleep."

Homat gaped at him. "But you are to be attacked! You must make preparations to defend yourselves."

"Maybe we won't have to fight, Homat."

"We'd better not," Lyra murmured uneasily. "Self-defense or no, if word ever got back to our sponsors that we'd engaged in a running battle with Class Four-B natives we'd never get another grant in our lives."

"Don't be so damned concerned for the welfare of the charming, considerate locals. What are you worried about? Is Homat going to appear before the Research Advisory Board to announce that we knew about the attack in advance?" After months of fighting with his wife, Etienne was more than ready to fight something else, and to hell with the regulations.

Besides, Po Rabi's deception grated on him. He remembered the ambassador's politeness, the warm feelings of contentment and achievement they'd felt just before setting out Upriver. If Homat's confession proved true, that meant all those kind words of help and assistance and talk of mutual sharing of knowledge was so much dung.

Maybe Changrit was the last city in league with Po Rabi, and maybe it wasn't. It wouldn't hurt to send a lesson not only to the Zanur of Po Rabi but to any other Mai who coveted the spirit boat, that the peaceful human visitors weren't to be trifled with. Yes, they all but owed it to the Mai to show what scholars could do when aroused. In so doing they might quickly discourage all future such assaults, thereby saving lives.

"It still bothers me to have to fight," Lyra said softly.

"I understand." He was quite willing to be understanding now that he'd made up his mind how to handle the Changritites. "But if it comes to that, it's self-defense. Anyway, by fighting we're only adhering to local custom. Remember how the rest of the fishing fleet cheered us on our way? Maybe some timorous board member would disapprove, but not the rest of the Mai."

She spoke in terranglo again while Homat looked on blankly, desperately wishing he could comprehend the alien babble.

"We could just use repellers."

"Dangerous if they managed to get a net or two on us.

[59]

You know how unstable the boat is on repellers. That's a last resort. Besides, if we don't invite some kind of reaction, we'll only have Homat's word about Irquit. What if she's no assassin, merely a guide? What if their orders are only to stand aside and let the Changritites do all the dirty work? Maybe he's just trying to shut her out of the bit of business he's working with us. By watching her reactions we'll have final proof of his words. If she doesn't make any threatening moves, once past Changrit we'll have a new problem to deal with."

Lyra sighed, shook her head sadly. "This is going to complicate the hell out of my notes."

"If that's all we have to worry about as we pass Changrit," he countered, "we'll be well off. Besides, think of the potential opportunities for studying the behavior of the Mai in battle."

She responded with a rude noise which even Homat could understand.

The following night on the Skar was equally cloudless and clear. As the sun began to shrink behind the distant ramparts of the canyon wall, Etienne peered through the cockpit bubble at an anxious Irquit. He nodded to himself as he studied her expression. Point one to Homat.

The guide was talking to Lyra, who stood watching the western shore.

"We are almost all out of meat, de-Lyra. I thought we were to stop here at Changrit." She gestured with a six-fingered hand toward the dots of light which marked the riverbank. "We will soon be past the harbor."

"We're not stopping tonight, Irquit," Lyra replied. "We have ample supplies of our own foodstuffs down in the hold. Maybe we'll stop in a couple of days. It's such a beautiful night, Etienne thinks we should enjoy the weather. I agree."

"But Changrit is such a wonderful place!" Irquit protested. "There is so much to see, so much for you to put into your records, de-Lyra."

"Oh, that's okay. I'm sure we'll find other places to stop that are just as interesting. We can stop and study there."

"None are so grand on this part of the Skar as is Changrit."

Irquit was glancing nervously past Lyra, apparently studying the river ahead.

"Something wrong?" Lyra asked innocently.

"No, no. I only wanted so much for you to see so powerful and beautiful a city. I felt that . . ."

Etienne tuned the pleading voice out and concentrated on the scanner by his right hand. He knew what Irquit was looking for, out there atop the dark water. The green screen was filled with bright shapes of many sizes strung out in three parallel lines across the Skar. It must have taken the Changritites weeks to gather the enormous flotilla.

He lost speed as he studied the scanner, looking for the place where the boats were spread thinnest.

There were more boats ahead than he'd expected, and the danger was greater. Some of his initial enthusiasm for a fight evaporated. The capture was no game to the local Mai, and despite superior technology there was something still to be said for commanding overwhelming numbers. He made certain the repellers were functioning, just in case they had to employ them.

Pick your way through, he suddenly decided, and take care not to get entangled in those damn nets and heavy wooden floats. Above all, don't let any of the locals on board. Surely they wouldn't have any *real* difficulty breaking through.

Irquit was failing at not looking Upriver. She knew about the ambush. That much of Homat's story was obviously accurate.

"Please, de-Lyra, it would be so much better to make port at Changrit tonight. I can shop very cheaply at first light and we can—"

"Go astern, Irquit," Lyra ordered her sharply. "We're not tired or hungry, we don't need to stop for supplies, and we're going on tonight."

The guide started to object again, then thought better of it and followed the rail sternward. Etienne wondered what she'd tell Homat, whom she still thought of as a partner in deception, and how well Homat would hide his true feelings.

Then he made out a dim irregular shape off to port, through the transparency of the cockpit bubble, and he no longer could spare the time to worry about the Mai already on board. None of the four moons were aloft yet and the river ran clear and unslivered beneath the hydrofoil's keel.

A half dozen tiny objects appeared suddenly on the scanner, heading for the hydrofoil. "Spears, Lyra!"

She dropped to her belly on the foredeck, behind the metal dome over the heavy-duty fishing equipment. A couple of sharp points whanged off the bubble and he flinched involuntarily. They did no damage to the tough plastalloy.

Large shapes hove into view, lying where the scanner had predicted their presence. Etienne turned off the sensitive audio pickups. They weren't necessary. He could hear the shouting and excited hailing of the boat's crews quite clearly in the still night air.

Arrows and warcries followed the first volley of spears, then something long and heavy flew over the bow and clung there as Etienne turned sharply to port to avoid a small fishing barge filled with gesticulating, wide-eyed bowmen. Arrows splintered or glanced off the clear cockpit bubble, but the larger affront remained. It was a heavy fishing net attached to huge bolts which had evidently been fired by several catapults or large crossbows operating in unison. Several such nets, flung one atop the other, could seriously obscure his vision. He could still run on instruments, but not if the thick mesh was entangled in the engine nozzle.

Putting the hydrofoil on autopilot and entering evasive orders, he took his pistol from its charging socket near the pilot wheel and headed for the stern. Lyra met him halfway through the cabin.

"Who's driving?" she asked curtly.

"Multiple K."

"Not good enough. Too many boats." She eyed the weapon in his right hand. "I came down so I wouldn't have to do that."

"It's to burn that net, not Irquit."

"What net?"

"You'll see when you take over." He pushed past her, slipping the safety off the asynaptic pistol.

He was halfway to the foredeck when something buzzed him like an apoplectic wasp. The fast-moving, elegantly agile hydrofoil made it difficult for the Mai marksmen to aim but occasionally an arrow or spear would *spang* against the hull or whistle past overhead. Despite their inaccuracy, the sheer volume of primitive projectiles made moving around out on deck dangerous.

Dropping flat and utilizing the slight inward curve of the metal gunwale for protection, he crawled toward the bow. Once alongside the cockpit bubble he rose and carefully began burning away the net that covered the plastalloy.

The bow section was aerodynamic so there were few projections for the nets to catch onto, and he had half of the net cleared away before a sudden burning made him glance down at his left arm. A small stream of blood dripped from where a passing arrow had dug. Etienne made a mental note to ask Homat if the Upriver inhabitants ever used poisoned barbs in their fishing. He turned back to the work at hand.

Lyra appeared to be fully occupied with the task of steering them through their assailants while causing as little damage as possible. She was darting rapidly from side to side, working with unexpected animation. He frowned, leaned close to the bubble. Yes, she was very active, and so was the second figure she was grappling with.

The hydrofoil lurched abruptly to starboard and nearly threw him overboard. Only his grasp on the remaining Mai net kept him from a fatal dunking. As he struggled to his feet he identified the second figure in the cockpit: Irquit.

But that was impossible. Because of Homat's warning they made doubly sure to lock the cabin door every time either of them entered or left. Irquit should have been stuck outside, on the stern deck where she slept with Homat.

Lyra was heavier than the Mai and probably a good deal stronger, but if Homat was to be believed Irquit was a trained killer. Lyra's experience ran to more genteel pursuits. From what he could see, his wife was having a hard time fending off a wicked-looking blade. He shouted at her, aware as he did so how useless his words were.

Without Lyra at the instruments and with the autopilot turned off, the hydrofoil was beginning to slow. That was a safety override, designed to keep a boat with a disabled crew from running into the shore. As the whine of the jet faded, Etienne saw shapes begin to close in on them. They'd run past most of the Changrit armada, but were still near enough to be overtaken by determined oarsmen. He could hear them chanting in the dark as they strained to overhaul the spirit boat.

If they were allowed on board, asynapts wouldn't be enough to cope with the sheer weight of numbers. His first thought was to get back inside. He could lock any boarders out, and with their primitive weapons they couldn't break in, but they could certainly disable the engine or clog the water scoops.

Bowmen were close now and suddenly found themselves presented with a relatively stable target. They kept him pinned down by the fishing dome, unable to move through the shower of arrows.

Suddenly he saw a third shape inside the cockpit. For a moment he despaired. If Homat had lied to them, if he'd been a willing ally of Irquit's and of the Zanur all along— he screamed Lyra's name.

But if that were the case, then why the trembling expiation last night up on the telescope platform? As Etienne watched he saw Homat edge carefully around the pinwheeling combatants, climb up into the pilot's seat, put both six-fingered hands on the wheel and nudge the accelerator.

Again he found himself thrown to the deck, only this time it was due to the hydrofoil's sudden leap forward. Shouts of dismay and anger reached him from the two fishing boats that were almost within boarding range. Two Mai actually made the jump and landed aboard.

The asynapt flashed twice in the darkness. There was a brief bright blue flash where each charge struck flesh, the smell of ozone in the air, and a single splash as the first victim tumbled overboard. The second fell near Etienne's sweaty face, curved knife locked in a stilled grip.

Etienne scrambled erect and ran to the nearest entryway. When Irquit saw the other human enter the cabin she broke free and rushed astern, trailing curses in her wake. He just missed her in the main corridor, collided with Lyra instead. It was a timely collision, since his impact knocked her aside and clear of the knife that whistled past them.

He fired wildly and seared a section of ceiling, as a funny, high moan sounded from the direction of the cockpit. Homat fell away from the wheel as Lyra moved to help him.

Another pair of fishing nets clung to the boat, and Etienne

pushed a few tangles aside as he cautiously emerged on deck. Irquit was unarmed, however, except for her mouth. She snarled something that Etienne translated crudely as "Death to the Faceless One!" Whether the curse was aimed at Homat or himself he had no way of knowing and likely never would know, because their former guide and cook threw herself over the side and instantly vanished astern. No doubt her Changritite allies would fish her out of the river and send her on her way Downriver toward Po Rabi.

Etienne was gratified that they'd put their trust in Homat. Certainly he had burned his bridges behind him. There was no way the Mai could ever show his face in Po Rabi again.

If he didn't live, though, it wouldn't make any difference. Etienne remembered that surprised moan as Irquit's knife sailed past his ear. With the Changrit flotilla rapidly falling astern, he turned and hurried back into the cool interior of the hydrofoil.

The pilot's seat was unoccupied and he slid behind the wheel, made a fast check of the instruments. The scanner showed only a few small logs floating to starboard, in contrast to the thick cluster of shiplike shapes behind them. In a minute or two those distant threats would slip off the screen altogether.

Homat was lying on the floor moaning. Lyra had pulled the knife out and was working to stanch the bleeding. The weapon lay near her right leg, a very large blade to have struck so small a humanoid. A couple of centimeters to the left, and they'd have found themselves continuing their journey without either of their guides. Lyra had removed her halter and bound it over the hole. The halter's air-conditioning system was still operating full blast, and he thought to ask why when it occurred to him that the cold would promote coagulation. On rare occasions it struck him that he'd married a woman of more than average intelligence.

With the flow of blood slowed she disappeared astern, to return a moment later with a handful of vials and spray cans.

"I don't know how well this is going to work on you, Homat. It wasn't designed to be used on a Mai, but it's all we have and I don't know what else to try. Can you understand me?"

He nodded slowly, his small sharp teeth grinding together in pain.

"You're fully mammalian and from what I've been able to learn your physiology's close enough to ours so that—"

"Screw the biology lecture, Lyra!" her husband snapped.

She glanced sharply up at him, but this time only nodded. Her unvoiced admission of his rightness gave him no pleasure. He was too worried about Homat.

The freeze spray on top of the effect produced by her halter's cooler stopped the rest of bleeding. Homat gasped at the chill and tried not to look at the intimidating alien machines they were using on his body. Then she took a small curved device that cupped the curve of her palm, adjusted it carefully, and held it over the wound as she removed the bloodied halter. As she passed the device over his shoulder and upper chest it hissed softly. A faint bright yellow light poured from its underside.

Homat writhed in pain, but when she pulled her hand away and snapped off the surgiseal he could see that the cut had been closed completely, and sterilized in the bargain. There would be a permanent scar, but Lyra was no surgeon and there hadn't been time to consult the computer.

"Any poison?"

"No, de-Lyra," Homat whispered at her, staring at his chest in amazement. "A clean knife for a clean death." Etienne received this information with relief. His arm had ceased bleeding and now he could stop worrying about his own wound.

"You'll be all right now," Lyra assured their guide. "Just take it easy for a few days and try not to use that arm too much." He was shivering steadily and it occurred to her it wasn't from shock.

"He'll freeze in here, Etienne." The cabin thermometer registered a temperature of eighty degrees. "We've got to get him back out on deck."

"Go ahead, we're well clear now. I'll help you." He allowed the autopilot to resume control of the boat and moved to lift Homat in his arms. The slim Mai was a light burden and once he had been placed on his sleeping mat, Etienne turned back to the stern gangway. It didn't take long to discover how Irquit had made her way inside to attack Lyra. A small wad of *sikreg* gum, a local product Irquit employed to help thicken her stews and soups, had been jammed between the center seal and the door, preventing the lock from functioning.

Thoughtful of Irquit, to have made such a study of how the doorways operated. Undoubtedly she'd been studying hard ever since they'd departed Steamer Station. It was their own damned fault, Etienne told himself. They were going to have to cease thinking of the Mai as ignorant primitives.

The thought made him frown as he turned to stare at Homat. Their remaining guide was sitting up now, propped against the low bar of the railing that ran around the top of the gunwale. The Mai had operated their boat!

"That was very quick thinking of you, Homat. Taking control of the boat while Lyra was fighting with Irquit. Another couple of minutes and the Changritites might have overwhelmed us."

"Yes, I was standing here watching them close on us, de-Etienne, and I thought to wonder what was wrong. I saw the door there by your hand swinging open, and with heart in hand crept inside despite the cold to see what was the matter, for I knew we should not be slowing.

"I have watched for a long time now, through the round glass, as you and de-Lyra ran the spirit boat. While I still have no idea what controls the spirits that make it go, it is not hard to see how you control those spirits. I told you that Irquit thought she could do it, so I saw no reason why I also could not do so.

"You turn the wheel to change direction and push the little button to increase the speed."

Etienne relaxed a little. "Put that way it doesn't sound terribly complex, does it? How are you feeling?"

"Your wondrous tools have delighted my side. Much better, all thanks from my ancestors and me to you."

Etienne nodded. "Did you hear what your former companion said as she took her leave of us?"

"No." He gave a shaky Mai smile. "I can imagine it was not very polite."

"Not very. Enough to insure that you'd better never go within a dozen legats of Po Rabi again."

"I had already committed myself to that. Did you not believe me?"

Etienne looked uncomfortable. "It is hard on a strange world to know what to believe and what not to believe, Homat. Forgive me if I seem insensitive."

"Do not feel so, de-Etienne. They say that the people of Suphum do not pause for midday rest but work straight through 'til sundown. That is also hard to believe. Truly is the Everything filled with wonders. I do not regret my decision, though I might have had I died under Irquit's knife, may her flesh rot in the river. I do not need a home, now that I have you and de-Lyra as my friends and protectors."

"Don't worry, Homat. You'll have your reward when we get back to Steamer Station." Lyra was adjusting a clean halter top. "I don't care what the regulations say. We'll slip you something that should make you wealthy for life."

In true Mai fashion Homat instantly pointed to the interior of the boat. "That machine you used to heal me. Could I have one of those?"

Lyra laughed. She hadn't laughed like that in a long time, Etienne thought, surprised at how sharply it pierced him.

"The surgiseal would wear out before very long and you wouldn't be able to have it fixed, Homat. There's nothing worse than a magician whose magic unexpectedly deserts him. Don't worry, we'll find you something suitable that will last."

"I am not worried," Homat replied calmly. He moved his arm gingerly. "Truly a delightful instrument, though."

"Hadn't you better check the autopilot, Etienne?"

"We're okay. We're back out in the middle of the river and the scanner will sound if there's anything ahead it can't deal with. Maybe we ought to start thinking about replenishing our stores. Irquit was right about our being low." He looked down at Homat. "You're *positive* Po Rabi's influence doesn't extend any farther Upriver than Changrit?"

Homat sighed. Sometimes you had to tell this peculiar folk the same thing several times before they believed you.

"The next major trading town beyond Changrit is Kekkalong, de-Etienne. I have never been there but I know it thrives independent of any ocean-city's rule. It lies some three thousand legats north of Changrit."

Lyra did some fast mental calculating. "Five hundred kilometers. We can hold off that long. Since it's a major port, maybe we can tie up there for a couple of days, take a rest. I can do some intensive research. I'm certainly not going to have the chance to do any work in Changrit."

"A most delightful major port," Homat agreed. "Not as big as Po Rabi or Losithi, but nearly as large as Changrit. Beyond Kekkalong all is unknown country, unknown to me and to any living trader of Po Rabi. None have journeyed so far Upriver from the Groalamasan."

"Then you'll be the first," Etienne said. He turned apologetically to his wife. "Two of them got on board. I had to use the asynapt on them. There was no time to shoot to incapacitate, Lyra."

To his surprise she didn't bawl him out. Perhaps Irquit's assault had made her a tad less protective of the people she had come to study.

"Only two? That's not bad. Probably not enough to start a blood feud with the Changritites."

"That's good, because when we return we might have to deal with the same situation all over again."

"Our return's a long ways away yet, Etienne. We'll worry about it months from now. By that time the Changritites may have grown bored with watching the river and sent Irquit on her way. At least we won't have to watch for any on-board threats." She glanced down at Homat, who was rubbing his miraculously healed shoulder.

"I apologize for doubting your story, Homat."

"No, no, no reason to apologize, de-Lyra. I would have doubted you if in your place. Doubt is healthy."

She stared out into the damp night. Occasionally a light from a house on shore would flash dimly in the distance, like a star. All was calm and quiet.

"I'm beginning to think that it is," she murmured softly.

〖 VI 〗

Kekkalong turned out to be all that Homat had promised.
A natural harbor had been scooped from the shore of the
Skar by powerful currents. As they entered, small fishing
boats and pleasure craft clustered like whirligig beetles in
the hydrofoil's wake.

As was the style in the great oceanic cities, half the buildings were contructed below the surface, the other half above.
There was the expected profusion of tall, thin towers. Unlike
the structures of ancient human cities, which they superficially resembled, these narrow cylinders reached deep into
the earth. Some served to convey cool water to the surface
while others allowed hot air to rise from the town's subter-
ranean levels. The Mai flourished in a brutally hot climate,
but they enjoyed a cool breeze as much as a human, even
if their idea of a cool breeze was a gust of damp air at ninety
degrees.

The townsfolk were friendly and did their best to restrain
their curiosity about their tall, hairy visitors. As Kekkalong
was ruled not by a single Moyt but by a coalition of merchants, there was something of a respite from the over-

powering urge to compete that drove the inhabitants of the southern cities. Lyra took notes as fast as she could address her recorder.

With the loss of Irquit, Homat's bargaining abilities were brought to the fore, and he proved himself an adequate replacement. As soon as he overcame his ingrained shyness he proved quite adroit at dickering for supplies in the marketplace.

They were walking through the central market, buying samples of the local carvings for their stock of primitive specimens, when Lyra called to her husband. As usual he'd left the trading to her and Homat, being more interested in the stones that had been used to pave the street.

"What is it? Lyra, did you know that some of this might have been quarried out of a pegmatite dike?"

"Sure I did," she replied sardonically, "but I'll try to forget it for now. Come over and listen to something."

She stood before a very old Mai. Trying to muster some interest, Etienne observed that the wrinkles on the Mai face formed whorls with age instead of lines.

"Only two hundred legats up the Skar," the oldster declaimed, "lies the place where it is joined by the great Aurang."

"He says," Lyra told him, usurping the old one's tale, "that the Tsla have a major town not far up the Aurang."

Etienne eyed her uncertainly. "How far is not far?" She gave him a figure in legats and he converted the native measurement in his head. "Between eight and nine hundred kilometers. That's a hell of a 'not far.' Our itinerary calls for us to follow the Skar to its origin, mapping and taking notes along the way. Nothing was said about making any major detours."

"It would give us the chance to study a wholly new race, Etienne, examine an entirely different culture. We have to make contact with the Tsla sooner or later."

"I thought the plan was 'later.'"

"But it's such a wonderful opportunity! I'm told the Tsla build very few centers and that this Turput is one of the main ones."

"It would still mean a radical change in our plans," he argued. "Lyra, not a day's gone by since we set down on this world that you haven't been able to wallow in your work, whereas I'm still waiting to reach the point where the Barshajagad narrows enough for me to do some serious research and studies in *my* specialty."

"If we go to this Turput, you'll have that chance, Etienne. They can't live in the river valley." She exchanged some rapid-fire chatter with the oldster. "His description of Turput's location fits what we've learned about their ecological niche. Turput's at least three thousand meters above the Skar. Apparently the Aurang hasn't cut nearly as deep a canyon. You should be able to dive into your studies sooner if we visit Turput than if we avoid it."

He considered carefully. "I know that we're supposed to make detailed studies of the Tsla as well as the Mai, but the plan was to do that during our return journey, after we'd attained the other major objectives."

"Etienne, my primary interest in coming here is to see how several entirely different cultures coexist side by side in separate habitation zones. To do this I need to observe how the Tsla live and react to the Mai."

"Can't it wait until we're on our way back?"

"We *owe* ourselves the detour. At three thousand meters above sea level the temperature will drop at least forty degrees from what it is here on the Skar, with a corresponding fall in humidity. For the first time since touchdown we can slip into real clothes and dispense with air conditioning. Doesn't that interest you?"

He had to admit that it did, but there were other factors she hadn't mentioned, possibly by design.

"From what this old one said, Lyra, Turput lies only eight hundred kilometers upstream from where the Aurang enters the Skar, right?" She nodded. "Okay. That means climbing three thousand meters up the canyonside over a short distance. Too steep a slope for the boat to navigate and too far to run on repellers."

Lyra pointed to the old trader. "Ossanj says there's a decent-size town at the confluence of the two rivers, called Aib. He says we might hire them to watch the hydrofoil as well as find porters to ferry supplies up to Turput."

"Really? Does he happen to have any relatives in Changrit?"

"Etienne!" She sighed with exasperation. "We're far beyond Changrit's influence. You know that."

"Maybe so. Pardon me if I seem excessively cautious. It's just that we haven't done so well where local help's been involved."

"Come on! You know we can take enough precautions to insure the safety of the boat."

"Granted that we can, I'm still not sure I'm ready for a three-thousand-meter hike. That's going to make hash of our itinerary."

"Our itinerary's not graven in stone, Etienne. If the weather's bad when we come back down the river we might not be able to make the climb at all. We can't pass on the chance. The weather's favorable *now*. Surely we can hire some kind of local transport so we don't have to make the entire climb on foot." She turned back to the trader. "Tell him about Turput, Ossanj."

"A most delighted wondrous place," declared the oldster. "Mysterious are the workings of the Tsla." He made a gesture to protect himself from any interested spirits. "Their fields climb the sides of mountains. They grow there delighted fruits and vegetables that wither here by the river."

"How do you know all this, Ossanj? I thought the lands of the Tsla too cold for your people to tolerate."

"With much clothing to keep warm, we can visit there for short times."

"And we'll be comfortable, Etienne," Lyra added encouragingly. "Doesn't that sound inviting?"

"Not as inviting as continuing Upriver."

"But that's just my point. Here's a chance for you to see some real topography."

"Lyra, I'm sick of river valley, you know that. But we ought to stick to our itinerary."

She drew away from him. "I see," she said coldly. "Fine. You continue Upriver with Homat. I'll take enough of the trade goods to tide me over until you return and I'll go up to Turput myself. Meet you on the way back."

He sighed. "Lyra, you know that's no good. What about the cultures Upriver from here? Am I supposed to do your fieldwork as well as my own?"

She shrugged. "Okay, then take a month or two and go

where you wish, study what you want, and come back for me. But I'm going to Turput tomorrow, Etienne, while I have the opportunity and while the weather's good."

"Damn you," he said quietly. "You know the dangers in splitting up. You get your way, as usual. I'll come with you. But I won't like it and you'll have to listen to me bitch about it all the way up the canyon."

"I'll suffer it." She smiled triumphantly at him. "Consider it serendipity instead of an enforced detour. Many important discoveries are made because of serendipity."

"Bullshit. You've just decided that you want to go *now*."

That prompted a glare that chilled the air in the market-place. She didn't speak to him for the rest of the afternoon.

Homat would have voted for staying on the river. Though he had eaten the produce the Tsla traded with the river dwellers and had heard much of their marvelous accomplishments, he'd never seen one and didn't care if he ever did. He thought that de-Etienne should have argued more powerfully with his mate, and if that had failed, given her orders. But it would seem that male–female relationships among the off-worlders were very different from those among the Mai. He spent a whole morning making signs and attempting to propitiate the proper spirits before they set off Upriver once again.

It wasn't long before the hydrofoil's instrumentation warned them of the approaching confluence of the Skar and the Aurang. Ahead, the Skar executed a sharp bend westward while the Aurang flowed into the main river from out of the north. Given the Aurang's immense flow and orientation, anyone not knowing which was which would have proceeded up the tributary, thinking it the Skar.

Making landfall on the eastern shore of the river just above the town of Aib, they dispatched Homat to inquire about the availability of transportation and porters. Despite the high rate of pay offered, engaging help turned out to be difficult.

"They are reluctant to leave their homes to travel to the land of the Tsla," Homat explained.

"Why is that?" Lyra inquired. "I thought that trade went on daily between Tsla and Mai, and has since ancient times."

"That is truth," Homat agreed. Behind them, fisherfolk

and farmers gathered curiously around the anchored hydro-foil, engaging in the usual futile hunt for sails and oars. "But that does not mean that the Mai are anxious to go up there." He held up something oval that resembled a cross between a grapefruit and a sick lime.

"This is a *gououn*. It cannot grow below the level of Turput." He bit into the shiny-skinned fruit with gusto and spit out several purple seeds. "This and much else can be grown by the Tsla alone. This makes many Mai fearful of them. And there are other things." He made hasty protective signs.

"The Tsla trade with the Mai, but they also trade with the Na of the Guntali."

"Then they're *not* rumors," said Lyra with excitement.

"Oh no, very real, de-Lyra. Too real." He shuddered. "Skins of strange creatures they bring down from the Guntali, and much *serash*." Etienne knew *serash* to be the word for the local equivalent of ivory.

"We Mai never see the Na, for we would freeze in moments in their lands. Their air is difficult to breathe and we would grow dizzy with fear.

"But some will come for hire. There are always some who will come, if the pay is sufficient," he said with assurance. "I wish muchly though, my *des*, that you did not have to leave the spirit boat behind." He looked at the curious to make sure they weren't being overheard.

"Aib is little better than a large village. The Oyts of such towns have few morals. Better to have left it behind in Kek-kalong."

Etienne made the Mai movement for negation, glanced sourly at his wife. "We're already taking too much time out of our schedule for this side trip, Homat. Leaving the boat at Kekkalong would've cost us several weeks of overland travel. Don't worry though. The spirit boat will be quite safe until we return."

Homat looked doubtful, still watching the crowd. "I cannot dissuade you, friends from across the ocean of night, but I do not think this a wise decision. Even the porters I have hired have come down to us from Upriver and not from Aib. I fear treachery."

"Relax. We'll have our weapons with us. No one's going

to bother the boat in our absence. You'll see." He indicated the fishing dock where they'd tied up. "Has not the Oyt of Aib promised us that he'll keep the dock sealed off and all the curious away? None will be permitted to come near and he's said he'll utilize his personal guard to insure that. We're paying him a handsome amount to see to it that any locals stay clear."

"The sum is not so handsome as the spirit boat itself," Homat grumbled. "As for the guard he will post here, would that it had come from Kekkalong. Still, if you are satisfied, Homat is satisfied." There was no satisfaction in his tone, however. He found it a struggle to understand these peculiar creatures. In many ways they were unimaginably sophisticated and in others, childishly naive.

"We know what we're doing, Homat."

"Could you not at least take it a safe distance up the Aurang?"

"And dock it in the middle of the river, exposed to unknown currents and high winds?" Lyra asked. "It's safer here. Besides, anyone who wanted to find it could do so just as easily a few dozen legats up the Aurang. We'll worry about our property, Homat, and you worry about the cooking and the guiding."

"As you say, de-Lyra."

In truth, he greatly enjoyed giving orders to the half dozen porters. It was the first time in his life he'd been able to exercise any power over his fellow Mai. Power gave rise to wealth, to new knowledge and capabilities. Power was the measure of an adult. He enjoyed himself so much he managed to forget his fears about the safety of the spirit boat.

The Oyt of Aib, a bucolic youth named Gwattwe who fancied himself something of a dandy, personally saw them safely on their way. He had his own spirit doctor cast a spell for their healthy return.

From Aib they would ride on lowagons northward until they encountered the Aurang's southerly flow, then turn northeast following the trading trail into the highlands.

"May you return in delighted safety," Gwattwe told them. "As one who has traded often with the Tsla, I would go with you myself to serve as guide and interpreter, but a village Oyt must watch over his people."

"We understand," Lyra assured him. "We know that you'll take good care of our property."

"Have I not sworn the oath?" Gwattwe looked injured. "Have I not given promise upon my mate and children and most of all, my fortune? Not to mention that I do not receive the second half of payment until you return."

I trust *that*, Etienne thought as he listened to the Mai's speech, more than any other assurance. Among the Mai, money was as blood.

As they turned to enter the waiting lowagons a bored-looking chorus of small children launched into an irritatingly atonal chant of farewell. They kept it up until the little line of porter-driven lowagons had moved beyond the first bend in the road, then scattered before the blows their chorus master dispensed impartially.

Gwattwe watched the strange visitors depart, then turned glittering eyes to the dock where the hydrofoil bobbed lazily at anchor, tethered to the landing by two wondrously strong metal cables.

"What do you think on all this, wise Enaromeka?"

The spirit doctor eyed the alien craft thoughtfully. "Give them six days before taking possession, Gwattwe."

"My purse itches feverishly. I don't know that I can wait six days."

"Better caution than confrontation. I do not think they suspect, but it would be awkward if they were to double back along the road to see what we were doing. Patience. We shall be masters of all the Skar. Even the oceanic states will do us homage... *if* we can make the spirit boat obey us."

"Even if we cannot," Gwattwe said, "we can make the hairy ones pay a huge ransom for its safe return. If they refuse, surely there are many items of great value within the craft that can be removed and sold. These are no wizards, no gods come among us, Enaromeka. Lightning does not fly from their fingers, no matter what the Downriver rumor-mongers would have us believe, and the rocks do not shake beneath their tread. They are like unto the Mai, save for their size and hairiness, and they have fewer fingers and toes to drive them through life. If cut, I am sure they would bleed,

[77]

and if they bleed, they will die. I understand them, and I think with care we can come to understand their spirit boat.

"Besides," he added with a smile, "they will be gone long to the city of the Tsla and long returning. We will have ample time to study and experiment with their vessel."

"It shall be a legendary triumph for you, Gwattwe," the spirit doctor declaimed with becoming unctuousness.

"And for you also, my good friend and advisor, for to you falls the honor of extracting the secrets of the spirit boat."

Enaromeka suddenly felt ill. "What? To me?"

"Are you not the smartest of the Aib?"

"The cleverest, but you, great Oyt, are the smartest."

"Your flattery is unnecessary. I know when I am beyond my depth."

Enaromeka looked resigned. "It will truly be a delightful great honor. I will enlist the aid of my most precocious students. In time, we will learn all that can be learned."

They observed and measured, discussed and debated for six long days. By that time Gwattwe was trembling with impatience to step aboard and claim possession of the spirit boat for Aib and his family line. Word filtered through the town that the day of Taking had arrived and many of the villagers put aside their daily chores to gather on shore above the dock. All wished to partake of their community's triumph, for all would benefit by the successful "repossession," as the town adjudicator had described it in a moment of florid rationalization.

The power and wealth that accrued to Aib would be shared by all, and the name of Aib known all along the river.

Enaromeka made certain everyone heard him clearly. "I claim the honor of being the first aboard." Gwattwe responded with a gesture of deference. This was as rehearsed and part payment to the spirit doctor for his services.

The gunwale was bumping gently against the wooden dock as he stepped gingerly over the side onto the exposed rear deck. Nothing happened. Enaromeka turned a slow circle, looking quite pleased with himself until a voice rumbled in perfect if slightly stiff Mai:

"Visitor, you do not belong on this boat. No permission for visitation has been granted. You have twenty *anats* in which to vacate this boat or you will suffer dire consequences. You have been warned."

Enaromeka stood as if paralyzed, while Gwattwe blinked and tried to see through the transparent bubble enclosing the cockpit. The warriors arranged nearby forgot their positions as they searched the windows for the invisible speaker. So did Enaromeka's assistants.

There was no sign of life within the boat. Nothing moved beyond the transparencies and the boat itself continued to bob on the breath of the current.

Enaromeka overcame his initial panic and moved cautiously to where he could look down into the boat. "I see no one."

"Nor do I," Gwattwe said from the dock.

"I will go inside and look." Enaromeka reached for the door handle and pulled. "I can't move it."

"That is to be expected," said Gwattwe. "It is not to be anticipated that they would trust us enough to leave their vessel unlocked. Would a long knife help?"

Enaromeka put his face to the window that comprised the upper half of the doorway. "It is strong. Little lights inside are blinking on and off, like the fires of hunting parties up the side of the canyon. Perhaps the lights have something to do with the lock. Fire spirits. Give me a *zhaloo*."

From within the ranks of warriors a heavy spiked club was passed forward. One of the spirit doctor's students handed it across to Enaromeka.

"Five *anats*," the voice announced dangerously. "Leave this boat *now*."

"I know what it is," Enaromeka declared suddenly, unwilling to abandon his moment of glory to an unseen specter. "A spirit voice locked within the boat, left here to frighten us." He spoke boldly. "I, Enaromeka, am not frightened by spirits. I will learn the secrets of this craft despite all the voices that shout at me. I am not afraid of voices!"

Taking careful aim with the club, he brought it down over the transparency covering the blinking lights. A brilliant explosion of light momentarily blinded the watching crowd and there was much screaming. Women and children fled for the safety of boulders and sun shelters. Several of the warriors lined up in stately procession along the dock broke formation to sample the cool waters of the Skar. Gwattwe had enough presence of mind to note their names and former rank.

When his sight had recovered somewhat from the effects of the unexpected flash, he turned back to the spirit boat. It still rode easily on its lines. Curled up on the rear deck was the object that an instant earlier had been his spirit doctor. Smoke rose from the skull and sides of the fetal shape while the leather sandals burned ferociously.

One of Enaromeka's students jumped onto the boat. Gwattwe held his breath but nothing happened to the scholar as he beat at the fire consuming his instructor's feet. With great presence of mind, the student yelled instructions. There was movement among the onlookers. A bucket was located, filled with river, and carefully handed over.

As the student dumped the water on Enaromeka's corpse, a solemn voice intoned, "Visitor, you do not belong on this boat. No permission for visitation has been granted. You have twenty *anats* in which to vacate this boat or you will suffer dire consequences. You have been warned."

"I'm not leaving!" the student announced, making a sign to ward off the most dangerous of unknown spirits. Reaching down, he picked up the ineffectual *zhaloo*, hefted it angrily as he moved toward the doorway that had defeated his instructor.

Gwattwe was not as surprised by the light this time. The student was barefoot, and the water in which he stood did not protect him from the fire spirits. His departure from existence was much more spectacular than Enaromeka's. Swallowed by the burst of energy, he gave a tremendous convulsive twitch and leaped or was thrown over the side of the craft.

Two warriors reluctantly doffed their armor and dove into the river to pull him ashore. Gwattwe examined the student's body with much interest. It was broken and distorted, though differently from Enaromeka's. The soles of his feet had been carbonized and black streaks ran up both legs. The smell of burnt flesh was strong in the morning air.

But there had been no fire, only a burst of light and a loud crackling sound. Pungiram, one of the elders of Aib, had come down onto the dock.

"It would appear, my Oyt Gwattwe, that the hairy strangers are not so dumb as they first seemed."

"So it would appear." Gwattwe showed no distress at having been abruptly deprived of the services of his spirit doctor. He eyed the boat with more interest than ever. "In this first test of trust and friendship, they have come out ahead. But I am persistent, old one. There must be some way to drive the protecting spirit out of this boat so that we can take possession of it."

Pungiram decided to speak up. "You will not find many ready to do battle with unknown spirits, especially spirits that slay as efficiently as do those guarding this boat."

"I am not afraid of spirits," Gwattwe said as he hastened to shield himself with a couple of quickly executed signs, "that are of this world, but it is a new thing to try to deal with a spirit that comes from beyond. However, I am not so sure that we are dealing with a spirit here. This boat is a thing of metal and other strange substances. It is not a proper spirit house."

"Do we have any idea what other spirits consider a proper abode?"

"Perhaps we may learn. I will not give up and walk back to my house." His gaze rose, turned to the trade road which had swallowed up the tall hairy ones. "A long way to Turput, a long way back. We have much time left to us."

The surviving students had clustered around the Oyt. He frowned at them. "What ails you?"

"We must do something about the Teacher." The speaker gestured toward Enaromeka's blackened body. "He must be given a proper burial."

"He must have his wood and his journey to the sea," another insisted.

"I agree," Gwattwe said. "Which of you will honor him by being the first to step onto the spirit boat to remove the body?"

Rapid glances were passed among the scholars. They decided it would be best to discuss the matter in depth before making any firm decisions. They drifted away toward the town, arguing vociferously among themselves.

His peace and quiet restored, Gwattwe again considered the object of his dreams. He had never been to any of the wondrous city-states that traders told of, had traveled only a short distance Downriver. But he'd visited Kekkalong and had admired its wealth. The spirit boat was no more than another new thing to be studied and understood, as he had come to understand power and wealth. He would make a massive effort to be patient. He would have to be or he would quickly run out of advisors.

He would make a speech praising brave Enaromeka. Then everyone would go back to work. Tomorrow he would consider the problem anew. That was all that was required; careful thought and sufficient tomorrows.

But he would have to cajole as well as order his advisors. The odor of a colleague's burning flesh was a powerful deterrent to curiosity.

〖 VII 〗

"De-Etienne, de-Etienne, we must stop and rest!"

Etienne halted, staring ahead to where the trading road climbed still another of the endless vertical walls in a series of laboriously cut switchbacks. The roar of the Aurang cataract was a constant buzz in his ears, even though it was out of sight far off to their left.

"We're nearly there, Homat. I don't want to spend another night on the road. Tell them no."

"It does not matter, de-Etienne." Homat gestured at the line of heavily laden porters behind them. "They say they will go not a step farther until they are given time to put on their warmest clothing."

Etienne made a face as he checked his wrist instrumentation. The air temperature was eighty-four and holding. Despite that, several of the porters made no attempt to hide their discomfort, and two were shivering. For his part, Homat was manfully trying to hide the chills that wracked his own body.

"Very well, but tell them to be quick about it. I want to reach Turput before dark."

"We should, we should, de-Etienne," Homat said grate-fully. He turned and relayed the information to the porters. They responded with a babble of thanks, dropping their packs with fine disregard for the contents in their rush to help one another on with heavy coats and hats.

Lyra watched with interest. It was strange to see a Mai clad in long-sleeved and long-legged attire. The cold-climate gear was made of double layered cottonlike fiber stuffed with some puffy plant material.

"In the land of the blind the one-eyed man is king," Lyra murmured.

"I don't see how that relates to our present situation," Etienne commented.

"In the land of the bald, the hirsute man is king."

"That's a lousy analogy."

"You never did have much of a sense of humor." She turned away from him.

The distant Skar was now only a faint silver thread lying against the western horizon. A considerable walk indeed. The fact that the air at three thousand meters was almost Earth-normal was a great comfort. Down on the Skar, they'd been forced to breathe mud. Or so their lungs had persist-ently told them.

The thinner air did not seem to have troubled the porters, but the drop in temperature had been affecting their perfor-mance for several days. Bundled up in their heavy clothing, they looked much more comfortable.

Etienne had to admit that he was enjoying himself. The multicolored strata they passed as they made the ascent were an unending source of wonderment. Tslamaina was an an-cient world, and its entire history lay exposed within the canyon walls. He wished only that he could see across the canyon, but at the confluence of the Aurang and the Skar it was still well over a thousand kilometers wide.

At least the road had been wide and clear, with no rough places, and they'd encountered few of the vertical walls with their leg-straining switchbacks. Wind and water had turned the steep walls here to a manageable slope.

For the first time he could see the edge of the Guntali Plateau, revealed in the distance from time to time when the high clouds cleared. The uneven rocky rim rose another three thousand meters higher than Turput, sharply defining the original surface of the planet.

At this altitude the *strepanong*, *dorril*, and *malming* became more than distant circling dots, their enormous soaring shapes resolving into living creatures with five- to eight-meter wingspans. The great scavengers rode the superheated air that rose from the floor of the Barshajagad and rarely scoured below the two-thousand-meter line. This according to the porters, who were nonetheless terrified of them.

They'd climbed past the last Mai village days ago and since then had seen only an occasional solitary hunting party swathed in heavy clothing. Etienne was enjoying the comparative silence.

"Billions of years," he murmured. "That's how long it took the rivers to cut those canyons."

Lyra turned from her study of the porter's cold weather gear to grin knowingly at him. "Then you're glad we made the detour?"

He was still unwilling to grant her the small triumph. "Certainly it's more interesting than the section of the Barshajagad we left, but I'd still prefer that we'd kept to our original itinerary."

"Can't give in gracefully, can you? You can't ever let me win. Why can't you admit when you're wrong?"

"I will, when I am wrong."

"Sure. You're the stubbornest man I've ever met, Etienne."

"Then why did you marry me?"

"Always the same question. Always testing, never content. One of these days I'm going to..." she turned and walked away, mumbling to herself. She always stopped before finishing that sentence, for which he was grateful. Or at least, it used to be that he was grateful. Ten years now she'd put off finishing that sentence.

Homat hurried up alongside him as they resumed their climb. "The porters pass on their gratefulness. They are still cold but it leaves their bones."

"Should be warm enough," Etienne snapped, unaware of the sharpness of his tone. "Took them damn near an hour to change clothes."

"They are not used to such cold, de-Etienne." Homat

tugged at the rim of his own hood, trying to cover as much of his bald pate as possible. "Nor am I. They dressed as rapidly as they could." He tried to see into Etienne's eyes. "Truly, you and de-Lyra are not cold?"

The geologist wore modified lederhosen and a heavier shirt over his mesh briefs. "Not only that, Homat, I'm still on the warm side."

Homat considered this. "Our bodies do not appear so very different, de-Etienne, and while you and de-Lyra have more fur, much of you still is bare skin, as are our bodies. I would not think that you would still be warm here."

"Different environments induce difference adaptations, Homat."

"Truly," Homat confessed.

"If you're through lording it over the natives," Lyra said in terranglo from her position farther up the road, "maybe we can make a little progress before nightfall?"

"I wasn't 'lording it,'" he shot back angrily, "I was just explaining to Homat that—" but she'd already turned away from him to resume her climb. When she did that it made him mad enough to spit wood. Short of grabbing her and forcing her to listen to him, however, there was little he could do, and he didn't want to engage in a shouting match in front of the porters. So he swallowed his anger, convinced it would go straight to the ulcer he was building in his gut, the painful cavity that had his wife's name written all over it.

It was early evening when they finally crested the last ridge overlooking Turput. Neither of them knew what to expect. A smaller version of Kekkalong, perhaps. They were pleasantly surprised.

Neat narrow streets paved with gray flagstone ran down to the fast moving Aurang and continued on the far shore. Both banks were lined with wooden water wheels that turned steadily in the swift current. Instead of the blocky Mai architecture they'd come to associate with civilization on Tslamaina, they saw buildings designed with flowerlike domes and elegant arches. Graceful winding walls connected the main structures, and fluted slate tiles drained rainwater from the roofs. Small observation towers bloomed amid the larger edifices. Excepting the towers, nothing rose higher than three floors.

Above the town the Aurang split into a series of gentle cataracts where dim figures worked with long fish sweeps. Terraces heavy with fruit bushes stepped toward heaven. At the far end of the formation Etienne identified as a hanging valley, a wide waterfall crashed into the riverbed.

Most magical of all were the sounds made by the profusion of bells and wind chimes that inhabited every house and shop, dangled from windows and rafters and projecting beams. The tinkling and clanging and bonging were audible even above the rush of the Aurang. There were bells of metal and ceramic, of glass and clay and wood, bone bells and stone chimes.

"Isn't it magnificent, Etienne?" Behind Lyra Homat made an impolite noise while Etienne elected to reserve judgment. Alien beauty could be deceptive.

"Very aesthetic appearance," he grudgingly admitted. But he found it hard to resist the multicolored town after the bland whites and yellows of Mai communities. It seemed as if every building in Turput was painted a different color. The town, like the air above it, was alive with rainbows.

They started down the ridge. As they neared the town they saw one could enter from any direction without encountering an obstruction. There was a single small gate, an afterthought of wooden logs and planks. One could walk around it as easily as through it. It also offered them their first Tsla.

Lyra and Etienne were not familiar with Tsla characteristics and so could not tell how old he was, but both scientists received an impression of age. In height he stood midway between Etienne's and Lyra's. The resemblance between Tsla and human, and for that matter between Tsla and Mai, ended there.

His toga-and-cape attire could not conceal the fact that he was covered everywhere save on the forearms and forelegs with a short, soft brown fur. The head rested on a neck that was curved forward, giving a false impression of age. Ears were short round stubs set atop the head. The six fingers were shorter and stubbier than those of Mai or human while the eyes displayed a dewy luster.

Most prominent of all the facial features was the quarter-meter long flexible snout like that of the terran tapir. It bobbed and dipped with an independent life of its own, no doubt conveying subtleties of expression discernible only to another Tsla. Twin nostrils were visible through the fur at the tip.

It strained Etienne's laboriously memorized Tsla to translate the Tsla's greeting. "I am Sau, Keeper of the Gate of Hospitality." To Etienne's relief the Tsla switched to fluent Mai. "Word of thy coming has preceded thee. You are the visitors said to come from another world."

Lyra nodded sagely. Her affinity for languages reached far beyond Etienne's, and she wasn't hesitant about trying the local dialect. "We are they, Keeper. Your gate must be of hospitality, for it protects nothing but air."

"A conceit." The Tsla spread both hands to the air, showing bare skin up to the elbow. "Most visitors seem to expect a gate, so one was made. Higher towns than Turput have need of real gates. We do not."

The language of the Tsla was slow and languorous, a startling contrast to the fast-paced singsong of the Mai. Etienne found himself impatient for the Keeper to continue.

"Thee are welcome here. We hope that thy visit will honor us."

Polite, open, with none of the double meanings the Mai attached to such phrases of greeting. Despite his initial reservations Etienne found himself developing a fondness for the Tsla. There was a graciousness about this creature no Mai had displayed, not even the obsequious Ambassador Ror de-Kelwhoang of Po Rabi.

"Follow me and I will take you to a place of rest. Thy friends," he added with a barely perceptible hint of distaste as he indicated the porters, "are also welcome."

"Most generous of thee," Lyra replied properly as the Tsla turned to lead them into the town.

Their escort kept up a fair pace, moving with deliberation so as not to tire the visitors. Instead of lifting each foot and then setting it ahead and down, the Tsla moved with a gait more shuffle and slide. The cape covering the creature's broad back was dark brown split by a single yellow stripe running down the middle. This simple motif was present on the toga as well. Etienne found himself unexpectedly pleased by the sight of another intelligent creature with hair. Baldness was the norm not only among the Mai but the thranx as well.

After they entered the town, each Tsla they encountered marked their passage by duplicating the Keeper's raising of hands, as if they were caressing the air. The Mai muttered among themselves and packed into a tight knot behind the humans. Etienne wondered at their paranoia, which was typically Mai. There was no suggestion of treachery here.

Clusters of Tsla children followed a polite distance behind, wiggling curious stubs of snouts as they took the scent of the peculiar strangers. Before too long the Keeper halted outside a long barnlike building with a gently curving roof. It resembled a broken olla set on its side against the earth.

"This is the Trade Place," one of the porters said. "I was here once before, though I did not stay long."

The Keeper beckoned them to enter. Inside it was dark and cool. Off to the right they found a row of interconnected chambers with skylights set into the curving ceiling. The glass was well-fashioned, with few bubbles. It was a good twenty degrees warmer in the room than it had been out in the hallway.

"For thy friends," the Keeper announced, "and for thee as well if you so desire."

"No, thanks." Etienne watched the Mai pile joyfully into the big room and stand with their faces turned up to the sunlight. They divested themselves of their burdens without being told. "I think we'd prefer the type of room you use yourselves."

"As thee wish." The Keeper took them back out into the hall and led them farther into the building to a smaller room full of the aroma of fresh incense.

"If this suits thee, I must leave now."

"It suits," Etienne said.

Lyra was running a hand over the near wall. "Look at this, Etienne. The entire inside wall is glazed, like a big pot!"

He let his fingers touch the slick surface. "Watertight and cool in summer, reflects the heat of a fire in winter." The single skylight did not trap the heat as did those in the porters' room. A window at eyelevel allowed a view outside to the paved street.

After a time a second Tsla joined them. He was taller than the Keeper and stood a little straighter while still displaying the curved upper spine. He wore a similar toga and cape arrangement, but this one was black with two gold stripes dividing it.

"I am Tyl. I have the honor to be thy host and guide during thy visit to Turput." He made no secret of his own curiosity regarding the strangers. "Anything thee wish thee have but to ask and if it can be provided it will."

"We can't stay long," Etienne replied, chosing to ignore his wife's radiant expression. She was in xenosociological heaven. "We left our boat down on the Skar and we have to return there soon."

"Never mind that now. Tyl, we want to see everything we can. It's true we have little time, but I want to learn as much as possible about thy people and their customs, their way of life. That is my job."

"Worthy scholarship," said Tyl. He had an unexpectedly deep voice that came rolling out in breathy, rounded syllables from beneath the flexible snout. "If thy time is constrained thee must listen close as well as look. Tomorrow, if arrangements can be made, I will take thee to the temple of Moraung Motau."

"Maybe we'd like to see something else first."

"Etienne! Don't be impolite. You've been too long among the Mai. I swear, you're starting to act like a riverfront merchant."

He was too tired to bicker with her, simply turned away and examined the wall while she continued to converse with Tyl.

"If thee prefer," their host said, "there is a little time left to the day. We could begin now."

"Not on your—thy—life." Etienne headed for a padded bench that obviously was designed to serve as a couch or bed or both. "I'm worn out."

"Well I'm not," Lyra snapped. "You may show me around if thee wish, Tyl."

"My greatest honor."

Etienne thought of a suitably sarcastic rejoinder but found

it hard to find a reason for spiting the Tsla's courtesy. He said nothing as they departed. The sound of chimes and bells was like a sedative and the couch-bed surprisingly comfortable. Before he knew it he was sound asleep.

Light from a candle set in a glass dish on a high shelf awakened him. No doubt it had been lit carefully while he slept by some conscientious servitor.

"Wake up, I said."

He rolled over, found himself staring up at his wife's excited face. He rubbed tiredly at his heavy eyes. "What is it?"

"Etienne, Tyl took me through half the town, by torchlight. The system of government these people have developed is unique to sentients in this technological classification! These Tsla are a xenological wonder. Do you know that the spiritual administrators—and they're not priests, more the equivalent of primitive psychoanalysts—actually hold half the seats of government?"

"That's interesting." He began to roll over but she put a hand out to restrain him. He looked irritatedly back over his shoulder.

"Etienne, *listen* to me! This social structure is unprecedented. This is a presteam civilization, yet the people are socially advanced enough to pay extraordinary attention to something as sophisticated as mental health. They don't define it quite like that, of course, but it comes out the same. They may be the stablest primitive alien society yet encountered, and they do this without holding any unwarranted illusions about themselves.

"No wonder the Mai fear and suspect them! The Tsla are so much better balanced. The Tsla have come to terms with the health of their minds earlier than most peoples do with the condition of their bodies. Even Martinson's work on Alaspin is proof of it. This discovery, Etienne, it's worth all the trouble of making the expedition." She stood and began to pace the room.

"The Tsla are special, unique. There's more than a chip monograph here, there's an entire volume."

"I'm thrilled for you." He let out a helpless yawn. "Do keep in mind that we have half a river left to explore."

She started to comment, changed her mind in midthought.

"You're exhausted, Etienne. We'll discuss this in the morning."

"You should be exhausted too."

"I know, but I can't hold back the enthusiasm. I'm running on adrenalin, Etienne, and I have to share this with someone. Who else if not you?" She hesitated and added in an odd tone of voice, "Tyl would be interested."

"Tyl strikes me as a good listener." Etienne pulled the light blanket up around his neck.

"He is, and a good talker as well. From all I was able to discern he's regarded very well by his fellow Tsla. I watched him perform his evening *prann*. Beneath all those robes and cloaks they wear, some of these people are very impressive physical specimens, Etienne. Much more impressive than the Mai."

"Makes sense. The climate up here's less benign and working steep terraces requires more strength than tending to a floodplain."

"Yes. Much more in the way of physical strength," she murmured.

"I'm glad you had such a profitable evening. Now if you don't mind, I really was enjoying my sleep."

"Sorry. Inconsiderate of me." She tiptoed backward from the room. "I'll leave you now, Etienne, and I'll try not to wake you when I return. I have to find Tyl."

"Sure," he mumbled, already half-conscious again, "go find Tyl."

He felt much refreshed the next morning. The sun was shining brightly through the skylight and window and a basin of clear cold water was waiting for him by the foot of his bed. It was the best night's sleep he'd had since leaving Steamer Station.

He splashed water off his face, dried himself with his shirt, and looked around.

"Lyra?" The other couch-bed was empty. He raised his voice a little. "Lyra!"

She entered through the arched doorway a moment later, already fully dressed and wide awake. He frowned at her.

"Didn't you get any sleep?"

"Sure did. Slept like Lazarus, got up at dawn. This is such

a wonderful place, Etienne. I know it's an unprofessional thing to say, but there's no comparing these people to the Mai, Homat being an exception. From what Tyl tells me there's next to no crime among the Tsla. We can leave our possessions anywhere in town without fear they'll be stolen. That's another byproduct of their concern for mental health. They've learned to cope with their baser instincts not only better than the Mai, but better than many people I know."

"That's quite a judgment to make on the basis of half a night's conversation with one native. Isn't it an unwritten rule that all primitive cultures have their hidden eccentricities? I'm sure the Tsla's will appear in due course." He hunted for his lederhosen.

"Maybe so, but I haven't seen any evidence of it yet and I've been looking. Hurry up. Tyl's waiting for us."

"Waiting for us? Why?"

She didn't try to mute her exasperation. "To guide us to the temple of Moraung Motau, remember?"

"Sorry. Still full of sleep. What about something to eat?"

"That's waiting too. I've already sampled the local cooking. It's blander than the Mai's but perfectly palatable. Don't worry about Homat and the others. They've already eaten and they're stretched out under their skylights, soaking up the ultraviolet."

The meal that was brought to their room was simple but ample. Tyl joined them, watching while they ate and sharing their enjoyment if not their table.

Etienne muttered a terse thank you, asked, "How far is it to this temple?"

"A day's journey. We will spend the night near there."

Etienne searched his memory, was unable to conjure up the sight of any large structures at the far end of the valley and told Tyl so.

"You did not miss seeing it, friend Etienne. I perhaps should have said it lies a day's ride from Turput. We will not use our own feet."

"Lowagons?" Etienne inquired, thankful for his feet.

"No. Those are tools of the Mai. We will ride *lekkas*. When thee are ready, I will take thee."

In the stable area behind the hospitality building they encountered their first *lekka*, a furry thin-legged creature

[93]

with an incongruously rotund body and a double tail that switched nervously from side to side. Blunt furry faces turned to glance curiously at the bearers of strange new smells. They waited with placid expressions and chewed their cuds as Tsla handlers attached reins to the base of high, forward-curving ears. The forelegs were longer than the hind, an unusual arrangement for an animal built to run. Etienne thought of hyenas and giraffes, though the *lekka* was bulkier than either.

In consequence, there was no pommel on the woven cloth saddles. Instead, each boasted a high backrest designed to keep the rider from sliding backward down the sloping spine. It was heavily padded. There were no stirrups. The handlers brought stepstools to assist in mounting.

The reins were simple and straightforward and both Redowls were mounted in minutes. Tyl turned his own steed, spoke comfortingly.

"One thing to be careful of. The *lekka* stands quietly, but they love to run. So be prepared." A stableyard gate was swung open ahead and he swung his *lekka* around.

As their guide shouted an indecipherable Tsla word, Etienne's mount made a sudden rush for the gap, reaching out with those long forelegs and nearly throwing its rider feet over head despite the saddle's solid backbrace. As it was he almost kicked himself in the mouth. Lyra's deep, vibrant laugh didn't make him feel any better. He threw her a murderous look which she ignored as she smoothly followed Tyl out the gate.

Etienne brought up the rear, furious at his own clumsiness and determined to master his animal. Before too long his hips adjusted to the odd reaching gallop and he was speeding up the wide dirt road as comfortably as Lyra.

The track ran parallel to the river. The Aurang here was some six kilometers wide, a mighty torrent but only a trickle compared to the Skar. At the far end of the hanging valley the river fell to earth in a broad waterfall, sparkling and most impressive. It was a good hundred meters high and reminded him of the great waterfalls trideed on the tropical thranx worlds that they some day hoped to visit.

He nudged his mount nearer Lyra and Tyl, called across to their guide.

"It is called the Visautik," Tyl informed him. "We will reach it by midday."

Etienne was studying the sheer wall that seemed to mark the end of the valley. "Then what?"

"There is a trail not visible from here, a trading road that climbs a rockfall on this side of the Visautik. It rises to the next valley. Many legats beyond lies the temple of Moraung Motau. And the Cuparaggai."

"What's that?" Lyra asked, simultaneously noting that the Tsla used the same unit to measure distance as did the Mai.

There was no way of telling if their guide smiled, since his mouth was hidden by the weaving proboscis, but Tyl nonetheless managed to convey a feeling of anticipation as well as delighted amusement as he said, "Thee will see."

⟦ VIII ⟧

They heard the Cuparaggai long before they saw it, and felt it before they heard it. It announced itself as a buzzing in the ears, a vibration in the bones. Its roar drowned out the rush of Visautik Falls before they crested the canyon wall.

The temple valley was not as large as the one in which Turput lay, and it appeared narrower and smaller still because of the height of the walls that enclosed it. Jewellike fields filled the valley, nourished by the Aurang's flow. At the far end of the valley lay the still unseen source of steady thunder, marked only by sunlit mist.

They paused atop the ridge and had an interesting lunch that consisted of some kind of local rolled meat and thick, sweet breadsticks. Then they remounted and rode on. Several hours later Tyl paused and extracted a handful of small round cottony pads.

Lyra examined the pair he handed to her. "What are these for?"

Tyl pointed to the small shapes atop his head, then pushed one of the pads inside.

"Oh!" Lyra hadn't noticed that they now had to shout in order to be heard over the nearing roar, but she was made aware of it as soon as she inserted the pads and silence returned.

Despite these precautions they were quite unprepared for the sight that greeted them when they turned a sharp bend in the canyon.

Several kilometers ahead, sheer rock walls met to form a vertical defile no more than four kilometers wide. For the first time since they'd left the Skar, Etienne forgot his irritation with Lyra. He was enveloped by wonder.

"How high?" she shouted at him, leaning close so that he could hear her through his earplugs. He'd already taken a sighting with the instrumentation on his wrist.

"Twenty-five hundred meters!" Only the fact that the spray did not rise half as high as the falls themselves enabled them to see the cliff where the Aurang River flowed over the edge of the Guntali Plateau. It was a frightening, magnificent drop and the result was a cascade of unmatched proportions, fittingly located on a world of geological superlatives.

It seemed impossible that the stone at the base of that torrent could withstand the impact of so much water falling from such a height without turning to powder. Just as it seemed impossible for the ancient multistorey edifice that clung to the cliff face just to the right of the waterfall to remain in place without having been shaken to pieces hundreds of years ago.

Tyl pointed. "Moraung Motau."

"How old?" Lyra shouted as they raced toward it.

"A thousand years, two thousand, who can say?" Tyl spurred his *lekka* on.

Hundreds of windows threw back the sun from the rambling, rock-climbing structure, which appeared more than large enough to shelter the whole population of Turput. Huge bas-reliefs covered the facade with writhing figures and decorative motifs. Only the fact that the building had been hewn from the raw stone of the cliff face enabled it to withstand the steady vibration produced by the immense waterfall nearby.

Several thousand years, Tyl had said, and Etienne had

no reason to doubt the Tsla's veracity. He had shown himself to be truthful in everything else.

As they drew near he saw that the thick green lines that covered the lower part of the cliff on both sides of the Cuparaggai were not sculpted and painted decorations but enormous vines, unlike anything they had observed growing on Tslamaina before. Tsla toiled among them, tending to roots and leaves. They wore longer capes of some shiny material which kept them from being soaked by the omnipresent spray.

Tyl reined in his *lekka* and the two humans slowed accordingly.

"Aren't we going any farther?" Lyra asked, shouting to make herself heard over the Cuparaggai's thunder. "Aren't we going inside the temple?"

Tyl gestured negatively and looked apologetic. "I am sorry, but it is not permitted. Thee are not initiates. Nor could thee stand it for very long. The monks who live and work at Moraung Motau are attuned to the old books and ancient ways. They are also quite deaf. It has always been so."

He led them through the gate of a nearby farm. Etienne could not tell if the stop had been prearranged, but the farmer and his two mates were as cordial and relaxed as if they'd known their guests for years.

There they stayed and spent the remainder of the day talking, or rather, everyone listened politely and attempted to answer Lyra's unending questions. She inquired about division of labor in the valley, family structure, monkish ritual, about trading procedure and education and what the Tsla expected of an afterlife until the poor farmer and his mates were exhausted. Eventually Tyl intervened.

"Much of what thee request of this family they can not provide for reasons of ignorance, inhibition, custom, or uncertainty. Nor can I. There is one who might sate thy endless curiosity."

"Then that's who I want to meet."

"Mii-an is Chief Consoler and First Scholar of Turput. His time he gives of but sparingly, for he is old and tired. But I believe he will consent to share himself with thee."

"That would be wonderful." Lyra put a hand on her husband's arm. "Wouldn't that be wonderful, Etienne?"

"Wonderful. You won't mind if I don't tag along?"

She looked shocked. "Etienne, this is a special opportunity. How can you?..." She caught herself, coughed. "You'd rather look at the rocks, wouldn't you?"

"That's right. I'd rather look at the rocks. You go ahead and sit at the feet of this Consoler." He glanced past her, to Tyl. "Provided it's no imposition."

"Friend Etienne, the sharing of knowledge is never an imposition, just like the sharing of self. It gives pleasure."

On their way back down to Turput, Etienne let his *lekka* fall behind Tyl's so that he could talk to his wife without shouting.

"Lyra, don't you think you're starting to view these people with something less than scientific detachment? Of all people, you ought to know better than to idealize a primitive race, no matter how superficially attractive their philosophy may seem."

"It's not superficial. You put too high a premium on technology, Etienne. There are other definitions of advancement, other kinds of higher knowledge."

He found himself growing angry. "Come on now, Lyra. The Tsla are nice enough, and they *seem* content within themselves, but that's hardly reason enough to go overboard about them. I never thought I'd see you romanticizing a bunch of elephant-nosed aborigines."

"I would not use the word 'aborigine' to describe them," she replied coldly. "They have advanced far beyond that stage. As for 'romanticizing' them, I don't consider you qualified to use the word."

Her whole attitude struck him as so absurd that the putdown missed its intended effect. "This is supposed to be a scientific expedition," he told her, "and we've been more than a little occupied with business. I'm sorry if I haven't found much time for romance, but I'm not used to strumming guitars beneath four moons, let alone one. Besides which it's a two-way street. A little encouragement on a second party's part might be in order."

She bridled at that. "I've given you ample opportunity."

"You don't say? How exactly do you define ample opportunity, and how does that have anything to do with encouragement? They're two different things, you know."

"If you don't know," she snapped, "I certainly can't tell

you." She spurred her *lekka* forward until she was cantering alongside their guide.

Etienne watched as the pair of them began an animated discussion of some obscure aspect of Tsla behavior. Infatuated, he told himself. A good scientist like Lyra, infatuated with a bunch of furry primitives. It was hard to believe.

Well, she'd get over it soon enough. Everything about Tsla culture was new to her, each bit of information a surprise and contrast to what they'd learned about the Mai. As soon as she worked it out of her system they'd head back down into the Barshajagad and life would return to normal. Let her rhapsodize about her work. He had plenty of his own to do for a change. If she tried to draw him into her discussions all he had to do was start talking enthusiastically about the amount of pyroxine in the local metamorphics and she'd leave him alone quickly enough.

True to his word as always, Tyl succeeded in obtaining permission for Lyra to have an audience with the Chief Consoler. From then on Etienne saw very little of his wife save at mealtimes. He lost himself in his own field studies, making as complete a record of the canyon of the Aurang and its formations as possible, estimating the age of various strata and returning several times to marvel at the power and majesty of Cuparaggai Falls.

It was only several weeks later, during one of their increasingly infrequent meetings in their room, that he remarked again on the amount of time she was spending among their hosts, and it was not something she said that prompted his comments: it was her appearance.

"Where did you get that outfit?" He stared at her and tried to withhold his laughter.

Lyra executed a slow pirouette for him. The brilliantly striped free-flowing gown and cape swirled loosely around her.

"Tyl gave it to me. Mii-an ordered it. It seems that he thinks very highly of me. We've been exchanging information, you see. He teaches me, I teach him. Mii-an lives for the sharing of knowledge."

"Glad the two of you are getting along so well. But really, Lyra—native dress?"

"What's wrong with it? It keeps off the wind, it's as warm

during the night as my long sleeves and cooler during the day. Eminently practical. They had to modify the shoulder area for me. We don't have that curvature of the upper spine, and my arms are longer, but it's such a tentlike garment little work was necessary. Mii-an insisted."

"Nice of the old boy. What enlightening discoveries have you made?"

"Everything I've learned to date only confirms what I originally suspected. The Tsla are the most sociologically advanced race of their class yet discovered. They have no standing army, no police force, and all citizens bear arms on the rare occasions when it's necessary."

"No crime at all, in a society this primitive?"

"There you go with your preconceived notions of what's primitive, Etienne. There's some crime, naturally. It's handled by the Consolers and Advisors. They treat the culprit like a patient, not a criminal. Cure and not punishment. According to the First Scholar there is perfection in everyone."

"You included, naturally."

"Me included." The sarcasm went right past her. "You included. The Mai and the Na included." Then she said something which made him sit up and take notice. "Etienne, I believe the Tsla may be mildly telepathic."

"Now that *would* be a discovery worth shouting about. There are no known telepathic races, only mutant individuals. What makes you think so?"

"Their remarkable perceptivity. They seem to have an instinctive grasp of what I'm going to say before I say it."

His initial excitement faded. "What makes you think it's anything more than that?"

She suddenly looked uncomfortable. "For one thing, Tyl has commented on more than one occasion that he doesn't believe you and I are getting along too well."

The sharp laugh that filled the room was wholly spontaneous.

"And you're basing your assumption on evidence like that? You don't have to be a telepathic native to see that you and I aren't exactly acting like the ideal couple. I'm sure you've shared that knowledge with this Mii-an also and he passed it on to Tyl."

"You just don't want to consider the possibility, do you?"

"Possibility? Show me some real evidence for telepathic ability and I'll consider the possibility. I'm starting to worry about you, Lyra."

"Save yourself the trouble." She turned to leave. "I should have known better than to confide in you."

"Lyra..." She hesitated. "Lyra, we've only been here a few weeks. The Tsla aren't natural wonders any more than they're living examples of Rousseau's natural man. They're simply a nicer group of folks than the Maï. For all we know they may make mass sacrifices every six months."

"I don't understand your hostility. Why this sudden antipathy toward the Tsla? They've been perfect hosts."

"There's no antipathy and what I'm saying has nothing to do with the Tsla. All I'm saying is that no conscientious researcher should jump to conclusions, much less make value judgments about an entire race on the basis of a few weeks spent among one group of villagers."

"I can agree with that, Etienne. A lot more study is needed to confirm my findings. There are several volumes to be composed. I haven't even had time to examine how the Tsla's position as middlemen between the Mai and the Na has affected their outlook on life and their social development."

"I'm sure someone will resolve all the loose xenological ends neatly some day." She said nothing and a sudden thought changed his tone. "Lyra, are you trying to tell me something?"

"Yes. I'm not ready to go Upriver again yet, Etienne. My work here is barely under way."

"When will you be ready to go Upriver again, my love?"

"Maybe in a couple of months. Certainly no sooner."

"That takes us into local winter. That wouldn't cause us any problems here, but up near the arctic circle the Skar may freeze solid. The hydrofoil's not equipped for ice skimming, Lyra. We can't wait two months."

She turned again, a swirl of brightly striped cottonlike folds. "I'm sorry, Etienne, but I can't abandon my work here. As you so aptly pointed out, I don't have sufficient evidence to support my numerous conclusions."

"Where are you going?"

"Evening meditation. I've been invited to watch and to participate if I desire. I'd ask you along but you wouldn't find a bunch of aborigines sitting around attempting to get in touch with their inner selves very interesting, would you?"

And she was gone. He stared after her for a long minute.

"Well, damn!" He would have kicked his bed if it hadn't been constructed of solid rock. He settled instead for slamming one fist into an open palm until the latter was sore.

Of one thing he was certain. No matter how vital Lyra considered her work here, they had to return to the Skar. That was the agreement. Similar agreements had kept their marriage together for twenty years and he was damned if he was going to alter that relationship because of a sudden infatuation on her part for a race of pseudolamaistic anteaters with soulful eyes.

She didn't come to the room that night. It wasn't the first time she'd stayed away all night, but it was the first time he'd lain awake long enough to notice it. It was very early the next morning when he strode purposefully down the hall toward the porters' quarters.

Like his companions, Homat lay asleep beneath a half dozen heavy woven blankets. Etienne estimated the room temperature at seventy degrees. He nudged the Mai hard.

"What is it, de-Etienne?" Homat inquired as he tried to clear his vision.

"Get up. Get everyone up. We're leaving."

"Leaving, de-Etienne? I thought—you did not say, and it is very early."

"There's been a sudden change of plans. You'll find out that we humans have a tendency to do things on the spur of the moment."

"I understand that, de-Etienne, but—"

"I'll be in the courtyard if you need me. Tell them to hurry it up." He left a very puzzled Mai behind him.

Evidently meditation was over, or else someone had roused his wife from her contemplation. She stormed out into the open courtyard, ignoring the strained singing of several lizardlike *puouts* on the main gate. Etienne didn't look up from his work. He was checking the supplies several somber Tsla were providing.

[103]

"Etienne, this is childish. You know how I hate it when you turn childish."

"Yes, I know, and you hate ultimatums even worse."

"That's because ultimatums are the worst manifestation of childishness. I thought everything had been settled last night."

"Settled to your satisfaction. Not to mine. I'm leaving." He tugged brutally on a backpack's straps.

She sighed deeply. "I told you that my work here is just getting under way, that I'm only beginning to make some real progress in understanding this culture, these people."

"Fine. I understand that." He moved to check another pack. Homat and the rest of the porters began filing sleepily out of the hospitality building, shivering in the early morning cold. Few Tsla were about this early and the sun was just peeking over the eastern wall of the canyon.

"You stay here, Lyra. You don't have to come down with me. If all goes as intended I'll be back in six months to pick you up. Stay and meditate like mad."

"You can't go north alone," she argued. "Two is the absolute minimum authorized for an expedition like this."

"Then from this point on the expedition advances without authorization, I guess. Homat's learned enough to assist me. Haven't you, Homat?"

The Mai guide's gaze shifted warily from one tall alien to the other and he found reason to work on the pack farthest away from them both.

Etienne started toward another bundle and Lyra rushed to confront him, blocking his path. "Stop it, Etienne. Stop it right now. I'm not in the mood for a fight."

"Why not?" he asked sarcastically. "Did I upset your morning devotions? And as long as we're on the subject of childish acts, how would you define someone who forgets eight years of higher education and goes native despite twenty years of arduous fieldwork that consistently proves such activities are counterproductive to good research?"

"I've explained before that the Tsla are a unique race deserving of special study. Sometimes to obtain the best results it's necessary to bend the rules."

"Not as far as I'm concerned it isn't." He waved expansively at the surrounding buildings. "But you go ahead. Stay and have yourself a deliriously good time. Bury yourself in native customs and habits. Inhale primitive wisdom, join the local religion, become a Tsla nun if they have such institutions—I don't care. I never put restraints on you, Lyra, despite all your talk of ultimatums.

"As for me, I intend to locate the source of the river Skar and study its history and geology from there to the morass of the Skatandah. Halfway along that journey of discovery I will make it a point to stop back here and pick you up."

"Etienne."

"What?" He stepped around her and bent to the pack with a will.

"Etienne, you know I can't let you go without me."

"Why not? What about your carefully timed research program?"

"We're a team, Etienne. We complement each other. Neither of us does our best work solitaire."

"We'll just have to adapt somehow, won't we?"

"No," said a new voice. Etienne frowned, looked toward the hallway. He and Lyra had been arguing in Tsla, using the local language out of habit.

The Chief Consoler and First Scholar of Turput stood in the portal. It was the first time Etienne had seen him and the Tsla's advanced age manifested itself in the streaks of silver that dominated his face, the wrinkled flesh of exposed forearms. Tyl stood at his right shoulder to lend support should it be needed. Mii-an leaned on a twisted cane.

"I was told of the disturbance," he said in a surprisingly strong voice.

"No disturbance," Etienne muttered, inspecting the packs. "Just a friendly domestic conversation, that's all."

"We do not mean to intrude," Tyl said. "It would give me much unhappiness if I thought that we—"

"Oh for heaven's sake." Etienne turned sharply to confront the newcomers. "Must you people always be so damned *polite*?"

"We're sorry," said Mii-an. "It is our nature."

Etienne threw up his hands.

"Such a disturbance cannot be allowed," Mii-an said.

"What do you mean it can't be allowed?" Etienne asked him.

"Discord among guests is not to be tolerated."

"Really? And what do you propose as a solution?"

Mii-an shambled across the paving to stand close to Lyra. He took her left hand in some strange alien grip Etienne hadn't observed in use before.

"Thee must go with thy mate. If thy duality is to be the price of thy studies, I cannot allow thee to continue. When all is resolved, return to study with us another time."

"But it was already settled," she protested. "I was to remain here and continue my research, learn your ways and—"

The Chief Consoler raised a six-fingered hand. "We will miss thee, for thou has a thirst for learning that all but matches our own. If thee could bring thy mate's work here all would be simplified, but mountains are difficult to move. It is more sensible for thee to accompany him. Besides, thee may still continue thy studies, for some of thy work can go with thee, a boon for which we would be most thankful."

"I don't understand, Mii-an." Etienne listened without looking. Apparently the First Scholar was taking his side and he was embarrassed by his early display of anger.

"Beyond the lands that lie Upriver from Turput are many that are unknown to thy Mai companions." He gestured to his right. "If thee will permit it, Tyl and four bearers will accompany thee. He has traveled extensively, knows many Upriver dialects and peoples. When you pass beyond his realm of knowledge, he will be there to see and to study for all Turput. And when not guiding thee he can continue to instruct you in our ways."

"You said you'd do that yourself."

"The instructor is not important. All that matters is the knowledge."

"It's not that simple." She glanced at Etienne, who carefully avoided her stare. "Looks like you win after all. I can argue with you but not with Tsla logic. That is, if you have no objection to Tyl joining us."

"I've no objection, but it's not entirely up to us." He rose from the pack he'd been inspecting so intently. "Homat?"

"You already have a guide, de-Etienne," he replied slowly.

"We do, and a fine one, but what the old Tsla says makes

good sense. Haven't you said that the river beyond this point is new to you?"

"Yes, yes." Homat was still reluctant to surrender any of his hard-won authority. "I see that you are right, de-Etienne. A Tsla who knows the way would be welcome." He tugged at the hood of his coat. "Anything would be welcomed that takes us quickly out of this cold country."

Etienne grinned. "I apologize. I guess I did kind of drag all of you out of a warm bed on your equivalent of an icy morning." He turned to the First Scholar. "We accept your kind offer. Tyl's been nothing but helpful since we got here and I see no reason not to share his company. How do you feel about this, Tyl? You haven't said anything."

"It is Mii-an's place to say, but I look forward to it. I will gain much knowledge. It is a unique opportunity for me."

"It's settled then, I expect." Lyra started for the hallway. "I'll go get ready. See what I mean about Tsla judgment, Etienne? They have enough sense to see that we're a team even when we don't."

He left the Mai to make final preparations and hurried to catch up with her. She was resigned to leaving, which was very different from being agreed.

"I'm sorry I had to force the issue like this, Lyra, but I was at my wits' end. I couldn't think of anything else."

"I accept that." She slowed and some of the hardness drained from her expression. "Maybe you're right, Etienne. Maybe I've gotten a little too close to my work here. The soul of a good working team is its ability to compromise. I'm compromising. Just remember, you owe me one."

"I promise, Lyra. On the way back you can spend as much time as you want. But we must make it to the turn-around point, the source of the Skar, before winter sets in up north. We've no idea what to expect, since the southern winters are moderated by the Groalamasan."

"So you keep telling me."

"What about this Tyl?" he asked, changing the subject. "You've been working with these people. He's a scholar. Do you think he's up to a difficult, dangerous journey? Physically, I mean. Mentally I know that he's ready."

"Don't worry about his stamina, Etienne. The Tsla are as adaptable as we are, not at all like the Mai. He'll be able to handle the heat down in the Barshajagad. We'll make space for him inside. There's plenty of room. He and his companions will manage."

"Companions?"

"You didn't hear the First Scholar's last words?" Etienne shook his head. "Mii-an doesn't want to send Tyl by himself. He wants to send him with four porters, to replace the Mai who will leave as soon as we reach the river."

"We don't need porters on the river."

"Mii-an has told me several times these past days that there will come a point where we'll have to leave the river, leave our boat."

"We can't leave the boat. You know that."

"I know it, yes, but Mii-an insists that without porters we'll have to turn back at a place scmewhere a couple of thousand legats Upriver."

"It's true." They turned around, saw Homat standing behind them. "I listen and hear many things, de-Etienne. The Tsla speak of this after you have come inside." He eyed Lyra with great interest. "Why do they say such things?"

"Mii-an talks about a spot far Upriver where the Skar undergoes...he called it a dramatic change of personality. It's like the Tsla to ascribe such traits to inanimate objects, and he was very clear in his description of this place. It's called the Topapasirut."

Homat's extreme reaction was unexpected. His eyes went very wide as he executed a half dozen powerful signs designed to ward off dangerous spirits.

"It means," Lyra told her husband, "Cleansing Place of all the Waters."

"That doesn't sound very threatening."

"I agree, but Mii-an insists we can't pass beyond it with the boat. Hence his insistence that we accept porters."

"Another waterfall? Satellite topographics don't show any large waterfalls in the northern region of the Barshajagad, though admittedly pictures are less than perfect."

"No, not a waterfall. Something else."

"Five Tsla, Homat?"

"I dislike the presence of so many strangers on board the spirit boat, de-Etienne, but it seems we must tolerate all to gain the knowledge of one."

Etienne Redowl considered, said finally, "Tell the one called Mii-an we accept his generous offer, but that all the porters are to be under your command." The Mai seemed to grow several centimeters.

"They won't stand for that," Lyra argued.

"Won't they? Surely your high and mighty Tsla can take orders from a mere Mai. Don't tell me they'll *argue* about it."

"Tyl is an important scholar."

"I said that the four porters would act at Homat's direction, not Tyl. You'll just have to explain to Mii-an that Homat's been with us a long time, that he's familiar with our boat and its workings, and that he's our right arm. Or left, whichever they accord more weight to."

"Neither. They're physically as well as mentally ambidextrous."

"We need a chain of command. It's going to be crowded on the boat. As for letting them inside the cabin with us, I understand the need but are you sure we can trust them?"

"I trust Tyl completely, Etienne. And the porters will look on their work as the Buddhaistic equivalent of making a pilgrimage for merit. So they'll work their hardest to make sure the expedition's a success."

"Tell them to hurry themselves along then, Homat. We have a long way to go."

"To the river, de-Etienne, and to *real* weather! I will hurry them with delightment!"

〖 IX 〗

Compared to the long climb up from the shore of the Skar, the descent was as pleasurable as an afternoon stroll through the gardens of New Riviera. In addition, the loads had been distributed among twice as many porters, the Tsla shouldering their new burdens alongside but separate from their Mai counterparts.

The Tsla joked amiably among themselves, their evident good spirits proof enough of Lyra's claim that all were willing volunteers. Whenever Tyl moved among them they deferred to him as they would a superior, but without any of the bowing and scraping common among the Mai. The porters recognized and honored him as their mental and spiritual superior. He, in turn, did not use his position to lord it over his fellows.

There was something of a subtle hierarchy among the porters, however, as if each one knew his place without having to be reminded of it. At the bottom of the pecking order was one exceptionally large, powerful, and mentally slow individual named Yulour. He hardly spoke at all and was often the butt of gentle, nonmalicious humor on the part of his companions, to which he invariably responded with a smile. It took a while for Yulour's slowness to manifest itself beyond a doubt, at which point Etienne slipped back from the head of the party to take Tyl aside.

"Yulour?" Etienne wished he could see if Tyl was smiling, but that weaving flexible snout concealed the lower half of his expression. "He was orphaned in the mountains, his parents slain by some carnivore he could not well describe to us. Perhaps the terror of that moment stopped his mind from growing." Tyl made a gesture Etienne did not recognize.

"He was raised a part of Mii-an's extended family, but it did not help him *here*." Tyl tapped the side of his head. "For all that he is a goodly soul, with a kind heart, and his back is strong if his mind weak. He will gain much merit from this journey, perhaps even enough to admit him to the afterlife."

"It's not my specialty, more my wife's province, but I didn't know that the Tsla believed in an afterlife."

"Not all of us do. I do not know if Yulour does, so I try to believe for him. He appears content with his lot, unfair as life has been to him. There are many I know who envy him his unshakable contentment. On this journey of discovery he is my greatest responsibility—save for thee and thy mate, of course." There was no guile in those warm brown eyes.

"If he were to wander away from us he would never find his way back. Indeed, though he has lived there all his life, he could not find his way back to Turput from this spot. He would not have enough sense to follow the road." Tyl waited and when no more questions were forthcoming, fell back among his fellows.

Everything Lyra claimed for the Tsla was borne out by each new experience. They were a kind, likable people. So why did he persist in trying to find a reason for disliking them?

He knew the answer to that one. Lyra was not fond of the Tsla. She was absolutely infatuated with them. But was that the root of his problem? He pressed on with his internal argument. No, it was something else. There was one Tsla in particular, one she spent all her spare time with, one she looked up to and turned to with every new question: Tyl.

Now there was a bizarre thought, he told himself. No question about it, Tyl was an impressive specimen of mammalian life. It wasn't the first time Lyra had grown personally fond of some object of study.

Patrick O'Morion's space, I'm jealous of an alien aborigine, he told himself. The shock of realization so numbed him he nearly wandered off the road toward a hundred-meter drop. Lyra noticed the dazed look in his eyes.

"Etienne? Are you okay?"

"Sure. Yeah, I'm okay." He blinked, extended his stride until he once more assumed the lead. Lyra stared at his back, shook her head in puzzlement and hurried to catch up with him.

The Tsla brought up the rear. Tyl stood next to Yulour, dwarfed by the porter's bulk. "Yulour?"

"Yes, Learned One?"

"What is the sign made by crossing the Oo and the Strike?"

The porter's brow did not furrow. There was no point in straining his capacity over the mildly complex concept.

"I do not know, Learned One."

"That's all right, Yulour. It's not important. Tell me, what do you think of our new friends?"

Yulour looked over the heads of his companions, at the two humans. "They are very nice, Learned One, though they have so little fur. And when they talk among themselves it is strange talk, neither like ours nor the Mai's. But they are nice."

"Yes, they are. Thank thee for thy opinion, Yulour." The porter made a movement with his trunk.

Tyl rejoined the objects of his interest. "Your curiosity induced me to chat with Yulour, Etienne. I put to him a question simple enough for a cub to answer, and he could not. It was beyond his simple powers of reason. Yet it struck me that he may be happier than we. While he is free of intelligence, he is also free of the pains and travails higher thought brings. Ignorance, frustration, envy: he is subject to none of these."

"You make him out to be a perfect saint."

"Sometimes I wonder. He is so content, and still there are times I do not understand him."

"We have a saying among our people, Tyl." Etienne struggled to translate it into Tsla. "Better a lucky idiot than an unlucky genius."

"Ah, this strange concept of 'luck' again. Lyra mentioned it to me. We have no such concept. You must explain it to me further." Etienne made an attempt to do so as they plodded steadily downhill toward the ever widening streak of silver that was the Skar.

Days passed and the heat intensified, rising past ninety degrees. As it did so the Tsla began shedding their clothing, capes and togas vanishing into packs, not to be used again until the climate of the far north was encountered.

It was the first time Etienne had seen a Tsla without the familiar cape-and-toga attire. They appeared quite comfortable without it, as if clothing was employed for protection against the elements and possibly to signify social standing, but not because of some primitive nudity taboo.

Not that they were naked in the human sense, since soft brown fur covered everything except forearms and forelegs. The only surprise was the unexpected presence of a tail, a short stub five to six centimeters in length. It made them look animalistic, though several intelligent races retained tails. The AAnn, for example, considered the retention of a tail as a sign of intelligence, not vice versa.

In other respects the Tsla were very human, if one discounted the six-fingered hands, six-fingered toes, and myrmecophagous face. There was one other aspect of their anatomy that interested him. He fully intended to question Lyra about it as soon as he could be sure she wouldn't misinterpret his curiosity. Undoubtedly she would have found his uncertainty amusing.

By the time the temperature touched one hundred degrees the Mai were shedding their cold-climate attire, able for the first time in weeks to luxuriate in the stifling heat and humidity.

They reached the bank of the Skar and turned toward Aib. Etienne was looking forward to a cool shower on board the hydrofoil. As soon as they'd cleaned themselves up they'd hand over the second half of the agreed-upon payment to the local Oyt and make preparations for resuming their journey Upriver.

That evening they were confronted by the leader of their

Mai porters. So rapidly did he talk that even Lyra had trouble following his words. It was left for Homat to interpret.

"It has something to do with the season of sowing," he explained. "They are all late to help and are anxious to be on their way. There is also talk of local taxes. They come not from Aib itself but from the outlying farming district."

Lyra nodded knowingly. "I understand. They want to skip with their payment before the local authorities can demand a cut. Perfectly Mai."

The porters organized a hasty ceremony of departure, took their payment, and left in a rush. Only slightly discomfited by the heat, the Tsla assumed the second half of the divided burdens. Larger and stronger than the Mai, they had no difficulty with the full loads.

Two days later they were nearing the outskirts of Aib when Etienne's eyebrows drew together. "That's funny."

"What is funny, Etienne?" Tyl asked uncertainly.

Etienne ignored the question. Impolite, but he was concerned with something besides alien concepts of courtesy.

"I don't see the boat, Lyra."

She strained her eyes. "Neither do I. Your eyesight's better than mine, Etienne, but you're right. I don't see it. Surely that's the dock where we left it moored?"

"Has to be," he muttered. "See, there's the basaltic outcrop the local ruler used for a dais."

"Something is wrong?" Tyl asked. "I feared as much. These Mai," he said evenly, not caring whether Homat overheard him or not, "will steal anything left unguarded for half an *anat* and consider it moral."

"We made an arrangement," Etienne explained even as his pace quickened, "with the head of this town to watch our boat for us. We paid him half the set fee prior to our departure."

Forbearing to say, "I told you so," Homat instead chose to put the best possible light on the situation. "Perhaps the people of Aib are not responsible for the disappearance of the spirit boat."

"You rationalize hopefully, Homat. What do you really think?"

The Mai's gaze shifted rapidly from one alien to the other.

It was a look Etienne had become familiar with and he hastened to reassure their guide.

"You have nothing to fear from us, Homat. We are your friends."

"You recall, de-Etienne, how I warned you against this possibility?"

"All too clearly." They were almost running now. The dock was an empty gesture protruding into the river.

"I cannot see, de-Etienne, how the spirit boat could have vanished without the Aibites knowing. If they did not take it themselves, they surely did little to prevent its being taken. I thought you said that it could not be stolen, that it would protect itself."

"That's what we thought," Etienne replied grimly. "It looks like we were wrong." He looked toward the town. "Let's pay our good friend Gwattwe a visit, shall we?"

The modest residence of the Oyt of Aib was guarded by a brace of well-armed but obviously nervous warriors. The Oyt, one of them explained, was not at home.

"Then you've no objection to our entering to lay tribute at his table?" Lyra replied.

"I was told to admit no visitors." The soldier looked very unhappy.

Tyl spoke. "This refusal gains your master no grace, to flagrantly flout the laws of hospitality concerning weary travelers."

"In addition to which if you don't let us inside, we'll call on our otherworldly spirits to blow the place down." This was more bluff than promise, since an asynapt wouldn't do more than scorch the stone wall before them, but the guard didn't know that.

The guard looked askance at the pistol riding Etienne's hip, having already assumed it was some sort of weapon. He had no desire to personally discover its capabilities. "I will find out what best be done." He turned and vanished into the domicile, reappearing after a lapse of a few minutes. A curious, hesitant crowd had emerged from other nearby structures. They milled about well clear of the travelers, staring at the pair of aliens and the five Tsla.

"You are to be admitted," the guard informed them, "but only if you leave your spirit callers outside."

"Our spirits come with us," Lyra informed him in no-nonsense tones.

The guard sighed. "I was asked only to request it. Enter."

The stone and wood edifice was something more than a house and a good deal less than a palace, but was no doubt the best a small town like Aib could afford. Although the matter of their boat's whereabouts occupied most of his thoughts, Etienne still managed to note the mixture of envy and distaste with which the local Mai viewed the Tsla.

As Etienne had expected, Gwattwe had been there all along. Etienne thought he looked unwell, as if all the traditional bravado had been knocked out of him. Strange. If he intended to bargain for the missing hydrofoil he was beginning badly.

"Where is it?" he snapped at the Oyt, in no mood for protocol.

"I do not have to guess to what you refer," said the Oyt tiredly. "Your spirit boat is not here."

"You stole it," Etienne growled. "We trusted you, we left payment as security for that trust which you betrayed. You promised that our property would come to no harm."

"I lied," said Gwattwe.

Venerable mastery of diplomacy, Etienne mused sardonically. But this wasn't what he'd anticipated when they'd entered the town. Something was wrong here.

"Where have you hidden it?"

"We do not have your spirit boat." Gwattwe executed a most profound gesture of regret and helplessness. Tyl was watching him carefully.

"I believed you when you offered us assurances. Why should I believe you when you offer disclaimers?"

"It matters not whether you believe me. We do not have your boat. We did not steal it. Oh, we tried to." His expression turned sour. "Most assuredly we tried. Your spirits slew my advisor and several of his students, one at a time." He paused, but if he was expecting some word of contrition from Etienne he was going to have a long wait. He continued.

"We tried everything that we could think of, but we never had a glimpse of the spirits that watched over your vessel, nor of how they slew." He rose from his couch and balding houris rolled clear of his feet.

"Then where's our boat?"

"It pains me to have to tell you that it was stolen."

"But not by you?"

"Not by us. Why do you think it pains me?" Clearly Gwattwe of Aib was distressed only because another had succeeded where he had failed.

"When I lost my best advisors in matters spirit-wise I finally resolved to contact the renowned Davahassi, who is head advisor to Langai of Hochac."

Tyl leaned close to Etienne and spoke in Mai. "Hochac is a very bad place. It lies a few legats north of the place where the Aurang flows into the Skar. We rarely trade with them, for the people there are mean of spirit and sometimes prefer to kill for what they want rather than pay for it as many Mai are wont to do."

Etienne saw Homat stiffen, but the guide held his tongue. He would have to convince Tyl to be a little more circumspect in his comments concerning the Mai whenever Homat was around.

"It was hoped that Davahassi might solve the secret of your spirit boat as he has traveled widely and gained much knowledge. He came down by boat with Langai himself and a large escort of advisors. I was suspicious then but didn't know what else to do.

"They studied your spirit boat for many days and buried three advisors of their own in the river before Davahassi hit upon his plan. The secret, he announced, was to leave the spirits that protected your vessel in place and not to intrude on their privacy, for clearly the craft was their home and they defended it as such from any intruder. But that did not mean that the home itself could not be moved, provided the spirits within were left undisturbed.

"Therefore at his instructions Langai had a great wooden cage constructed. Many spells were then placed upon the spirit boat as the cage was placed around it and bound in place. It was then dragged from its home, the water, and placed on a platform whence it was transported to the center of Aib. It sat right there while we all celebrated." He pointed toward the town square outside the official residence.

"During the celebration our spirits were high. All would share in the profit from this action. We relaxed with our good 'friends.' Davahassi, may his entrails entice parasites, drugged our fine wine. When we awoke the next day it was found that Langai and his advisors had slipped the spirit boat back into the river. The wooden platform on which it had been placed apparently made a most delighted raft that they used to carry their booty homeward, like carrion eaters.

"We pursued, but too late, and Langai had stationed soldiers in the hills between here and Hochac. Certainly we could not have approached by water in time to intercept them." He concluded his tale of woe and lost opportunity with the Mai equivalent of a disgruntled shrug.

"You see, we did not steal your boat, but it was not for want of trying."

"How noble of you to say so."

"A wooden cage," Lyra murmured. "Wood's a rotten conductor. Once out of the water they'd be safe enough so long as they didn't make contact with the hull."

"'Left the spirits in peace,'" Etienne repeated. "That explains what happened. Nothing's wrong with the ship's defensive systems. They just avoided provoking them. I never thought the locals would have enough sense to move the whole boat without trying to get aboard and at the controls or contents." He turned back to Gwattwe.

"We'd like your help in recovering our property. You can compensate for your own attempted thievery and earn your fee by providing us with a troop of soldiers to help us assault Hochac."

"Would that such a thing were feasible," Gwattwe murmured. "I would do it for the chance at revenge alone, but Hochac is not Aib, hairy one. It is not much larger but it is far stronger. It would take many more soldiers than Aib could provide to overcome it, for Hochac is a walled town and heavily defended. Otherwise it could not withstand the attentions of its neighbors, whom it makes a practice of bullying and defrauding. The Hochacites are known for their love of battle. We of Aib are a peaceful folk."

"Sticky fingers and now sticky feet." A hand came down gently on his shoulder.

"Perhaps," Tyl whispered to him in Tsla so that Gwattwe could not understand, "it might be better for us just to go. The Hochacites may be expecting a big attack. If we approach with patience and caution, we may surprise them. But do not inform this one of our intentions. Like all his kind, he may yet find profit in selling such information to those who have already stolen from him. Feuds are like chaff to the Mai, and as permanent as their promises."

Etienne turned back to the waiting Oyt. "As we apparently have lost our craft and cannot recover it, we must return Downriver to the Groalamasan and our base in order to obtain another. You owe us for what we already have paid you."

"I do not deny that. Business is business," Gwattwe readily admitted.

"We will accept recompense in the form of a couple of riverworthy sailing craft so that we may safely return Downriver."

Gwattwe looked relieved, if not downright pleased. "That is fair," he said quickly. "The craft you wish will be provided. And may you have a safe journey Downriver."

Safe it would be, Etienne mused, but they had no intention of heading south.

Having no reason to ply the Skar, the Tsla were not very good sailors. But Homat felt right at home. With his help, both small boats managed to make their way slowly Upriver.

They anchored well out in the river away from the walled harbor of Hochac. Occasional fishing boats drifted past and their crews hailed the newcomers. Etienne and Lyra stayed out of sight belowdecks while Homat fielded the passing inquiries. The sight of the Tsla raised curious stares, but many of the drifting fisherfolk were from farther Upriver. Their questions were not threatening. Only a few of the curious called Hochac home port. To them the sight of Tsla on the river was unusual, but hardly cause for alarm.

Langai of Hochac and his advisor Davahassi might know that the alien owners of the stolen spirit boat had gone to visit with the Tsla, but that wasn't reason enough to connect the off-worlders to these furry fishermen. As far as Langai and the rest of Hochac knew, Etienne and Lyra Redowl were far away.

So no soldiers rowed out to inspect the fishermen and the two boats were able to move safely inshore on the heels of nightfall. As soon as it was dark, Etienne and Lyra crept out on the upper deck and produced daynight scopes from their kits.

"Must be used to attacks." Etienne squinted through his monocular. "The stockade's made of wood instead of stone, but its good and high. Too high to scale easily. You can see places where the individual logs have been scarred by fire. The top is flat and lined with broken glass. Cute."

"What sign of thy spirit boat?" Tyl asked softly.

"I can't see a thing besides the stockade, but there's a helluva lot of light from the center of town." He touched a switch on the side of the scope and the tiny long-range microphone amplified sound along with the light. Homat jumped at the unexpected rush of noise while the Tsla drew back and made signs. Lyra reassured them.

As soon as Homat had overcome his initial suspicion of the scope, Etienne asked him, "What do you make of this?"

The Mai moved hesitantly nearer the source of the sounds. "Drums, pipes, flutes, high chanting: they sound as if they are celebrating." His face lit with recognition of a particular chant. "That is what it is. A gathering to celebrate their great triumph over the Aibites and their successful theft. I did not recognize it at first. Many of the words here are different from in Po Rabi."

"Then we have a chance to surprise them while they're partying."

"I don't think so, de-Etienne. They will have the spirit boat carefully watched, lest some of their own fellows try to steal it and sell it Downriver. Anyone clever enough to steal the spirit boat would not be so stupid as to trust his own people."

Etienne touched the asynaptic pistol riding his hip. "Then we'll just have to walk in and make a polite request for the return of our property." He glanced at his wife but this time Lyra had nothing to say about the prospect of wreaking havoc on the natives.

Another source did, however. "The taking of lives would be most regrettable." Tyl wore his most soulful expression.

"I'm sorry too, Tyl, but we have to get our boat back and I'm in no mood to be nice about it. Not only would its loss mean the end of our expedition, but there are devices on board that could be a real danger to the Mai themselves if they ever managed to figure them out." He wiped sweat from his forehead. The temperature was still over a hundred and ten and the humidity hovered around ninety percent.

"There's another factor to consider. Lyra and I could probably obtain transportation back down to the Skatandah Delta, but we couldn't take months of this heat."

"I do not dispute the need to recover thy property, Etienne. I only abhor the necessity of taking lives through violence."

"We'll do as little shooting as possible."

"A very exuberant celebration." Homat was still listening intently to the amplified sounds coming from beyond the stockade as the two boats slipped into the harbor. "Siask!" he suddenly snapped, dropping to the gunwale. Etienne and Lyra immediately flattened themselves below the seats.

"What is it? What's the matter?"

"A patrol, I think. What do we do now?"

"If I may be permitted?"

Etienne glanced down toward Tyl. "You have something in mind?"

"You and thy Lyra must remain concealed, for on sight of thee the alarm will surely be raised, but thy friend Homat will only be questioned, especially if we show ourselves. It is unusual, as you know, for we of the Tsla to come down to the river. These warriors should be intrigued by our presence but not alarmed, for it is well known that we love peace and harm no one."

"Good idea, Tyl. You put them off their guard long enough for Lyra and me to get close enough to bring them down."

Tyl's proboscis twitched with amusement. "That would be too risky, would it not?" He gestured toward his companions. "We will undertake the necessary action."

"Wait a minute." Lyra looked confused. "What about what you just said, Tyl, about loving peace and not harming anyone?"

Etienne shushed her. "Don't confuse our guests. Let's see what these pacifists can do when they want to, shall we? Think of it as an interesting footnote to your research."

She gave him an angry stare, but said nothing. They hid themselves beneath a section of sail as the Tsla rowed the boats into shore. He had a sudden crazy urge to pinch her but managed to suppress it.

At first the patrol ordered both boats to stand off, but on sight of the Tsla they allowed them to dock. Etienne listened hard. At any moment he expected the sail to be thrown aside and to find himself eye to eye with a long spear.

Then there was the sound of muffled struggling and he and Lyra emerged from their temporary cocoon with pistols at the ready. They might as well have relaxed beneath the cloth.

Tyl and the porters had no trouble with the patrol. Yulour in particular distinguished himself, exercising his great strength with a caution that was frightening to see. Etienne made a mental note to leave the teasing to Yulour's companions.

The entire patrol had been neatly silenced. Etienne was full of newfound respect for their philosopher-guide as he helped him and the other Tsla slip the guards into the river, but he couldn't help but wonder at this facile contravention of established Tsla tenets. Time enough later for social analysis, he told himself curtly. First order of business was to get their boat back, not discuss Tsla motivation.

Having gone ahead to scout out the approach, Homat now beckoned them forward. Soon they were standing next to the impressive palisade of logs that girdled the town. There were plenty of slots cut in the wood through which archers could aim and fire on attackers. The openings near the harbor showed only the backsides of buildings, but as they made their way around the stockade, gaps appeared which permitted a view deeper into the community.

Eventually they located a small pedestrian gate. It was unguarded and swung wide at Homat's touch and they stepped inside, concealing themselves behind a square storage building.

From the slurred shouts they could now hear clearly, it was evident that plenty of drinking and drug-taking was going on. As they moved toward the center of the town they had a glimpse of unsteady revelers falling down in unexpected places, and nearly tripped over several who had celebrated themselves into unconsciousness.

Ahead lay the town square, a place of ceremony and

money-making among the Mai. Smack in the center of the paved square, surrounded by celebratory bonfires, was the Redowls' hydrofoil. The fires were maintained at a reasonable distance from the boat, not out of any fear of harming it but to ensure the safety of the wooden cage in which it rested. The chanting was loud now and terribly off-key. Etienne looked to his wife, saw with disgust but not surprise that she was furiously whispering a description of the celebration into her note-taker. That was his Lyra: if the locals ended up boiling her in fish fat she'd spend her last moments jotting down the recipe for posterity.

"What now, Learned One?" Apparently Tyl had exhausted his limited store of strategic knowledge. Etienne felt a perverse satisfaction over the Tsla's use of the honorific.

"How can we free thy boat, Learned One?" asked one of the porters. "It seems secured most strongly."

"Doesn't matter," Etienne told him. "All we have to do is get within shouting distance. We're close enough now, but I'm worried that all this loud chanting might drown us out."

"*I* understand," said Homat confidently. "You plan to call upon the spirits that watch over your boat."

Tyl eyed him distastefully. The Tsla were not heir to the plethora of superstitions that infected Mai culture.

"How will thee regain control of thy craft, Etienne? And more important, perhaps, how are we to transport it from the center of this unfriendly village to the water's edge?"

"You'll see," Etienne told him. "Homat's not far from the truth." Their Mai guide chose not to look down his nose at the skeptical Tsla, probably because in any such exchange he was bound to come off second best.

Etienne idly noted the architecture as they worked their way closer to the central square. No grand stone towers here. This wasn't Po Rabi. Most of the buildings were of wood, thatch, mud, and adobe, though several did soar to the impressive height of three stories. He did not admire them, however. Hochac's prosperity was tainted and it throve by taking from its neighbors. Perhaps tonight they could redress a few of those wrongs, make the inhabitants reconsider their methods. He hoped he'd be given that opportunity. Lyra would disapprove of his attitude, he knew, but

[123]

right now he didn't much care. He watched her coolly making notes and couldn't help but admire her. If they died here tonight, no one could say they'd neglected their research right up to the final moment.

They were halfway to the central square when they stumbled into a pair of sober locals. They looked very young and Etienne regretted having to pull his pistol. He was too slow and could have saved his regrets. Once again Tyl and his companions did their work with quiet efficiency. There were no screams and no deaths, though a single brief warning shout was lost in the shouting and chanting.

They were surprised when the arrow thudded into Swd's side. The short thick fur absorbed some of the arrow's force, but not enough to keep the porter from staggering up against Tyl. He struggled with the shaft as they sought cover beneath the overhang of a large house.

The archer stood on the porch of a building across the street. He was waving his bow toward the square now, jumping up and down and screaming high and steady. To Etienne's chagrin, Homat stepped out into clear sight to return the local's steady stream of expletives. While personally gratifying, this was a lousy tactical move. The celebrants in the square heard the row, turned to see the odd assortment of intruders, and had enough presence of mind left to scatter and sound the warning throughout the village.

A few located their own weapons and began to advance. Bows and arrows and spears might be primitive, but as the unfortunate Swd could attest, they were often as effective as any modern weapon. The differences between asynapt and arrow were neatness and convenience, not lethality. Add to that the fact that in seconds they were likely to be heavily outnumbered and there was little humor to be found in Homat's foolhardy posturing.

Wishing he was closer, Etienne cupped hands to mouth and yelled at the top of his lungs, "Execute Command Red-Ten!" Then he lowered the muzzle of his asynapt and fired at the feet of the nearest onrushing Hochacite. The Mai let out a yelp and fell on his face, paralyzed from the knees down.

That halted the charge for a few seconds, long enough for an answering rumble to rise from the central square. The rest of the attacking villagers turned and stared over their shoulders.

Lit from beneath by the dancing bonfires, the hydrofoil made a most impressive sight as it rose four meters into the air on activated repellers, lifting the wooden cage with it. It executed a slow pirouette until it was facing the direction from which the command had been given, locked in on Etienne's eyes, and started to move toward them. As it did so the downward facing air jets on which it hovered blasted flaming fagots of wood in all directions, scattering fire and natives alike. The movement caused the wooden cage to begin to break up, showering logs and planks down on the scurrying Mai.

〖 X 〗

Those Hochacites who were sober started screaming about spirits and devils as they flung their weapons aside and bolted for the nearest cover. Homat retreated to rejoin his companions, his eyes wide and locked on the hovering bulk of the spirit boat as it drifted toward them.

Lyra had to give him a shove to start him back toward the stockade gate. "Back to the harbor, everybody, before they get over the shock!"

Moving as fast as possible without conveying the impression of a hasty retreat, the intruders fled with studied dignity. Now and then a face would peek out at them as they passed along the street, but a burst from an asynaptic pistol would cause doors and windows to slam shut quickly.

They reached the narrow gate and filed quickly through it. Unable to quite clear the crest of the palisade, the hydrofoil made a satisfyingly loud smashing and crackling as it splintered several of the massive logs.

Etienne and the Tsla remained behind to guard the landward end of a pier while Lyra directed the boat over the water before retracting her husband's order. The hydrofoil settled gently into the Skar. Bending low to avoid an intact section of wooden cage, she stepped aboard.

From his position facing the town wall, Etienne was gratified to hear the start-up growl of the engine as power was transferred from repellers to jet. A few armed Mai had pushed through the gap in the stockade, but hadn't gained the courage to charge. As soon as word came that the boat was acting like a boat once more, some of the initial terror of its unboatlike behavior would fade and the Hochacites would try to recover it. Etienne had no intention of giving them that kind of time. "Now, Tyl! Get your people on board before the Mai have time to regroup!" Even as Etienne backpedaled to cover the Tsla's retreat, the bolder villagers slowly advanced.

Lyra made a quick head count and spun the wheel as she nudged the accelerator. The hydrofoil *varoom*ed out into the safety of the Skar, but not as fast as Etienne wanted. The unwieldy remnants of the cage prevented the boat from rising up on its hydrofoils. Distant shouts sounded from Hochac's harbor; pursuit was being organized.

Among the ship's tools was a heat stitch that could cut and weld. It made short work of the leather thongs that bound the sections of the wooden cage together. As Etienne sliced the thongs the Tsla heaved the heavy timbers over the side, and a few arrows *thunk*ed against the rear of the boat. Finally, with a loud splash the undersection of the cage gave way and drifted astern. The pursuing Mai were still within insult range but by now even Homat was too tired to respond.

Etienne stumbled to the intercom. "We're clear, Lyra. Raise her up."

The rumble of the electric jet became a whine as the boat rose above the surface on its twin foils and rocketed Upriver at a leisurely sixty kph, leaving the Tsla whispering their wonderment to one another and the frustrated Hochacites far behind.

"Wonderful, delicious," Tyl muttered as he peeked hesitantly over the side. "The boat flies over the water. You must explain to me how it works."

Etienne stiffened, relaxed almost as quickly. Tyl's words had sparked bad memories of Irquit and the ease with which she'd mastered the hydrofoil's security system. But there was no deception in this philosopher-teacher. Etienne felt guilty at his instinctive suspicion.

"Be happy to, Tyl. You're entitled to learn about what you've just rescued. I'll try and explain the principles to you and you must tell me more about what we're likely to encounter Upriver, especially this Topapasirut that has you so concerned."

"I will gladly do so, Etienne. But as for the Topapasirut there is little to say. It must be seen to be understood."

"Still certain we can't surmount it?"

"I still think so, yes, but after seeing what you have achieved tonight I am less certain than I was before."

That is faintly encouraging, Etienne mused. Further discussion would have to wait until morning. He longed desperately for the softness of his air-conditioned bunk. Lyra could drive for another half hour. Then they'd be far enough Upriver from any lingering pursuit to put the boat on autopilot.

At last they were on their way again, though he felt no pride in the thoroughly unprofessional but necessary diversion for which the inhabitants of Hochac were responsible. With any luck that would be the first and last interruption of its kind.

As for allowing the Tsla into the cabin, that was a necessity. They would be much more comfortable inside, where the temperature approximated that of their home. There was no fear in him. For one thing he was too tired. For another, he'd slept peacefully among the Tsla for weeks. They'd earned his trust. Besides, he and Lyra could always lock themselves in their cabin, and no curious Tsla could disengage a locked autopilot.

The morning dawned bright, hot, and stinking humid but Etienne sat comfortably alongside Lyra in the little dining nook. Tyl squatted on the floor nearby. The porters ate farther astern, in the storage area that had been turned into their living quarters. They could have joined the humans but chose not to. Etienne asked why, confident it would have some bearing on his question.

"They're ashamed," Tyl explained.

"Ah." Lyra looked satisfied. Apparently she'd been thinking along similar lines. "Because they had to fight?"

"Oh no." Tyl nibbled at his bowl, his stubby six-fingered hands probing for solid morsels. The Redowls had already overcome their distaste at seeing a Tsla rummage for food with its long snout. "They are ashamed because they were not permitted to fulfill their intentions."

"But they did," Etienne argued. "We're safe and we recovered our boat."

"Yes, but no thanks to us."

"You dispatched that patrol at the harbor."

"It was our intention to assist thee during the entire process, Etienne. Yet we could only stand helplessly by and watch while this wondrous craft," and he tapped the metal floor, "did more to save itself than did we."

"But you couldn't have done more than you did," Lyra told him. "We barely had enough time to activate the voice pickup."

"That is not the point. We know we could not have carried this boat to the river on our shoulders, but we did not have the chance to *try*. Therefore merit was lost because we did not have the opportunity to vanquish our enemy."

Lyra looked uncomfortable. "It's my understanding that your society is a pacifistic one."

"Of course, that is true."

"Then how can you talk of gaining merit by fighting?"

"Like a storm or rockfall, a declared enemy is an agent of nature. As an enemy it removes itself from the considerations of civilization."

Etienne was enjoying his wife's discomfiture enormously. "But your enemy is only acting in what he considers a civilized manner."

"He must be judged by civilized standards."

"You mean, by Tsla standards."

"Naturally. You do not think that we would adopt the standards of the Mai?" He sounded politely outraged. "A truly civilized people instinctively know what constitutes civilized behavior."

"Sounds like expediency to me."

"Not at all. Our moral standards are not nearly so flexible."

"Then you feel remorse when you kill an enemy?"

"Naturally. An enemy is one who has freely abjured his soul. How else could we feel but sorry for him?"

"That wouldn't, however, have prevented you from killing every Mai in Hochac who opposed you?"

"No, it would not. By opposing us in the recovery of your property they would have demonstrated disregard for civilized behavior, thus removing themselves from consideration by those who adhere to such behavior. I see no contradiction in this."

"No contradiction at all." He glanced at his wife. Lyra's note-taker was running and she didn't look up at Tyl. "Just wanted the point clarified."

"I thought," Lyra said quietly, "that the Tsla considered it sinful to kill."

"To kill any civilized person, yes, a terrible sin. But there is no moral restraint against defending oneself from the hostility of an uncivilized person any more than it is sinful to raise a roof to keep out the rain."

"All perfectly clear," Etienne agreed. He was content. It was clear that his initial worries about the safety of the Tsla were unfounded. For all their vaunted pacifism they were quite capable of taking care of themselves should the need arise. Killing a civilized person is a sin. Anyone who assaults me is uncivilized. Very neat.

Neat enough to quash Lyra's romanticized notions of Tsla society. Her beloved mystics were no more or less bloodthirsty than any other primitive folk. Well, that wasn't quite fair. But it was evident they could slaughter with a clear conscience so long as their victims fell below civilized standards. When you set those standards yourself it gave you considerable flexibility in establishing a defense.

Lyra continued to press Tyl for information, hoping to bolster her fading thesis of Tsla nobility. Etienne left to check the autopilot and then to see what the other Tsla and Homat were up to. He also wanted to tell the porters that, in his eyes at least, they'd acquired a great deal of merit for what they'd done in Hochac.

They were more than three thousand kilometers north northwest of Steamer Station and the distant Skatandah Delta. Cloud cover was increasing daily though it brought little relief from the heat and humidity. The Barshajagad was beginning to narrow sharply, towering walls shortening the daylight on the river. Both sides of the canyon could be seen now though the edge of the Guntali Plateau was still faint with distance. But for the first time it felt like they were sailing up a canyon.

Ahead lay another major tributary of the Skar, the river Gaja. Beyond this confluence, according to Tyl, the Barshajagad's walls drew toward one another with breathtaking suddenness, closing in to seal off the place where river devils were born, the Topapasirut. Beyond the Topapasirut lay lands unknown even to the wise men of Turput.

One thing Etienne no longer had to concern himself about was Lyra's tendency to adopt Tsla habits. After Tyl's breakfast explanation of adaptable battlefield philosophy he never again saw her in Tsla cape and toga.

They reached the place where the Gaja flowed thick and muddy into the clear Skar. The Tsla records were accurate. It was immensely wide and tinged a pale rust in color. The Gaja was another Amazon, just another tributary. He felt no amazement. Tslamaina had already exhausted his store of geological superlatives.

Beyond the Gaja the Skar narrowed rapidly. As it did so the current intensified. Submerged mountains and hills began to produce some white water, the first they'd encountered in their long journey Upriver. The cloud cover was thick overhead and Etienne saw why that section of the river had not been accurately mapped by the single orbiting satellite.

Seven thousand meters overhead, the edge of the Guntali glistened with ice and snow. The rim was now a mere two hundred and fifty kilometers distant to east or west, descending toward the bottom of the canyon in a series of steps and escarpments. Through the telescope Etienne examined one sheer wall some four thousand meters high.

One day they were cruising slowly so that Etienne could check the standard subsurface water samples. Lyra sat at the controls while Etienne was working in the lab astern. Several Tsla were watching the logging procedure with interest while Homat lay half asleep on his mat on the rear deck. Suddenly the boat tipped wildly, almost knocking

Etienne from his feet. Something had bumped the right side of the hull.

"What the hell was that?" Etienne yelled forward.

"I don't know. Something hit us from below."

"What's with the scanner?"

"Nothing. It didn't come from Upriver."

He did some fast thinking. Whatever had nudged them un-gently hadn't shown up on the scanner. Therefore it hadn't slipped down toward them. Therefore it must have come up *behind* them.

Therefore it sure as hell wasn't a rock.

Homat was shouting hysterically from astern and Etienne and the Tsla piled out through the rear door into the hot, damp air. Even as he emerged Etienne caught himself wishing for his pistol.

Not that it would have done him any good. He was staring at a slowly rising cliff black as polished obsidian. Within the cliff was a cavern, filled with acres of dripping blueblack streamers like baleen, only thicker and more widely spaced.

"Lacoti!" Homat was blubbering in fear. Etienne immediately understood how they'd missed the creature on the scanner, since it was programed only to acknowledge submerged objects which might be dangerous to the boat. The device would blithely ignore anything organic flattened out along the river bottom. The current provided food for the Lacoti, which doubtless rested contentedly in the mud of the Skar, mouth agape to receive whatever nourishment the river chose to provide.

Unless something disturbed it, of course.

If the Lacoti had eyes, they were hidden somewhere back of that vast cavernous maw. It was moving toward them, a fact that he perceived right away. He shouted toward the intercom, unafraid but having no wish for a closer view of Lacoti gut. It might be a slow swimmer but it might also be capable of a last second burst of speed. "Lyra, there's something back here that's about half the size of a starship. Move us out of here."

"What do you think I'm trying to do? I can see it on the rear screen!" Her voice was frantic. "We've got a short or something. I can't get any speed up."

"Oh hell," he muttered. "Tyl?"

The Tsla wore a fatalistic expression. "We are not river dwellers and have no experience of such creatures. We can pray."

Etienne let out a curse and dove into the cabin. Behind him the towering gullet was drawing slowly nearer. Part of the problem stemmed from the fact that it was sucking in water at an enormous rate, creating a suction the hydrofoil was hard put to counter. If they didn't lift up on foils and make some speed they were going to go down the Lacoti's throat like a cork in a sewer. He had no idea what had prodded it out of its bottom lair. Maybe the hydrofoil's engine produced a discomfiting vibration. No time now for study.

He reached the cockpit and shoved Lyra aside. She didn't protest.

"Emergency override?"

"I tried it already!"

He fumbled at the instrumentation. The stern screens were dark now and he could hear the echo of water rushing down a monstrous throat.

The familiar high whine of the jet filled the air. Lyra was thrown against a wall and the backrest of the pilot's seat pressed hard into Etienne's back. For an instant Etienne was sure he could see a thick black lip overhead as the boat slid down that endless throat. Then they were out in the light again and the stern screen showed the immense mouth receding behind them. It closed and the Lacoti sank like an island. A quick check of the scanner showed it was not pursuing, just as it revealed rocky outcrops, mudpoles, and vegetation growing atop the massive back. The thought that something the size of the Lacoti required camouflage was sobering. The sooner they reached shallower water the better he'd like it.

He rechecked the readouts before allowing himself a long, relieved sigh. "Go check our passengers."

"Don't give me orders," she snapped as she pushed back her hair and adjusted one fallen halter strap. "I know what to do. I'm just not as mechanically inclined as you, that's all."

He spoke very carefully, conscious that she was treading a fine line between anger and hysteria. "When you tried the

[133]

accelerator you forgot to disengage the secondary lock on the autopilot. That's why the emergency override didn't work either."

"I know that," she murmured. She was mad at herself, he saw, not at him. "I saw that thing in the screen and I got scared. I guess...I panicked a little."

"It could have happened to anyone," he said softly. He didn't want to say that. What he wanted to do was let off tension by calling her a stupid, senseless little fool. But he didn't. He was gentle and understanding. It was possibly the most intelligent thing he'd done since they'd stepped off the shuttle at Steamer Station many months ago.

What really confused him was that he didn't know why he did it.

"I'm going to run a complete checkout," he told her. "That thing coming up underneath our keel gave us a pretty good jolt. I want to make sure it didn't bust something loose."

She nodded. "I'll have a look in the hold."

She was gone for several minutes, returned sooner than expected. Her expression was grim.

"Etienne, we've suffered a fatality."

"What?" He spun the seat around and stared at her in disbelief. "How? We made it clear in time."

"One of the porters. Her name was Uon. When you hit the accelerator I was thrown against the wall. Everyone out back was knocked to the deck. But Uon was standing up top, near the mast. When we shot forward she lost her footing and fell. Cracked her skull, looks like. She's dead."

Fingers tightened on the back of the seat. "I didn't have any choice," he growled. "Another second's delay and we'd have become a meal."

"I already explained that to Tyl and the others. They understand completely. They've...made a request."

He didn't look up. "What do they want?"

"They'd appreciate it if we could stop hereabouts for the night so they can give Uon a proper sendoff. I didn't get the details but apparently there's a lot of ritual involved. They want to anchor somewhere inshore."

"I suppose we can find a quiet place. Least we can do. I'm really sorry, Lyra."

"It was my fault as much as anyone's." She smiled slightly.

"They've accepted it with somber grace. They adjust to death very well."

Now he looked up. "Maybe better than we? If that's a sign of social maturity I'm willing to concede the point."

But his concession didn't make her feel any better.

They found a small cove, no more than an oversized pothole that the Skar's swirls and eddies had etched into the riverbank. The night sky was a dull starless gray thanks to the solid cover of clouds that stretched like a fluffy awning from one rim of the Guntali to the other.

Lyra overcame her sorrow by burying herself in her studies, trying to record every slightest nuance of the Tsla funeral ceremony which was performed on the open rear deck of the hydrofoil. This involved the use of torches, some special powder carried by Tyl, and much chanting and singing. Having no desire to participate or watch, Homat had relinquished his bedmat for the privacy of the bow. He lay there murmuring spirit rhymes as he leaned over the side to watch the phosphorescent motocrullers, tiny, superfast clamlike bivalves that made whirlpools of light beneath the shade afforded by the ship.

Having considerably less interest in native rituals than his wife, Etienne had retired to the comfort of their cabin. The expression on her face when she burst in on him startled him out of his reading. She stumbled against him and he put both hands on her shoulders to steady her. She looked ill.

"What's wrong, Lyra, what's the matter?" She'd left the door open behind her and the steady chant of the Tsla filtered in to the bedchamber.

"Sendoff ritual," she whispered, choking on the words. She pushed past him, toward the head. The recorder dangling from her neck bounced against her chest.

Curiosity overcame his apprehension as he left the cabin and headed astern. The rear deck was lit by the flicker of torchlight, illuminating the source of Lyra's distress. His reaction was less violent than hers. Not that he was delighted by the sight, but since he held no high hopes for the Tsla he was far less disgusted and disappointed than his wife.

The Tsla were deeply engaged in the funeral ritual and only Tyl broke away long enough to greet him. He looked concerned. This was mitigated somewhat by the blood dripping from his mouth and snout.

"Lyra left us in a hurry. I hope we did not offend her."

Etienne summoned unsuspected reserves of diplomacy. "My wife sees you and your people as being nobler than any of us have a right to be. It's a failing many humans are heir to."

Tyl's nose twitched and those big soulful eyes turned toward the doorway. "I see. But you feel differently?"

"After a fashion. I don't approve, but neither do I condemn. Neither would Lyra, if she hadn't lost sight of her scientific training."

"I am sorrowed," Tyl continued. "It is part of the ritual. It must be done the same day, as soon after death as possible, because otherwise..."

Etienne cut him off. "The reasons are self-explanatory, Tyl." He was unable to keep his eyes from the scene on the deck. "It's only that the customs are very different among my own folk."

"I can sympathize." He gestured backward with a hand. "Uon was much loved by her friends. We could not think of sending her soul on to eternity without properly displaying that affection."

"We feel likewise, only among our kind we choose to express such love for the departed in more metaphysical and less immediate terms."

"Customs are different among all peoples. Now if you will excuse me, I must participate or Uon's soul will not count me among its friends."

Etienne pointed. "You have blood on your face."

Tyl wiped at it. "The result of ritual contact. She struck the deck very hard."

Etienne left the ceremony to return to the cabin, closing the door behind him. Lyra sat on the bed, staring blankly at a xenological chip unscrolling on the viewer. He doubted she saw the words. He sat down behind her and put both hands on her shoulders.

"I know how you feel," he said helplessly. "It's never pleasant to have one's illusions shattered."

"Such hopes," she muttered disconsolately. "I had such

hopes for them. They seemed to have progressed so far without the corresponding technological traumas."

"They *have* progressed far," he found himself saying, to his own considerable surprise. "But it's still an alien culture, Lyra. You can't let yourself lose sight of that, let your scientific observations be compromised by your feelings for them personally. You can't anthropomorphize their culture any more than you can their physiognomy."

"If I did that," she replied, "it was out of hope."

"I realize that, which is why you're going to make your report on Tsla funeral custom as detailed and informative as any other part of your records. The balance it will provide is important. It will help confirm your objectivity. Otherwise all the rest of your work among these people will be disregarded."

"You're right, of course." She put the chip reader aside, fiddled with her recorder as she leaned back against him. "I don't have any choice, do I?"

"As Lyra Redowl you do. As visiting xenologist representing the interests of every xenologist who couldn't make this trip, you do not."

She nodded, then stood. "It was unprofessional of me to run away like that. I know better. Among the new one must always expect a shock or two."

"It's easier for me. Rocks are rarely shocking."

She smiled, not because his sally was funny but because he bothered to try and make it so.

"We're only human, Lyra."

"Yes, and the Tsla are not. For a moment I'd forgotten that. I won't forget again."

"Don't let this push you too far in the other direction. Whatever you think personally about their customs, they're still good people, and our friends. Tyl is what he's always been: a learned and compassionate friend."

"Among his own kind, yes. Etienne, you've been right and I've been wrong."

He turned away, embarrassed by her admission as he often was when he won some small portion of their private war. There was a contradiction there he didn't understand.

She started toward the hall and the stern deck, muttering as she went. "After all, one can make the argument that ceremonial necrophilia is no more barbaric than any of a half dozen other funeral rituals observed among pristine primitive cultures. Among the Canuli, for example..." Her voice faded as she slipped further into scholarly preoccupation.

He felt sorry for her at the same time that he was glad he hadn't chosen to share her discipline. He made a mental note to inform Tyl sometime soon that in the event he and Lyra should meet with a fatal accident, they were to be buried in accordance with human custom only.

Still, several days passed before Lyra could bring herself to talk with Tyl or any of the surviving porters. They sensed her distress and kept their distance, no easy thing to accomplish within the confines of the hydrofoil. They busied themselves with learning the art of trolling, something they could not do on the unnavigable waters of the upper Aurang.

They were now five thousand kilometers north of Steamer Station, with an unknown distance yet to cover. Unknown because the satellite responsible for the photogrammetric mapping of Tslamaina had rather neglected this portion of the northern hemisphere in favor of detailing the much more heavily populated areas around the equator and the Groalamasan Sea.

The temperature had fallen to the point where Homat was obliged to don long clothing in order to be comfortable in the ninety degree heat of midday. Of greater concern was the sharp narrowing of the Barshajagad. Towering walls had closed in on the river, compressing its volume into a much smaller channel, and the increasingly swift current was becoming powerful enough to slow their progress even though the water could gain a grip only on the two submerged hydrofoils. They encountered no white water, however, and the scanner indicated the river bottom still lay far below their keel.

But Etienne found it difficult to concentrate on such things; he was hypnotized by the canyon walls, seven thousand meters that dropped in places sheer to the river, a gorge unmatched even on gas giants with surfaces solid enough to withstand continual erosion by high winds. All that remained of the sky was a narrow strip directly overhead, masked by perpetual cloud cover, a faint gray band delineating the limits of the real world.

Each time the river bent, the rock cliffs seemed to swallow any hope of retreat. The hydrofoil seemed very small indeed as it fought that steadily intensifying current. The Redowls worked in relays now, unable to trust navigation to the autopilot. If they lost speed while they both slept and the river caught hold of them, it would crush the duralloy hull against one of the granite walls as easily as eggshell.

[XI]

Two days of this saw their speed dangerously reduced. Lyra entered the cockpit rubbing her eyes, took one clear look at her husband's and said, "Etienne, we can't keep this up. We're both exhausted and we've no way of knowing how much longer this stretch is."

He coughed into his fist. "I thought the damn track would start widening out again by now. It doesn't make sense. This much water moving downstream at this speed ought to have worn a broader canyon. But it hasn't."

"What's the current reading currently?" She half smiled, half yawned as she squinted toward the instrumentation, wishing it could produce a cup of post-Ethiopian *katfe*. Unfortunately the nearest cup of *real* hot stimulant was light-years distant.

"Have a look for yourself." He touched a button without taking his eyes off the river.

She blinked at the readout. "That's incredible," she said quietly.

"Yes, incredible. No boat was ever designed to travel against such a current."

"What about continuing on repellers?"

"Don't tempt me. Sweet of you to suggest it, but it's too risky. We could try it for a few hours, but that's all they're designed for. Hopping rapids and avoiding waterfalls, not steady travel. We'd run down the batteries and probably find ourselves stuck in an identical position farther Upriver. Can't chance it." He muttered an obscenity.

"We can't quit here! We've come too far."

She leaned against the console. "I know how much this meant to you, Etienne. But it's not worth risking our lives for."

He looked at her then. "You think we have a life?"

A new voice interrupted them. "I overhear. There may yet be a way. I have had long to think on it and would not have thought it possible, had I not seen what thy spirit boat can accomplish."

Etienne didn't turn to confront their visitor. "What way, Tyl?"

"Do thee remember the crevice splitting the east wall, that we passed the previous day?"

"No. I was too busy looking over the bow to do any sightseeing."

"I was working on my notes," Lyra added.

"I have been watching the Barshajagad, marveling long, but always watching. There was a trail along the east wall. It terminates at this crevice. I have been this way once before. I saw no reason to mention the trail, to distract thee from thy work. We were to travel by boat, not by foot. But now I see that I must mention this other possibility or all will end."

"A trail? I didn't . . . no, wait a minute," Lyra murmured. "I did see something. I thought it was an old high-water line."

"It is a trail, Learned Lyra. A trading trail."

"Where does it go?" she asked him.

"Up. Up to a high plateau. Not the Guntali. Higher than Turput but lower than that. High enough so that Tsla can live upon it. Up above the Topapasirut. The trail is steeper and more dangerous than the one that climbs to Turput."

"How much more dangerous?"

[141]

"Enough to restrict travel. But it rises beyond the To-papasirut."

Etienne gestured ahead, at the narrow, impossibly deep canyon. "I thought that this place was the Topapasirut."

Tyl executed a gesture full of amused negativity. "No. If you would take the measure of the adversary that still lies ahead, thee must climb beyond its reach. That is, if thee think thy spirit boat can go no farther."

"Point of diminishing returns, Etienne," Lyra reminded him. "Every hour we're using more power to cover less distance. Can't you calculate how long it will be before we reach the break-even point and find ourselves making no progress even at full power?"

"Soon enough. You say there's a way to get around this Topapasirut, Tyl?"

"Above, yes. Beyond, I do not know. I have not been to that place. But I have gazed on the Topapasirut. If thee would do likewise, thee must leave thy boat behind, at least until thee see for thyselves."

"Leave it where?"

"Turn back to the trail end. I would not have thought there was a place, but thy boat can rise like a bird from the water."

Etienne looked at Lyra.

"It's your decision, Etienne. You're the geologist."

"Hydrology's not my specialty, though. But it's starting to look more and more like we've come to a dead end, at least as far as this section of the river is concerned." He looked back at Tyl. "The east wall, you said?"

The Tsla nodded. Etienne turned back to the instruments. Unwilling to risk turning the boat broadside to the current, he lifted it on repellers and turned it neatly in midair before setting it gently back into the water.

There was a sharp lurch as the river caught the hull. He used only enough power to maneuver, letting the cells recharge as they raced back downstream.

"This is our best chance, Etienne. We have to see what we're up against."

"I know that, dammit. The canyon *has* to widen out somewhere above this. It can't be like this all the way to the arctic line. Too much erosion. There's a geological anomaly some-where ahead of us."

"And it has a name, apparently. Could it be another big waterfall, like the Cuparaggai above Turput?"

"No. I'm sure of that much, anyway. The water here isn't acting like that and there's no indication of a sharp rise in elevation at this point. The photogrammetrics are solid enough on that score. That's why I don't understand this intensified flow. But if this Topapasirut's only the narrowest part of the canyon, we'll see how much farther Upriver it lies. Maybe we *can* pass above it on repellers."

By midday they had returned to the section of cliff Tyl had spotted. Etienne again lifted the hydrofoil on its repellers, set it down on an exposed beach out of reach of the river's grasp.

The crevice to which Tyl had alluded turned out to be much more than that—it was a break in the Barshajagad wall, a sizable side canyon rising toward the sky. And the winding line against the rocks that Lyra had thought was a high-water mark did indeed show signs of use. It snaked along the granitic wall and started up the side passage.

"Now we climb," said Tyl confidently.

"For how long?"

"Several days, at least." He turned his gaze upward.

"Homat won't be glad to hear that," Etienne murmured.

"Why not leave him to watch over the boat?" Lyra suggested.

"Sensible. We'll leave one of the porters with him and carry our own supplies. I don't imagine he'll regret missing the chance to view the 'birthplace of all river devils.'"

"I will come with thee and leave the others behind, for I do not share thy trust of the Mai," Tyl said.

"Homat's been invaluable," Etienne replied. "Without his aid we wouldn't be here now."

"His kind are not to be trusted."

"In this instance I think you're wrong, Tyl," Lyra said. It was the first time Etienne had seen her openly dispute the Tsla's opinion.

Tyl responded with a gesture of indifference. "Then I will direct Swd to remain behind by himself. While recuperating, he will keep watch over thy property—and its other guard."

A small stream trickled down the branch canyon, which was indeed steeper than anything they'd climbed thus far. As the meters dropped behind and below them, so did the temperature. The Redowls were obliged to wear their long-sleeved and long-legged attire while Tyl and the porters re-donned their capes and togas. Since they didn't expect to find any villagers to trade with, they carried a full stock of rations.

They ascended to the cloud. At five thousand meters Lyra was having some trouble breathing, though this was due more to the unaccustomed exertion than the altitude. Due to the denser atmosphere, five thousand meters on Tsla-maina was equivalent to thirty-five hundred meters or so on Terra.

As they crested the trail head, the clouds momentarily parted. Ahead rose the peak of a steep-sided mountain that towered above them and the nearby edge of the Guntali. As they rested, Etienne took a sighting on the peak.

"Eleven thousand meters, most of it frozen."

"Aracunga," Tyl said. Etienne noticed that all the Tsla now wore their sturdiest clothing. They stood some two thousand meters higher than Turput, at the upper limit of the Tsla ecological zone. They could climb higher still, but not comfortably.

After several days of climbing to the east, they set off northward. Etienne expected Tyl to continue in that direction, but he was wrong. On the second day they turned slightly to the west, and by that evening the Redowls could feel thunder again.

They expected another waterfall, perhaps one that plunged the full five thousand meters to the river below. But it was no waterfall Tyl led them toward. It was the Topapasirut.

Must be the father of all waterfalls, Etienne mused, still unconvinced by Tyl's denials. By the fourth day the thunder had become so loud they could communicate only by signs.

The Redowls could tap out messages on their wrist computers, but the Tsla possessed no such wondrous devices and had to make their intentions known through gestures.

It grew damp around them, the rocks treacherous and slick. Yet as they hiked now through the perpetual mist, the sky overhead remained clear.

Etienne searched in vain for signs of the expected cascade. When they finally reached the lip of the abyss, all was explained.

It was raining upward. Forced into a narrow throat of the Barshajagad, the entire volume of the Skar suddenly made a sharp and unexpected bend from south to west. As a result, the swiftly flowing river cannonaded into the north cliff face that formed the base of the mountain Aracunga, five thousand meters below their feet.

This produced a spray that rose on disturbed air to drench the puny observers clinging to a granite overhang. The solid bedrock trembled under the river's impact. Tyl communicated with gestures, but any description was superfluous before the stupendous sight below.

Etienne knew that this was the Topapasirut, the birthplace of all river devils. He knew that Tyl had been more than right when he'd insisted no boat could pass through this place. The hydrofoil could not rise high enough on its repellers to clear the maelstrom.

Across the canyon, rising from the opposite side of the abyss, was a metamorphic mass that dwarfed even Aracunga.

"The Prompaj!" Tyl screamed into Etienne's ear. He took another sighting.

"Fourteen thousand two hundred meters," he informed Lyra via wrist computer. "An impossible mountain. I think the two peaks were once closer than now. See how the river bends sharply to the west before turning south again? Tslamaina's seismically stable now, but a few eons back there must have been one hell of an earthquake in this part of the world. See the signs of slippage?" He pointed to particular strata down in the roaring canyon.

"This section of the surface slipped eastward. South of here the land went west. The result was the displacement of the northern third of the Skar several kilometers to the east. I'm glad I wasn't around then."

Lyra tapped out a reply. "I'm not real happy to be here now. Let's get away. I'm cold and wet."

They lingered a few moments longer so he could chip a few more pictures, take some final measurements. Then they headed back toward the trail head, leaving the clouds and hillsides to swallow up the Topapasirut, its thunder, and the brooding massif that was called Prompaj.

They made camp that night in a small cave, drying themselves and their clothes before a large fire. Etienne watched with interest as the porters groomed each other's fur.

The Redowls said little. There was no point in belaboring the obvious. Their expedition had reached its end. They'd run up against not a brick wall but a watery one.

When the porters had finished and dressed themselves once more they gathered close around the warmth of the fire. Tyl spoke while his companions ate.

"What will thee do now, Learned Etienne? Does the spirit boat possess some magical power we have not seen that would enable it to pass through the Topapasirut?"

"It does not," Etienne replied glumly. "We do have other machines which can fly through the air and put any bird to shame, but we don't have one here. We chose to travel by boat. It's all we have. You were right, Tyl. I apologize for doubting you."

"You had not seen the Topapasirut, Etienne. No one believes until they have seen."

"That's it, then." Lyra was not as disappointed as her husband, though she strove to sound as sympathetic as possible. If they could no longer go onward, they would have to go back, and she still had work to do among the Tsla.

"You've been stopped by a geological phenomenon, Etienne. What better way to conclude your report? Think of the reaction among your colleagues when you describe this place. Maybe some day we can come back up here with an aircar."

He'd been staring at the floor of the cave. Now he looked up, determined. "They'll be fascinated, but it won't be the end of my report."

"Etienne," she said gently, "we can't get through that chute. You've already acknowledged that."

"I won't be stopped by the very river I've come to survey."

She sighed, leaned back against the inflated sleeping pad. "Maybe you'll accept it by morning."

"Maybe."

He did not, nor did he admit defeat during the long descent to the Skar. He kept to himself and brooded, causing Tyl to move next to Lyra.

"What ails Etienne?"

"He's unhappy because he knows we can't go on. That means he'll have to leave his work here unfinished."

"But it is not his fault. Nothing passes Upriver beyond the Topapasirut. He has no control over that. It is not as if he were beaten by something in himself."

"He knows all that, Tyl, but he is persistent, Etienne is. Always has been."

"I see. A Tsla teacher would accept the inevitable; such constant worry is harmful to the mind."

"True, but sometimes it can lead to solutions where none seem possible. I've seen him do it before. Within our fields, Etienne and I are well respected. We've achieved success where others have failed. It's one of the reasons we were allowed to make this expedition while other applicants were rejected. Sometimes, Tyl, blind persistence can succeed where everything else has failed."

"I still do not understand why you would sacrifice peace of mind. I can admire such tenacity, but I cannot empathize with it."

Down on the river there was a brief but joyful reunion with those left behind. Homat didn't try to conceal his relief over the safe return of his human protectors.

"All these days," he whispered to Lyra later, "trapped with that Tsla, and him mumbling and chanting to himself all the time. It was enough to drive a sane person crazy. Did you find a way to pass this Topapasirut?"

"No, we did not." To her surprise Homat looked downcast. "I thought you'd be pleased. That means we have to go back Downriver now, back to the warm lands of the Skatandah. Don't you miss them?"

"Very much so, but I have joined myself to your purposes and therefore am disappointed for you."

"That's a very nice thing to say, Homat." She hadn't expected such depth of feeling from the Mai. Nor was it a ruse. He was genuinely distressed that their journey had come to an end.

She looked past him, frowned. Etienne was deep in discussion with Tyl and looking more animated than he had in many days. She strolled over to join them.

"What's all the excitement about?"

"You tell her," Etienne suggested to Tyl, his features alive with enthusiasm.

"On the eastern flank of Aracunga Mountain," Tyl explained, "lies the Tsla trading town of Jakaie. I have not visited it myself but it is known to Turput. It is said that beyond Jakaie and the mass of the mountain, the Barshajagad once more becomes a navigable river. If thee could but convey thy craft to that place, thee might safely resume thy journey—if the story is accurate."

"An impossible if."

"Maybe not," Etienne murmured. He was tense with possibilities. "Maybe we could portage around."

For a long moment she just stared at him. Then she let her gaze trace the lower section of the steep trail that wound its torturous course up the side canyon.

"Sure we could. We'll just hoist the boat onto our shoulders and haul it five thousand meters straight up. Lost your mind?"

Her skepticism didn't even slow him down. "No, I've just found it. Look, the hydrofoil's made of ultralight material. The hull's a carbon filament honeycomb. And we can surmount the rough spots on the repellers."

"With what power?" she argued. "We'd burn out the cells."

"We would not. You're not listening. We'd only use the repellers to get over real steep places. The rest of the time we'd rely on muscle power. Porters, Lyra! Mount the boat on some kind of platform and pull it up and over."

She did some quick figuring. "I admit the hydrofoil's light, but it's a relative lightness. You'd still need a thousand Mai or Tsla to drag it up a thousand meters."

He looked back at Tyl. "Tell her."

"There is a draft animal," the Tsla explained, "that the Mai use all along the river. It is called a vroqupii. The Mai use them in teams to pull trading boats Upriver against the current. They are strong." He eyed Homat. "Well, Mai?"

The guide looked thoughtful. "We passed many trading villages below this place. Each should be home to a few vroqupii. The animals used hereabouts must be unusually powerful because the current is so fast."

"Do you think we could find enough to do it?" Etienne asked.

"I do not know." Homat gazed at the intimidating trail.

Lyra's dreams of returning to tranquil Turput were slipping away. "Assuming we could find enough animals to do the job, could we hire enough? Would their owners consent to such an undertaking?"

"If they were promised enough money, certainly," Homat replied, looking at her as if she'd just disputed a fundamental law of nature.

"What would we pay them with?"

"Our trade goods," Etienne said. "We have some left."

"If we use up our remaining supplies we won't have anything to give any natives we meet beyond this point."

"If we don't get beyond this point the question becomes moot." She had no comeback for that. Etienne turned to Homat. "Would these vroqupii be able to climb as high as Jakaie?" He translated the relevant measurements into Mai terms.

Homat looked uneasy. "We go that much higher than the home of these Tsla who accompany us?" Etienne nodded. "I am not sure. But these Upriver tribes are proud. They might see such a proposal as a challenge."

"They wouldn't freeze. It's not *that* high," Etienne said.

Tyl agreed. "Many Mai hunters hike beyond Turput in search of prey, and their blood continues to flow."

"How many vroqupii might we need?" Homat wondered. An intense discussion of weight versus capabilities ensued, before the Mai felt comfortable in announcing a figure.

"Thirty at least. Forty would be better, fifty best, and sixty delightful, but I do not think we can find that many willing to try, not even for a share of off-world treasure."

"We must try," Etienne told him.

"Then I will do my best to convince the Brul, as they who handle the vroqupii are called." His bald skull glistened in the reflected cloud-glare of afternoon and he smiled ingenuously. "That is my job, is it not?"

Etienne nodded once. "Let's get started. Lyra, are you sure you're willing to go along with this?"

She shrugged. "If you're determined I couldn't stop you anyway, Etienne. I think it's a mistake to sacrifice the rest of our trade goods on a scheme that has a good chance of failing, but I can't argue that it's your last chance to go on. Our last chance," she added with a faint smile.

"I promise," he told her, "if it looks like we're not going to make it, we'll turn back and return to Turput. I know that's what you want."

She almost said, "I want what you want, Etienne," but did not. Their relationship was based on more powerful bonds than artificial acquiescence. They did not give in to each other; they agreed on things. She agreed now and having agreed, considered how best to help.

"Tyl, do you think it can be done with thirty vroqupii?"

"I have watched them pull heavily laden ships Upriver," the Tsla replied thoughtfully. "They are very strong. But it will require more than mere strength to achieve this thing. It will take cooperation among the Mai who are involved. The vroqupii can, I think, pull thy spirit boat up to Jakaie, but not if the Brul fall to quarreling among themselves."

"They'll cooperate!" Homat declared angrily. "I'll see to it that they do."

"And why should they listen to thee?" Tyl replied without malice. "Thee are a runaway from one of the far city-states that border the Groalamasan. The river folk do not trust those who come from the lands that lie against the Sea."

"I am not of the city-states," Homat said proudly. "Not anymore. I am of," he hesitated to glance sideways at Etienne and Lyra, "I am of these folk." Etienne suddenly felt very good.

"Don't include me in that mental family," Lyra said sardonically. "I'm going along with this insanity but I don't believe in it. If Homat wants to consider himself as one with Etienne, that's fine. Idiocy knows no species boundaries." Everyone smiled.

"We'll do it, Lyra," Etienne told her, putting an arm around her shoulders. "You'll see. We'll do it! We'll get the hydrofoil up to Jakaie, around the Topapasirut, and down to the river on the far side. Then we'll be on our way again."

"Sure we will," she said softly. She inhaled deeply. "Well, I guess we'd better get on with it. The sooner this is begun, the sooner it will end."

"That's right," he replied with a grin, "but not the way you think it will."

Word was passed down the river, the call going out for the bravest of Brul mahouting only the strongest of mounts. Meanwhile the carpenters of the village of Taranau, which was the last sizable town near the narrowing of the Barshajagad, set about under Etienne's and Lyra's instructions building a platform to hold the hydrofoil. It was to be light and strong, with double-wheeled axles fore and aft. These could be bound to the platform which in turn could be attached to the two hydrofoils. Not only would the skeleton frame provide a maximum of support with a minimum of weight, the open woodwork also would not block the downward exhausts of the repellers.

Though they talked as rapidly as their brethren, the Brul turned out to be less loquacious and argumentative than their urbanized relatives. They formed a tightly knit society with rules all their own and wore their pride on their faces. It was not quite group arrogance.

Lyra learned from Homat that most of the Brul lived outside the villages in isolated clusters or in single dwellings with only the immediate family for company. Their lives were devoted to the care and handling of their vroqupii.

As it turned out the Redowls did not have to exhaust their store of trade goods. Once the nature of the enterprise became widely known, Brul arrived from distant locations not to serve for pay but simply to pit the strength and endurance of their animals against those of their competitors.

Still, the expedition was fortunate in engaging forty of the massive animals and their owners. After some discussion among the Brul the vroqupii were yoked to the boat in ten ranks of four abreast. They walked on pile-driver legs and their bellies scraped the earth. The vroqupii was all traction and muscle, its short square head set on a bull neck. A line of horny plates ran along the upper jaw and swept back to form a low ridge above each eye, downcurving to shield the throat.

It was a startling assembly, not the least because with a

few faintly yellow exceptions, the vroqupii were clad in short, bristly, rose-hued fur. They grunted and heaved against their harnesses, anxious to get moving. The Brul sat on the soft saddle behind the neck frill, alternately joking with and taunting his fellow drovers.

With the rushing roar of the Skar for counterpoint, the expedition finally got under way. At first there was nothing but good-natured jostling for position as each Brul strove to prove that his animal was the strongest. Eventually the drovers settled down to work, conversation fading as each concentrated on the task at hand.

The vroqupii plodded onward in comparative silence, even when they reached the branch canyon and the way turned steep and difficult. They were used to pulling against the constant pressure of the river, and the incline did not seem to cause them any unusual problems. Etienne knew the real test would come during the final thousand meters, when the air turned cold and thin.

Days passed and their speed slowed only slightly. What did drop off considerably was the amount of joking among the Brul, as the difficulty of what they were attempting began to sink in. Etienne had Homat weaving in and out among the Mai every night, listening for talk of discouragement or dissent.

The tension was hard on everyone, and when they finally passed the four-thousand-meter mark, four-fifths of the way to the top, humans, Tsla, and Mai were as tired as the patient vroqupii. It had been days since any joking had passed among the Brul, and the increasingly cold air was beginning to bother them if not their animals.

A few quit under the strain. One was killed when, shivering from the chill, he fell from his mount and was crushed under the heavy feet of the team behind him before it could be halted. But even those Brul who gave up left their animals in the care of friends, admonished them to return the precious creatures in good condition when the final goal was achieved—if it ever was. Forlorn and disappointed, they straggled back down the trail by ones and twos.

It was the cold that discouraged them more than anything else. By the time the temperature had fallen to sixty degrees the Brul were so wrapped up in heavy clothing it was all they could do to cling to their saddles. A steady breeze tumbled from the flanks of nearby Aracunga, and soon even Etienne and Lyra had to bundle up.

"Do you think we'll make it?" Lyra asked her husband one day as she finished the latest count of the remaining Brul. "It looks like we just might, if we don't lose too many more drovers."

"Don't you go getting confident on me just when I'm starting to have doubts," he told her. He blew into his hands. If the temperature fell much further they would have to dig jackets out of the hydrofoil's storage lockers. The Tsla also looked uncomfortable. It was chillier than it had been during their climb to the Topapasirut.

As Tyl had explained, Jakaie lay at the uppermost limit of Tsla habitation. Above that level even the hardiest Tsla crops withered and died, though one could survive by foraging and hunting. Or so it was said.

Forty-five hundred meters, forty-six, and as Etienne's nervousness increased, Lyra's spirits rose.

"We're going to make it, Etienne. You were right all the time. We're going to make it."

"I'll believe it when the boat's sitting in Jakaie's central square," he told her. "I wish I knew why you get more enthusiastic the closer we come to a crisis point, while I get more and more worried."

"We complement each other, remember? When I'm down, you're up, and vice versa."

"I thought all you wanted was to get back to Turput."

"I never thought we'd get this far. Now that we have, I'm dying to see how the Tsla of Jakaie have adapted to their harsh environment. There should be different architecture, methods of farming, cooking, everything. Society as a function of altitude. There's a whole paper in that."

"Must be a very close-knit population."

"I agree, but what makes you think so? You usually don't speculate in my field."

"They have to be close. It may be the only way to keep warm."

"Anytime you think it's getting a little chilly, Etienne, just consider the poor Mai." She gestured toward the long team of vroqupii and Brul as she and Etienne marched alongside

[153]

the hydrofoil. "I wonder how low the temperature has to fall before they become susceptible to frostbite?"

"To freezing, I'd expect, but you'd never know it to look at them now. Half of them are so cold they can't shiver anymore. Too numb."

Not one Brul had quit for several days now, however. For those who remained the climb had turned into a grim contest. None would give up so close to the goal for fear of being derided by those who stayed on.

As for the vroqupii, they could not voice any complaints, but they seemed to adjust to the colder weather much better than their masters. Their pace was slower now, more measured, but none had fallen by the wayside. Undoubtedly their short brightly colored fur afforded some protection against the changing climate. It also helped that when a particularly steep spot was reached, they were unhitched while one of the humans lifted the boat and its wheels to the next level on repellers. The Brul looked forward to such respites with relief.

Forty-eight hundred meters. Forty-nine.

"Tomorrow morning." Etienne spoke as he crouched across from the portable heater they recharged every couple of days from the boat's batteries. He longed for the comfort of their heated cabin. They slept outside at Homat's insistence. If they did not, he warned them, they risked losing the respect of the Brul. "We'll reach the top of the canyon tomorrow morning."

He put down his self-heating cup of tea and slid beneath the thermosensitive blanket. The covering was warm but the ground beneath the sleeping pad very hard. A glance showed the temperature to be fifty-three.

Tomorrow, vindication, he mused. After that, two days of steady travel overland to Jakaie. There they would find friends, shelter, and fires large enough to warm even the Brul.

Lyra still sat in front of the heater, staring at her husband. "You never would know when to say no, would you, Etienne? A bad habit, one that'll be the death of both of us one of these days." She smiled. "You dragged me all this way when I'd just as soon have quit and turned back toward home."

"Home?" His eyebrows lifted.

"Well, back toward Turput. I've come to think of that as kind of a home away from home."

"In spite of the inhabitants' unpleasant burial rituals?"

"I didn't spend much time consorting with the dead. I get to do that on the boat every night."

"Very funny." But she was still smiling. Tyl sat nearby, leading his fellow Tsla in their nighttime chant. Etienne watched her as she listened to them without reaching for her recorder. Light from the porters' fire lit her profile, burning away the years.

Ten years together. She'd been very beautiful a decade ago. Now she was hardened, toughened by fieldwork, by adversity, by too many hours spent away from the comforts of civilization—and still beautiful. All the poison in her spirit, all the acid in her voice could not change that.

She grew conscious of his stare and turned back to him. "I owe you an apology for wanting to turn back."

"How about a kiss instead? I haven't had a kiss in a long time. Apologies I can live without."

She eyed him uncertainly for a moment, then walked around the heater to bend next to him, touching her lips to his. They were warm against the night.

Then she pulled away, sooner than he wished. Too brief, too considered, not spontaneous enough, he thought. But something, it was something. It had been a long time since they'd had even that.

He turned over beneath the blanket, feeling much warmed inside—and not by the heater—anxious for morning to come.

【 XII 】

Screams, shouts of panic, and the hoarse trilling cries of the vroqupii woke him, the latter a sound he hadn't heard since the start of the long climb up from the Skar. Gesticulating silhouettes rushed past his sleep-filled eyes like the shadows of ghosts. Only the heater was alive, a steady glow in the darkness.

Trying to force himself awake he sat up, hunting for the source of all the disturbance. Suddenly he found himself rising from the ground. Something had placed tight steel bands around his shoulders and the back of his neck. He screwed his head around so he could look overhead, thinking how strange it was to meet a denizen of hell five thousand meters away from the center of the planet.

Four long wings beat at the air, protruding from a thick, flattened body. Wind and a fetid, corrupt odor assailed his face. Not far from his eyes, altogether too near, was a mouth full of sharp hooks. A pair of saucer-sized bright blue eyes glared down at him. The pupils were huge and yellow.

The odor of carrion was overpowered by a sudden sharp smell of ozone. The monstrosity shivered. Lyra fired again and Etienne found himself falling. He landed heavily on his blanket and sleeping pad instead of the naked rock. With two holes burned through one wing, the creature had had enough. It lifted skyward, emitting a cry very like the sound the devil must make when gargling.

Etienne rolled over and clutched his right elbow, which had absorbed the brunt of his fall. It throbbed painfully. He was fully awake now.

Lyra jostled him as she slid on her knees next to him. Her eyes were still on the night sky. "Here," she said, handing him his pistol. "Others are still around." She gave him a hand up.

Guarding each other's backs they stumbled through the confusion and screaming, Etienne handling the asynapt with his left hand. The most immediate danger came not from the nocturnal carnivores but from the bellowing, stampeding vroqupii.

Etienne fired and fired. Though there was no recoil, his fingers grew numb simply from gripping the pistol. Eventually the night was scoured clean, however, and he let the weapon fall to his side. The stars returned, except off to the north where the air was filled with vast dark shapes, rapidly receding.

The Redowls returned to their campsite, set the heater back on its base, and sat down. All around them panic was giving way to muttered curses and exclamations in excited Mai.

Homat joined them, almost invisible in his cold-weather gear.

"What were they?" Lyra asked him. Etienne massaged his elbow, still looking to the north where a last straggler fled after its companions on ten-meter-wide wings.

"Monsters." Homat was shivering despite his bulky attire. "Very rarely do they come down to the river. They must be more common up here, where the land is better suited to monsters and Tsla!"

Other eyes joined the conference. If Tyl had overheard Homat's last words, he chose not to comment. "Strepanong," he declared, gesturing heavenward with his flexible proboscis. "Scavengers and killers." He paused. "They took two of the Brul. They rarely bother us in the fields, and never in the towns. Never have I seen so many in one place at the same time. The presence of so much meat must have drawn them."

"A bad omen, bad omen," Homat was muttering. "Perhaps we should turn back, de-Etienne."

A small invisible needle pricked his elbow and he winced. "Not after making it this far, Homat. I'm not turning back now."

"The Brul may grumble once they restore calm among their animals," Homat warned him. "They do not come this far to fight with monsters."

"Tyl, repeat what you said about never having seen so many in one place before. The chances of this happening again before we reach Jakaie are insignificant, aren't they? Tyl?"

The Tsla spoke mournfully. "I can guarantee nothing, Learned Etienne, though it would be most unlikely."

"One strepanong is too many," Homat argued.

"We drove them off," Lyra reminded him, gesturing with her pistol. "We injured several of them, maybe fatally, threw a real scare into the entire flock. I don't imagine they'll come after us again. You tell the Brul that. And from now on Etienne and I will alternate standing guard at night so we're not surprised anymore. If there is a next time they'll feast on strepanong, not the other way around."

"That is no consolation to the families of the two who were taken." Homat shuddered at the thought.

"Their families will be compensated," she promised. "Tell the Brul that if they turn back now because of a bunch of carrion eaters they're no better than children, crying for their mothers. We're only a couple of days, maybe less, from our goal, where there'll be warm shelter and safety for all."

Tyl assumed an uncharacteristically haughty air. "That much can be assured. Tsla hospitality refuses no one."

"You can also tell them," Lyra continued with a sudden burst of inspiration, "that if they insist on turning back now, we'll have to find Tsla help to take us the rest of the way."

Homat smiled at this slyness. Truly de-Lyra was becoming knowledgeable of Mai ways. "All your assurances would not convince them, but an insult to their reputations!—yes, I will tell them that. I do not think we will have any trouble."

He turned and disappeared in the direction of the vroqupii corral.

The Redowls were left alone. Lyra indicated her husband's right arm. "What's with your elbow?"

He forced a wry grin. "It thought it was a foot. I landed on it, but I don't imagine it's broken. Just feels like it. Couldn't you have managed to shoot the damned thing before it got me off the ground?"

"Sorry," she said dryly. "Be thankful we're camped on a relatively wide section of trail. You might've been dumped over a precipice."

"Wouldn't that have made for an interesting dive? Time enough for forty-eight twists with a couple dozen triple gainers thrown in. Unfortunately, I don't think I would have survived long enough to enjoy the judging."

"I'll try and come to the rescue a little sooner next time."

He was suddenly solemn as he eyed the sky. "I hope there won't be a next time. Insult to their professionalism or not, I don't imagine the Brul will stay if we're attacked again. Did you get a good enough look at our visitors to classify them? I wasn't much interested in their taxonomy myself, and I didn't have the best view."

"It wasn't a bird. I'm not even sure it was mammalian. Looked like a cross between a condor and a centipede."

"Sweet critter. I think we'll forgo any opportunities for up-close study." He grimaced as he tried to straighten his arm. "I saw enough to know it spends most if not all of its time in the air."

"I've never seen a quadruple wing arrangement like that before," she added, "except on insects, and the strepanong's no insect despite its appearance. It had feathers, and plenty of 'em."

"I know. I had to smell them." He looked toward the circle of Tsla. Tyl was watching them, the fire bright in his wide, sad eyes. "You're positive we're not more than a day or two march from this town?"

Tyl performed an elaborate gesture with his nose. "I am positive, Etienne. A passing of the sun once or twice across the sky will see us in Jakaie. I look forward to it myself, for I am curious to see how my brethren have adapted to so isolated a home. Life must be harder than in Turput."

"But not so hard they won't be able to aid us?"

"Learned Etienne, the more difficult a Tsla's circumstances, the more generous he is with his hospitality."

Lyra confirmed this declaration, as Etienne knew she would.

There was much grumbling and many more complaints than usual among the Brul the next morning as they mounted their vroqupii. That was only to be expected. Etienne thought he saw several expressions of hatred directed at himself or his wife, but Homat assured him it didn't matter whether the drovers disliked them or not. Only that they respected them.

Several of the vroqupii displayed new scars, evidence of attempts by the marauding strepanong to carry them off. At least the weather had decided to cooperate, and the grumbling rapidly died down. It was almost warm as they set out up the trail.

They reached the top of the canyon and paused for a brief celebration, which helped to raise the drovers' spirits considerably. That night they slept easy, reassured by the sight of one of the Redowls patrolling alertly with asynaptic pistol in hand.

By the following day nearly all dissension had faded away. The trail now crossed level ground and the Brul paused in their shivering long enough to study a land they'd never visited before. They realized they were pioneers of a sort and a few found they were enjoying the journey.

They were two days in from the trail head. The vroqupii surmounted the occasional ridge with ease. The beauty of the lower plateau captivated the travelers, from the rushing streams beginning their long race down to the Skar to the stunted but wide-spreading evergreens.

Lyra was particularly interested in a convoluted pile of brush that Tyl called an *aroyt*. Covering as much as half an acre, the *aroyt* was a single growth that defended its highly edible trunk with an impenetrable armor of centimeter-long thorns. There were also clumps of high mossy fungi that rose to their knees and held melt water like a sponge. Not that water underfoot was a problem. Most of the trail had been cut from solid rock. Soil was a precious rarity at this height.

They were approaching a saddle between a finger of Aracunga and a low hill when the two lead Brul who had disengaged themselves from the team to serve as advance scouts returned at a gallop. That in itself was extraordinary, since it was the first time the Redowls had seen a vroqupii move at anything faster than a walk.

Homat hurried to meet the outriders as the procession slowed. The scouts were chattering loudly to their companions as they traveled down the line.

"Maybe they've spotted Jakaie over the ridge line," Lyra suggested hopefully. Too hopefully.

Homat rejoined them quickly, his fright apparent in his expression. "The Brul are taking their animals out of harness."

"What?" Etienne looked toward the front of the team, could see the drovers working with the harness. "What the devil's wrong?"

"Exactly," Homat replied. "Many devils. Demons." His eyes were wide.

"More strepanong? Or some other animal?"

"Not animal, not animal," Homat insisted. "Demons!" Etienne could see he was far more terrified than he'd been the night of the scavenger attack.

Etienne started up the line. "They can't unhitch and quit now! We're almost there." As he spoke, several vroqupii were already moving out of file. "You've got to make them stop, Homat."

"They won't stop, de-Etienne. The strepanong they can understand, but no one can fight demons."

Desperately, Etienne turned to Tyl. "What's going on? What are they so frightened of?"

"I am not sure," Tyl murmured, "but I fear what I may know."

"Demons are in Jakaie," Homat went on. He turned to point toward the saddle just ahead. "Jakaie lies just over that ridge, but the demons are there. The Brul will go no further, de-Etienne. They say they are going back to their homes as fast as their mounts will carry them. They complain that nothing was said in the contracts about dealing with demons."

"What kind of demons?" Lyra asked, trying to make some sense of the Mai's panic.

"Ice demons!"

"Ah, it is as I fear." Tyl turned and began talking rapid-fire to his companions, the words flying almost as fast as if he were speaking Mai.

"Not the Tsla too," Etienne snapped angrily. The first retreating vroqupii were passing the boat now, heading back toward the Barshajagad. He stepped toward the nearest.

"You must stay!" he shouted in Mai. The Brul ignored him. He walked to the next in line. "You can't leave us here like this. We have a contract, an agreement." He struggled to recall the words Lyra had used to hold the drovers the night of the strepanong. "What of your commercial honor?"

"To flee from devils is no disgrace," the Brul announced with dignity, even as he looked back over his shoulder to make certain no demons pursued. And that was all any of them would say.

In less than thirty minutes the last vroqupii had disappeared over the slope behind them, its Brul urging it to greater speed. Etienne and Lyra considered their boat, marooned on a rocky plain, yoked to nothing.

"Ice demons," Etienne grumbled. "Didn't they see how easily we drove off the strepanong?"

"These are not strepanong," Tyl told him. "Thee must see to understand as thee had to see the Topapasirut to understand it. I sorrow for thee, Learned One. As for ourselves, we must go on to aid our brethren in Jakaie."

"Hey, what about us? Are we supposed to just sit here and wait for the next flood?"

"Etienne," Lyra said gently, "you're not thinking clearly. You never do when you lose your temper."

"So enlighten me."

"This town lies just over the ridge ahead." She stared meaningfully at the hydrofoil.

Realization brought embarrassment with it, though the Tsla did not perceive it. "Just ahead. We have plenty of battery power and we don't have to lift too high." Lyra nodded, turned to the Tsla. "These ice demons. They wouldn't happen to be the Na, would they?"

"What other demons of the ice are there? I thought thee knew." Tyl gestured toward the boat with his snout. "Thee will use thy spirit boat to help us?"

"To help you, yes, and ourselves, since we have to get it into Jakaie somehow. You know what to do?" Tyl nodded and moved with the porters to climb aboard. The Redowls followed.

"You wanted to see this legendary third race, the one that inhabits the Guntali," Etienne reminded her as they mounted the ladder. "Looks like you're going to have your chance."

"I'm not sure I like the circumstances, but it doesn't appear we have much say in the matter."

They checked out the boat's systems carefully. It had been several days since the repellers had been used. But the hydrofoil lifted easily off the ground and started forward on its cushion of air. The wooden platform hung beneath the hull, the huge heavy wheels spinning aimlessly. Bindings groaned but held.

Jakaie had better be as close as the Brul had indicated, Lyra thought as she guided them toward the notch in the rocks. Otherwise they'd have to squat down somewhere until the cells recharged the batteries.

Jakaie was built into a flank of Aracunga. The architecture was similar to Turput's but much heavier construction seemed to be the rule. The buildings boasted fewer windows. At that altitude the Tsla needed to conserve heat.

Off to the north lay irrigated fields filled with soil laboriously collected from notches and arroyos where it had gathered. The wall was the most obvious difference between Jakaie and Turput. It was an impressive wall; a good six or seven meters high but not especially thick.

Apparently Jakaie was high enough for creatures of the Guntali to mix with those of the Tsla ecological zone. Including, it seemed, the Na. He tried to visualize the Na in his mind's eye, using variations of the Mai-Tsla pattern—a bipedal, mammalian type. And that much was true. But the ways in which the new form diverged from those previously encountered caused the small hairs on the back of his neck to tense.

Several gates broke the town wall and no more than two dozen Na battered away at the largest. That two dozen Na would take on an entire town said more for their ferocity and disposition than all the fears expressed by the Brul.

Jakaie was large enough to harbor anywhere from five hundred to a thousand inhabitants, all of whom not only were on the defensive but appeared to be losing the battle. Tsla bodies were visible outside the wall. There was no sign of dead Na though one individual did sit some distance away from the fight. A big male, it was festooned with spears and arrows and was busily engaged in plucking them from his body as if they were so many bee stings.

As they watched from the straining hydrofoil, the gate gave way under the steady pounding from rocks and small trees. The Tsla inside scattered as the Na rushed in among them, and screams of terror pierced the clear mountain air. "Thee must hurry, Learned Ones, or many will die!" Swd called from the foredeck.

"We're moving as fast as we can," Etienne told him through the speaker membrane. "This boat wasn't designed for rapid travel out of the water."

Many primitives would have paused at the sight of so alien an object as the flying boat coming toward them. Not the Na. Either they did not possess sufficient imagination to be fearful of strange new shapes or else they were too confident in their own irresistible strength. A few bellowed in the hydrofoil's direction as it crossed over the wall, but the assault continued.

The hydrofoil bucked and rolled uneasily as they began to pass over homes and streets. It wasn't designed to compensate for such uneven terrain. Everyone aboard was glad when Etienne finally set the boat down in a parklike area near the center of Jakaie. A few anxious faces, flexible snouts aquiver, peeked out at them from shuttered windows and portholes. The noise of fighting could be heard clearly. Etienne checked his pistol as Lyra urged him to hurry. "What, in a rush to shoot some more natives?" he chided her. "How are you going to justify that in your report?"

"If this town's devastated we won't be able to find the help we'll need to get us down to the river again."

"What makes you think the Tsla here have any interest in helping us? This isn't Turput." He scrambled down the boarding ladder.

"Because we're going to endear ourselves to them by helping to repel this attack. Not that I wouldn't help them anyway." She started toward the broken gate and he had to hurry to keep up with her.

Anxious to protect her precious Tsla, he mused. But she was right about one thing: they'd do it if they had to or not. Tyl and the porters had become more than natives during the journey Upriver from Turput. They'd become friends.

Tyl and the three porters were offered arms by oldsters and adolescents. Only Homat did not accompany the reinforcements. He remained with the hydrofoil because between his bulky clothing and the temperature he'd have been useless in a fight.

It was not as if they hadn't encountered violence on Tslamaina before Jakaie, but it was still a shock to stumble onto the decapitated body of a female Tsla lying in the street. The head was nowhere around and the sounds of combat were very close.

After the Na broke through, the Tsla retreated to their strong buildings to harry the invaders with spears and arrows. Etienne and his party rounded the side of one such structure and halted only a few meters from a cluster of ten or twelve farmers who were trapped against the wall by a pair of Na. The farmers were holding the attackers off with long pikes and sharp tools, yet it was apparent that if something wasn't done quickly the Na would pick them apart one by one.

Etienne had no time to admire Tyl's bravery as their guide darted forward, weaving with the waddling gait of his kind, to cut at the leg of one Na with a curved blade. It did not penetrate the leathery skin very deeply and he had to retreat in a hurry, leaving his weapon behind.

But the Na had felt it, grunted, muttered something unintelligible, then reached down to pluck the weapon from its ankle. The creature was four meters tall and covered with a thick, shaggy pelt. Its clothing was crude—heavy sandals of some unknown leather, a leathery vest and breastplate, and a kilt of some similar material. A bone knife hung from a cord tied around the waist, the blade almost as tall as Lyra. As its main weapon, the Na clutched a club which had once been a tree of respectable size. It was panting heavily and a dark tongue lolled from a corner of its mouth.

[165]

That made sense. An inhabitant of the Guntali would have little use for sweat glands.

Without a word Etienne moved to his left, Lyra to the right. As he ran he fired. Thick hair was burned black on the back of a pillarlike thigh. The Na howled and turned its attention away from the desperate farmers.

The creature's forehead was very low and its blunt snout seemed incapable of advanced expression, but there was no mistaking that snarl of hatred. It displayed four canines, two upper, two lower. The remaining front teeth appeared to have been filed to sharp points. One did not have to be an experienced biologist to realize the Na did not exist on a diet of vegetables.

It uttered something in words of single syllables as it brought the massive club down faster than Etienne would have guessed possible. He dove wildly behind a small wagon piled high with some kind of vegetation. The club made kindling of the wagon and splinters bit at Etienne's exposed face. As he rolled to his feet he thought suddenly, *What am I doing here?* I should be behind a desk at a university, grumbling over sophomoric student reports and wondering who's going to show at the next faculty get-together.

There was no time for regretful contemplation. The club swung parallel to the pavement and he heard it *whoosh* as he ducked and it missed the top of his skull by centimeters. Then a big hand was reaching for him, six treelike fingers with hooked nails at the tips.

He stumbled backward, away from that menacing grasp, firing as he fell. The bolt passed between the forefinger and first thumb to strike the Na in the left eye. It let out a thunderous howl, dropped the club and fell to its knees, shaking violently. The Na was dead by the time it hit the ground.

Etienne tried to rejoin his companions, only to find his path blocked by the other Na. It charged forward and brought its own club down with both hands. Etienne barely missed being pulped by diving behind a nearby wall.

Freed of the need to ward off two attackers, the farmers fanned out behind the survivor. Pikes and spears and scythes stabbed and cut at muscles and tendons. The Na roared and bellowed, frustrated in its attempt to locate the snoutless Tsla who had slain his companion. As a great tendon was finally cut, the beast fell to one knee swinging the club in a wide arc to kill a pair of Tsla who'd closed too quickly.

But now that the Na was down it no longer seemed so massive or invulnerable. Etienne took careful aim and fired at the base of the skull. The bone was so thick that it prevented the charge from penetrating to the spine, but the shock was sufficient to temporarily paralyze the creature and send it tumbling the rest of the way to the street.

It did his heart good, though Lyra would surely not have approved, to watch the peaceful, philosophic Tsla jump all over the body and start hacking it to pieces. Knowing that his help was needed elsewhere, he left the surviving farmers to their butchery.

He needn't have worried. The Na were in full retreat, harried by the persistent townsfolk. He spotted Yulour atop a crop-loading ramp and climbed up beside him.

"You don't fight here, Yulour?"

"No, Learned One," said the slow-witted porter. "I want to help, but Teacher Tyl tell me no. He say, I would only end up hurting myself."

Etienne nodded, commending Tyl's good sense. He picked his way back down the ramp.

The fleeing Na carried huge bales of some kind of dried meat from a storehouse they'd broken into, while others hauled off unknown booty in huge leathery sacks. The Tsla pursued them only as far as the ruined gate.

Etienne saw only one other Na corpse. Perhaps word of the two deaths he'd had a hand in had been enough to frighten the rest of the Na into giving up the assault. Or perhaps they'd gained what they'd come for. He could speculate on motivation later. Right now he was exhausted and more than glad to see them go.

Another folk might have pursued in an attempt to recover their stolen stores, but not the Tsla. There was no room in their philosophy for active military pursuit. And out on the open plain they would be at a disadvantage against their opponents, whose size and maneuverability would not be restricted by stone walls and narrow streets.

He slowed as he approached the shattered gate, to stare after the retreating Na. A group of curious locals began to gather around him. Smiling and making Tsla gestures of friendship, he forced his way through them to find Tyl deep in conversation with a silver-furred elder.

The guide introduced him. "This is Ruu-an, First Scholar of Jakaie. Ruu-an, make greeting to the Learned Etienne, a scholar from a world other than ours. He comes here to learn about us . . . and as thee have observed, sometimes to help."

"I am gladdened by thy presence," the elder said. His accent differed from that of Tyl and the other Tsla of Turput, but the words remained comprehensible. "Also that thee saw fit to put aside thy studies long enough to aid us in a most desperate time. I have been informed that thee helped to bring down two of the Na and thereby to hasten their flight."

Etienne holstered his pistol. "Does this happen often? From what I saw of the fight I don't see how you could survive repeated attacks."

"The Na assail us infrequently, and usually with less loss of life. Many times we will simply fall back against the mountain and let them take what they will. They are not indiscriminate thieves and never take more than they can carry. But it has not been a good time for us and it was decided this time to resist. I do not think the choice wise."

"They come to steal your food?"

"When the time is hard on us, it may also be hard on them. Nor do they know how to grow food of their own. Despite their appearance, they have a hunger for the fruit of the soil. When it is scarce on the Guntali they will sometimes come down among us. I suppose they cannot be blamed. The life offered by the Guntali must be very hard."

"You sound like you're ready to forgive them," Etienne said, eyeing the bodies scattered both in front of and behind the ruined gate.

"We always do," the First Scholar told him. "Have they not souls just as we? They are more to be pitied than hated for their ignorance and weaknesses."

"I didn't see many weaknesses, but I've already learned that you Tsla are more forgiving than we humans." Already the townsfolk were busy removing the dead. That sparked an unpleasant memory.

"After the . . . funeral ceremonies . . . are concluded, what do you do with the bodies of your deceased?" He could not look at Tyl as he said this. Sensing his discomfort, the guide discreetly allowed the First Scholar to answer.

"Here we cremate the bodies and then scatter the ashes upon our fields, so that as tillers of the soil those who pass on may help the next generation to grow better crops."

"So they can be stolen again by the Na. You ought to put a stop to it."

"That would be a fine thing," the elder said, "but alas, a thing not possible. We cannot chase the Na up to the Guntali. It is too cold for us and the air too thin for us to fight in. Up there, they are the masters.

"Similarly, they cannot fight long down here. The thick hair which protects them from the Guntali's cold soon causes them to grow too hot to exert their great bodies, and they must retreat."

"I'm glad I don't have to depend on the weather for my defense," Etienne replied. Not that it was within his province to criticize the way these Tsla managed their lives.

"Actually," the elder continued, surprising his human audience, "there are times when we trade peacefully with the Na."

"I'd been told the Tsla served as a conduit between Mai and Na, but for some reason it just slipped my memory."

"You must not judge them only by this unusual attack," Ruu-an advised him. "There are many times when the Mai also prefer to fight instead of to trade."

Etienne was glad Homat was still back at the boat. "Listen, I'm standing here taking in all this information and it isn't even my department. Lyra's the one who should be making a record of your ways." He looked past them, making a perfunctory survey of the battlefield. "Where is she, anyway? I haven't seen her since we split up to try and flank the two Na we first encountered."

"Ah, Learned Teacher Lyra," Tyl murmured.

"Yes. Didn't she stick with you, Tyl?" Suddenly he was very cold, the kind of coldness that comes from inside the body and makes the muscles of one's arms and legs start to cramp.

"No. We became separated during the fight. I have not seen her since. Perhaps we ought to return to the place where we began the combat." He sounded concerned.

[169]

There was no sign of Lyra. Not where Etienne and the farmers had slain the two Na, not in the streets nearby, not before the gate. The word was passed among the townsfolk. Surely they'd know her whereabouts. An alien fighting among them would stand out immediately.

When the word came it was devastating in its finality.

⟦ XIII ⟧

The expedition's aims, his hopes for a personal rapprochement, the papers they planned to present to various scientific societies, the acclaim and acknowledgment and honors, all suddenly meant nothing beside the hollowness in his heart. Ten years of hard work had been shattered like that gate which had so ineffectively protected Jakaie.

Several of the townsfolk had seen the alien female disappear into a Na sack. They were positive she was alive at the time. Two or three Tsla had been stuffed in the sack with her.

Etienne and Tyl, accompanied by the First Scholar, rushed to the narrow street near the gate, following the lead of two young Tsla. A quick search turned up several raggedy fragments of Lyra's shirt—and something more significant. Battered but still functional, her pistol lay dark against the paving stones where she'd dropped it.

Asking without wanting to ask, he looked despairingly at Ruu-an. "Why would they take her alive?"

The elder glanced at Tyl, who knew the strange creature

better than he, but no enlightenment was forthcoming. So he answered.

"I told thee, Learned Etienne, that when times on the Guntali are difficult the Na come here to find food. They are not selective in their diet. Meat is meat to them, whether recently killed on the Guntali or traded to them by some merchant...or the merchant himself. They take live captives to prolong their supply of fresh food, as we do with our domestic animals."

The sudden irony of it made Etienne want to laugh, but he couldn't, any more than he could cry. All he could do was stare silently through the broken gate toward the rampart marking the rim of the Guntali, more than a thousand meters higher than Jakaie.

Lyra was up there somewhere, no doubt occupying her thoughts with the unprecedented opportunity granted her to study the culture of the Na at close range. Probably she was bouncing around in her sack with her fellow captives and cursing the lack of a recorder. She'd be doing exactly the same thing when they slipped her on the spit. Her last notes would detail the eating habits of the Na. He was sure it would be a paragon of scientific explication and his wife's final thought would be regret over the fact no one else would be able to read them.

"Damn them," he muttered. "Damn her!" He let all his anger and hate and frustration flow out over the stones and an occasional curious onlooker and when he finally concluded the tirade he was ashamed of himself, because there still were no tears.

As he turned back to the patient Tyl he discovered he could speak with extraordinary calmness. It was the peace of the resigned.

"Do you think they will eat her soon, or save her for a while?" How easily the words came now, the absurd words.

Tyl looked to Ruu-an instead of replying. "It is hard to say. Certainly they have sense enough to wonder at the differences between her and us. If any among this tribe has ever seen a Mai, they may think she is kin to them, albeit from a larger tribe. They may want to sample this new food right away, but I think they may choose to make a special feast around her. Thus they would save her for a last meal."

"I have to proceed on that assumption."

Tyl eyed him curiously. "What can thee do, Learned Etienne? I am wounded for thee. I was very fond of Learned Lyra. I learned much from her and enjoyed our sharing of customs and knowledge. Both pupil and teacher she was, but there is nothing to be done for her now."

"You and your damn fatalism! She's my wife, damn it, and as long as there's the slimmest chance she's still alive I have to go after her. It's her own damn fault for being so careless and putting me in this position, and she knows it. She's probably laughing over my predicament right now knowing that I have to come after her or risk everything going down the drain. Months of work, years of preparation all at risk because she didn't have a care for her fat rear and let some big dumb cretin of a native stuff her in his shopping bag. Lost her pistol, too." He shoved the other asynapt into his belt.

"I'm going to go back to the boat for our cold weather gear. Lyra'll be lucky if she doesn't freeze to death before she finds herself on the menu. Or maybe she won't be lucky. It depends on how right your assumptions are and how fast I can move up there." He scanned the rock wall.

"One thing I can tell from here; I'll have to hike it. No way the repellers will last long enough to get me up that. What about trails? Are there foot trails leading to the plateau, or do they just follow the easiest route down?"

"Always they follow the easiest," Ruu-an said. "That is their way. They make no attempt to hide themselves, for they have nothing to fear from us. But I do not understand what thee intend, Learned Visitor. The captured are already lost. Whether alive or dead this moment matters not. Thee saw how the Na fought here in our homeland, constrained by our walls and overheated as their bodies were. Think what they will be like to confront on the Guntali, where they are at home and in comfort. I will meditate on thy mate's behalf."

"Thee meditate thy butt off. I'm still going after her." He turned to their guide. "Tyl, you'll come with me, won't you?"

"As the First Scholar tells, the captured are already lost to us. In any case we can do nothing against the Na in their own land. To do so would only be to add to the rolls of the departed."

"How do you know you can't do anything if you've never tried?"

"Logic, Learned Etienne, and common sense, dictate our actions. We are calm because we are sensible, content because we understand our role in the scheme of existence." He reached out to try and comfort his distraught hairless friend.

"Please, Etienne, friend, thee must continue with thy work. Thy Lyra would have wished it. Thee must not grieve for her."

"I'm not grieving for her, you gutless wonder. I'm going after her because she may still be alive." Then, more quietly, "I mean no insult, Tyl. I won't grieve for her unless I know for a *fact* that she's dead."

"If thee wish to perish alongside her, why, that could be understood," said Ruu-an, attempting to make some sense of an alien reasoning that flew in the face of all logic.

"I've no intention of committing suicide."

"That is what thee will do if thee persist in following the Na onto the Guntali," Tyl insisted. "I am sorrowed, Etienne, but I cannot follow thee. My teachings, my beliefs, will not allow it. You may ask of any others thee wish." He did not add that such a request would be a waste of time.

Etienne forced himself to reply as courteously as possible. "I respect your beliefs, Tyl. I don't understand them and I don't sympathize with them, I don't even like them, but I can respect them. But I'm wasting time standing here trying to convince you." He wondered what Lyra would say if she could hear Tyl's refusal.

"I'll go after her myself."

"Thee will not return," Tyl warned him.

"Oh, I'll come back. Look at it like this: I'm going to acquire additional knowledge. It will be a learning experience."

"Death is learned soon enough," Tyl said. "They who—"

"I will go with thee."

So intent was he on his mental preparations and his frustration with the Tsla that Etienne didn't hear the voice.

Again it said, "I will help thee."

[174]

"Who said that?" He turned, to find himself confronting one of the porters. The last porter anyone expected to say anything: Yulour.

"If thee will have me, Learned One."

"Have you, yes, and glad of it." He didn't think Yulour could think fast enough to be of much help in a fight, but if supplies could be piled on that willing, powerful back they would make much better time. And it would be good to have company. In that respect the porter's slowness did not concern him. He doubted he'd be much in the mood for extended conversation atop the Guntali.

"Why? Isn't it against your spiritual principles?"

"I have no spiritual principles, Learned One." Yulour fought with the large Tsla words. "I do not have sense enough to have them." He looked hesitantly past the human. "Teacher Tyl must allow. I am bound to him."

Tyl was staring curiously at the porter. "I cannot allow myself to go, nor would thy companions, but if thy conscience is clear and committed."

"What is conscience?" Yulour asked innocently.

Tyl sighed. "No matter." He turned to Etienne. "He may accompany thee as he wishes. I cannot stop him, though I would if it were in my power. All beings have free will. Remember this, though: thee will bear a heavy responsibility if he dies. It will be on *thy* conscience."

"I'll remember that." Etienne faced his one volunteer. He'd had little personal contact with Yulour, indeed, with any of the porters, preferring to give them their instructions through Tyl.

"Thank you, Yulour. I accept your offer of help. It would be better understood among my own people."

The porter shook his head sadly. "I do not understand, Learned One."

Etienne clapped the Tsla on one muscular shoulder. "It doesn't matter. All that matters is that you're willing to help."

"I *like* Teacher Lyra," Yulour said with simple sincerity. "I want to help her."

"If we can, we will, Yulour."

They hurried back to the hydrofoil, ignoring the crowd

of curious Tsla which had gathered around it. Homat was waiting to greet them.

Etienne caught his breath as a blast of superhot air rushed out of the main cabin. Inside the temperature reached for the hundred-degree line, forty degrees warmer than the air outside. Homat's reaction was exactly the opposite of Etienne's. As cold air poured inside he retreated to the pile of blankets he'd assembled on the floor of the cockpit, curled up beneath them, and peered out apologetically as Etienne strode in after him.

"Please do not be angry with me, de-Etienne," he pleaded. "Only I was left behind, and I remember how to work the device that makes the air inside the spirit boat hot or cold. I could not resist. It's the first time in many times I have been truly delightful warm."

Etienne had to smile. "Relax, Homat, it's all right. I'm not mad at you." The smile quickly vanished. "De-Lyra has been taken by the Na, by the ice demons."

Homat began to moan and Etienne hastened to cut him off. "Yulour and I are going after her."

Homat's nearly bald head emerged from the smothering blankets. "After the demons?"

"After the Na, yes."

"You will not come back."

"I really appreciate all the support I'm getting," he mumbled absently as he started rummaging through a storage locker in search of needed supplies. "I never thought I'd see the day when Mai and Tsla were in perfect agreement on anything."

"After the demons," Homat whispered. "I—I would come with you if I could."

Etienne threw him a surprised look. "That's delightful of you, Homat, but you know how much use you'd be. The temperature atop the Guntali's probably somewhere just above the freezing mark. I don't think you could handle that for very long. No Mai could. The climate here in Jakaie's at the upper limit of your tolerance."

"I wish it were not so, de-Etienne. It is wondrous that you can move so freely between the comfortable weather of the Skatandah and the roof of the world."

"Our special clothing helps to make that possible, Homat."

He held up a thermal coat just excavated from storage. "I'm more concerned about the atmospheric pressure above the six-thousand-meter line. The air will be thicker than at a corresponding altitude on my home world, but thinner than I'd like. We have some methods of compensating for that, too."

Into the large backpack went a half dozen supplementary breathers. Each consisted of a facepiece designed to fit comfortably over mouth and nose and flexible metal tubes that fit over the ears and behind the head to hold the contraption in place. The tubes contained pure O_2 under pressure and would serve equally well under water. For high altitude use they'd last much longer, since their full flow wouldn't be required.

Two ascents from the bottom of the Barshajagad had prepared him for the coming climb. All that he feared was the possibility of having to do some running at high altitude. He wondered how Lyra was handling the thin air and low temperatures. She was wearing long clothing when the Na had attacked, but that wouldn't suffice if the nighttime temperature dropped below freezing. It might be that all that stood between her and freezing to death at night was the warm presence of her fellow captives.

"Yulour, will you be warm enough?" he asked his sole companion when all was ready. The porter wore several layers of toga and two capes, in addition to a cloak pulled tight over his head.

"I will be fine, Teacher. Please not to worry about me. It upsets me when I see anyone worrying about me."

Tyl and Ruu-an waited at the main gate to see them off. With typical Tsla matter-of-factness, masons and carpenters were already hard at work repairing the broken barrier. Ruu-an presented one stocky villager who would guide them to the base of the incline the Na usually employed for their travels.

"Do they ever leave a rear guard behind, or anything like that?" Etienne asked the First Scholar.

Ruu-an made a negative movement with his trunk. "They have nothing to fear from us since we never pursue them."

That sense of invulnerability should be my greatest ally, Etienne mused. Once safely back in their own territory atop the Guntali the Na would relax. Counterattack would be the last thing they'd expect. The shock should be considerable. But he didn't delude himself into thinking that they'd run off in panic. The Na weren't the type to run.

No, he'd have to rely on surprise. Even with two fully charged pistols he doubted he could hold off an entire tribe of the giants for more than a couple of minutes.

"We're wasting time." He led their local guide toward the wall beckoning to the east, moving as rapidly as practicable. Yulour fell in step behind, the big pack bobbing easily on his broad shoulders.

Tyl and Ruu-an watched them go.

"What a strange folk," the First Scholar declared. "I listen in amazement to the accomplishments you tell me they have achieved, and then something like this is done, something which a child of but a few years can see is useless."

"They are full of contradictions." Tyl's gaze was still on Etienne's retreating back. "One moment they are very wise and the next, foolish as little Mai. I think their souls must be in perpetual confusion."

"Thee believe they have souls, then?"

"I am convinced of it, though other teachers of Turput argue otherwise."

"It may be that their minds are variable, that they are adults one moment and cubs the next. Very strange folk. I am glad I was able to meet and talk with one of them before they died."

"Yes, I will miss them. The female came to me day after day and asked endless questions, which allowed me to make a close study of her and her ways. Now that they have left us we will have only that to remember."

He turned and helped the elderly Ruu-an as they started back toward town, continuing the discussion as they walked.

There were plenty of switchbacks which over the years the Na had developed into a recognizable pathway, so the climb was not as difficult as Etienne first feared. He still had to stop at regular intervals to catch his breath. Common sense insisted on calling regular halts while his nerves tried to force him to greater haste. The supplementary breathers wouldn't last forever and he tried to ration the flow of the one clamped over his face.

Despite the frequent pauses they reached the plateau sooner than he'd dared to hope. Gaps in the thick clouds afforded only an occasional glimpse of Jakaie and its valley sitting far below and behind them. Above the rest of the real world brooded the mountain called Aracunga. A thick cloud of ice crystals trailed southward from its crest, looking like smoke flowing from a volcano. In the distance rose a white ghost, the impossible bulk of the sky-scraping Prompaj Massif.

A few trees stood ready to greet their arrival, thin wispy branches applauding their achievement at the behest of a steady wind. Nearby, green-brown bushes clung to the ground. Etienne bent to examine the nuts they produced, found them hard to extract from the poor soil. They hugged the earth with hooks of wood.

In the light dusting of snow they saw tracks of animals that walked on broad but delicate feet, with long strides. Etienne visualized something tall and thin running fast. As they left the rim they encountered larger spoor, indication that a large predator had recently passed.

Whenever their course was in doubt Yulour would drop his head toward the ground and employ his oversized proboscis to sniff out the scent of the Na.

"Not far," he told Etienne by the end of the day.

"No reason for them to cover ground." Etienne squinted into the growing darkness, an occasional snowflake tickling his skin. "Probably they've picked a comfortable spot to relax and reminisce about their attack on Jakaie. If they have that much sense, that is. We should come up on them soon, then?"

"Yes, soon." Yulour straightened. "Then what we do?"

"I'm not sure. Depends on how they set their camp."

They saw the glow from the earth before Yulour caught the scent of the tribe. The fire itself wasn't visible because it lay in a depression. Heeding Etienne's request for silence, Yulour followed the Teacher as they crept up the side of the low ridge and found themselves looking down into a small crater in the rocks. It was deep and offered excellent protection against the wind. On the far side, stone overhung part of the depression, and the alcove was packed with sleepy, sated Na. Only a few of the primitives were moving, mostly to tend to the roaring fire. The odor from the burning chips was strong.

For the first time Etienne saw Na females, along with two-meter-tall cubs. Unlike the children of most species, the offspring of the Na were not cute. They moved nervously in their sleep, their bare feet kicking toward the warmth of the fire.

Vegetation was unusually abundant in the depression, not only due to the presence of nutrients unintentionally supplied by Na but also because the hollow served as a watertrap. The pool lay directly below Etienne, the fire on the far side. A large pile of dried animal dung helped to reflect as well as freshen the blaze.

Yulour pointed and whispered with childlike excitement. "Look there, Teacher, look there!"

Etienne's gaze traveled to the right of the fire. Stone and bone had been heaped together to create a crude kitchen. Attached to a long bone suspended over a smoking fire was a shape that he didn't immediately recognize. It took him a moment to see that it was a dead Tsla shorn of its fur. He glanced sideways at his companion. There was no fury, no hatred in the porter's face.

"It doesn't bother you?"

"What bother me, Teacher?"

Etienne gestured toward the firepit. "They're cooking one of your own kind down there."

"Everyone must eat," Yulour said ingenuously.

Etienne turned away. Obviously a great deal more research would have to be performed before they could fully understand the Tsla.

Of more immediate interest was the cage that rested against the far right-hand base of the depression. It was made of the curving rib bones of some big creature, lashed together with cured sinew. Four—no, five—Tsla were clustered together within. Along with one figure clad in bright blue. His pulse raced, threatening to set his fingers trembling.

Lyra was alive and apparently intact, from what he could see. The collar of her shirt was buttoned all the way up over her neck and her long hair was wrapped around her face.

The Na had left their carrying sacks in with the prey, and Lyra lay beneath one for further protection from the cold.

A single young male squatted sleepily in front of the cage, idly tossing pebbles into the fire and ignoring his charges.

"Soon he may sleep, Teacher," Yulour said of the guard.

"He'd better." Etienne checked to make sure both pistols were readily accessible, along with the supplementary breathers. Then he backed carefully down the slope and circled the depression.

When they climbed up again they topped the rise directly behind the cage. Then they waited.

It was well after midnight when Etienne stirred himself for another look down into the hollow. Tslamaina's moons were masked by cloud and most of the light in the depression came from the central bonfire. He watched the motionless guard for another half hour before he could be certain the Na was asleep.

"What must I do, Teacher?" asked Yulour.

"Just stay here and keep quiet, and wait for us."

"Be careful, Teacher."

"I will, Yulour."

"I will come down if thee need me," he added anxiously as Etienne slid on his belly over the top.

"I know you will. You're a good friend, Yulour."

"I thank thee, Teacher," whispered the porter, overwhelmed by the compliment.

Etienne half-slid, half-crawled down the incline. The tribe dozed like the dead beneath the rocky overhang. He checked his wrist. It was twelve degrees below freezing. He was quite comfortable but he worried about Lyra. If the temperature fell much further she would have difficulty walking until he could get her into her own thermal suit, which was stuffed into Yulour's copious backpack.

He reached for a purchase only to see the rock tumble down the slope. It came to rest against the back of the cage. The guard did not stir. Etienne followed the stone as rapidly as practicable, assuming a kneeling position behind the cage.

"Lyra," he whispered intently, shifting his gaze from her to the guard and back again. Bodies stirred within the cave but no one rose from sleep.

"Lyra!" Her head jerked around in the darkness and she shoved her hair aside.

"Etienne?"

"Who the hell else would it be?" He pulled one of the pistols and carefully adjusted the setting after quickly inspecting the lashings holding the cage together. "I'm going to try and burn through the material holding these bones. Be ready, for God's sake!"

He started working, the pistol's faint hum absorbed by the wind overhead and the crackle of the central fire. Lyra moved quietly to wake her fellow prisoners. They had enough presence of mind to keep quiet, save for one who whispered in surprise, "It is the mate of the stranger who is with us!" Lyra shushed him.

"Here, as Etienne cuts these loose, take them up and lay them somewhere aside." The Tsla moved silently to comply.

He smiled to himself. Fatalistic in philosophy the Tsla might be, but clearly that didn't extend to sitting dumbly by if the chance of escape presented itself.

"Etienne, what the devil are you doing here?"

"Saving fair maiden from an incipient barbeque." Another lashing split and he started on the bonds above it. One of the Tsla males gripped the base of the loosened section to prevent its falling.

Lyra sat clear of the humming pistol, shook her head. "Somehow I never thought you capable of the heroic gesture, Etienne."

"Lyra, shut up. I'm busy." Another series of sinews gave way and he started on those holding a second bar as the Tsla carefully removed the first.

The second bone popped clear easily and again the Tsla moved it aside. Lyra was first out and Etienne caught her as she stumbled. Her muscles were numb from cold and confinement.

For an instant he thought she might have suffered some unseen injury. She quickly dispelled that concern.

"I'm in one piece, though I thought I'd suffocate in that damn stuffsack." The Tsla were filing out wordlessly behind her, looking around in bewilderment. "We're up on the Guntali, aren't we? The sack was opaque, so I couldn't get any bearings." He nodded. "No wonder I'm so cold."

"Fill me in on the details later," he advised her, looking anxiously past her toward the dozing guard.

"We are grateful," said the senior Tsla among the captives.

"Be grateful when we're safely back in Jakaie," Etienne admonished him. "Follow me and stay *low*." He started up the slope on his belly, glancing back once to make sure Lyra was on his heels. "You need any help?"

"No. It just feels good to be moving again."

As soon as they dropped over the dark side of the depression he extracted her thermal suit from the supplies. She was so cold it took her three times as long as normal to climb inside.

"I am gladdened to see thee, Teacher. We feared for thee."

She looked at Yulour in mild surprise, peering past him to see the others who had come with her husband. Her disappointment in the darkness was evident.

"Etienne, you wouldn't believe the habits of these Na. Their cruelty isn't studied, of course. It's simply their way. But their victims suffer needlessly. As a matter of fact I'd have to say that based on preliminary studies which admittedly were not carried out under the best of conditions, they have no redeeming social characteristics whatsoever."

"You'll think of some as soon as you get warmed up. You'll end up with a balanced report. You always do."

"Maybe, but I don't feel I'm in a very balanced mood right now."

When the last of the Tsla captives reached bottom Etienne addressed them hastily. "As you know, I am Learned One Lyra's mate. We're going back to Jakaie. Stay together and no talking unless it's absolutely necessary. We have to travel as rapidly as possible. If anyone gets lost or falls behind for any reason..."

"We know what we must do," said the senior Tsla. "But we do not know the way back to our home."

"We do, so stay close by us." Holding Lyra's hand tightly in his own he turned to follow Yulour. The rest of the Tsla trailed behind in perfect silence.

〖 XIV 〗

They shambled on through the cold and wind all the rest of that night, following Etienne's lead. He glanced constantly at the instrumentation on his wrists, but was glad he could rely on Yulour's sense of smell for confirmation of their course. The rising sun was welcomed not only for the warmth it provided but as a further aid to direction. Aracunga was a more reliable beacon than any readout on a tiny screen.

They were well down the trail toward home when a boulder the size of a small house fell past them in awesome silence, to pulverize a basaltic outcrop below. It missed Etienne and Lyra by a few meters.

Instinctively he pressed his back against the cliff. "Landslide," he muttered.

Yulour made a quick, sharp gesture of disagreement, looked upward. "Na slide."

A glance toward the Guntali showed a single enormous hirsute shape leaning over the edge, gesticulating angrily and stomping the ground. The mouth made sounds that were swallowed by the wind. Then the figure vanished.

"Coming after us," Etienne commented with unexpected

calm. "I'd hoped they wouldn't. I wonder how many of them there are." He pulled on Lyra's hand. "Can you run?"

She clutched her pistol firmly, nodded.

"Remember now, hon, we don't want to harm any more of the native population than is absolutely necessary," he said dryly.

"Pardon my lack of objectivity. The rotten cannibalistic bastards."

"No time for gory details, love."

Trying to make as much speed as possible, they raced down the pathway. No more small mountains crashed down around them, but by the time they reached the base of the cliff they could hear bellows and roars behind them.

Twists and turns in the descending trail made it impossible to tell exactly how near their pursuers were. Voices could carry a long way in the clear mountain air. Then they broke out of the talus at the base of the cliff and found themselves running along a well-beaten road.

The Tsla who'd joined Lyra in escaping shouted warnings to the farmers who toiled in the fields. Tools were flung aside, seedlings left in pans as everyone ran for the safety of Jakaie.

Yulour put a hand on Etienne's shoulder, bade him turn as he pointed with the other. "There, Teacher!"

Etienne saw, no raiding party this time, but the entire tribe stumbling down the cliff face in pursuit. Females and awkward adolescents brought up the rear. Evidently the rescue was an outrage sufficient to infuriate the Na beyond reason.

They ran slowly but with ground-eating strides. Out in front and much too close behind were males hefting clubs bigger than a man.

"Come on, move it!" he shouted at the farmers who had begun to lag behind.

"We'll make it with plenty of time, Etienne." As Lyra spoke her right foot located the only hole in the road and she went down in a heap, immediately rolling over on her back to clutch her ankle. Pain replaced confidence on her face as she cursed her clumsiness.

"Not broken," she was finally able to gasp out.

"I know that, stupid," he said as felt gingerly of the already swelling knot. He looked past her. He couldn't tell if the Na had seen her go down. The farmers and escapees were nearing the town wall now.

"Hurry, Teacher," Yulour implored him. "There's little time."

"Get up, Lyra," Etienne ordered her. She threw him a look of anger mixed with determination. Using his shoulder and an arm for support, she struggled to her feet. They limped toward Jakaie. The agony in her ankle started her crying silently, but she didn't stop.

Etienne did so, however. "Too slow. We'll never make it." He bent under her and her pain gave way to startled surprise.

"Etienne!" She was across his shoulders. "Put me down! You'll end up killing both of us."

"Lyra, you talk too much." She bounced awkwardly on his shoulders as he ran. There was no pain, but the considerable weight soon had him panting heavily. Without the supplementary breather's steady flow of pure oxygen he couldn't have done it.

"Teacher, can I help thee?" Yulour waddled alongside them. Something went *whomp!* against the earth off to their left, smashing a small bush to kindling. The Na club was much larger than the unlucky shrub.

Etienne wanted to look back to see how close their pursuers were but he couldn't spare the wind. The city gate was very near now, the repaired entrance gaping invitingly. This time armed Tsla waited on the walls, waving and shouting to urge him on. Encouragement was one thing he didn't need. Already his legs felt like lead determined to sink toward the center of the planet and Lyra, lovely sweet Lyra...if only she were a little less voluptuous.

Something struck the small of his back and he almost went down. But he staggered, regained his balance and ran on. A dull flame began to burn just above his coccyx as waiting hands reached out to relieve him of his burden.

They set Lyra down alongside him as he sucked at the last of the breather's air, breathing like a man who'd just finished a long underwater swim. Shouts and yells penetrated his exhaustion.

"I'm too tired to sit up," he wheezed. "What's happening?"

"Don't ask me. I'm the one with the sprained ankle, remember?"

"Pity you couldn't have sprained your mouth."

"Be of good cheer, Teacher," said the solicitous Yulour. "I will find out." He moved toward the gate.

Long moments passed with Lyra massaging her ankle and Etienne slowly regaining his strength.

"That was a dumb thing to do," she finally told him. "You could have gotten a hernia."

"Excuse me," he said between gasps. "Next time I'll drop you."

"Next time I shoot myself before I let them take me." She saw the expression on his face and looked away. "So it's bad xenology. I can't help it. I have feelings too. What on earth made you try something like that, anyway?" When he didn't reply she pushed at his shoulder. "Roll over. I want to see your back. I saw the tail end of that club hit you."

With an effort he turned onto his side. Her fingers moved across his waist, making him wince.

"Could have busted your spine," she murmured gently. "You've got a hell of a bruise."

"I can tell. Where's Yulour?"

She looked toward the gate. "I don't see him, but so far it looks good. There's still a lot of yelling and screaming on the walls, but the new gate looks much stronger than the old one." Her eyes returned to him. "You're an idiot, Etienne. You saved my life."

"That was the idea."

"Why?"

He slowly rolled back, stared blankly at the sky. "Damned if I know." His face contorted as the fire in his back spread to new nerves.

"It never ceases to amaze me, Etienne, how often you can do the right thing and then say just the opposite. Stay there. I'll get something from the boat." She started to rise, flopped back heavily. "I forgot. I can't walk."

"What a sensible, always alert pair we make," he murmured. "If only our sponsors could see us now." He would have laughed if he hadn't been so tired.

"Thank you for saving my life, Etienne, whatever your motives."

"Anytime. Don't mention it. Do you think you can help me sit up?"

"Be careful," she warned him.

Several faces were suddenly staring down at them. One was familiar.

"Hello, Tyl." Etienne clasped his knees toward his chest, trying to alleviate some of the pain in his back. The nerves there argued with every millimeter of effort.

Tyl executed a most profound sideways Tsla bow. "We did not expect thee to return, Learned Etienne. Thee were in the right and we in the wrong, and most grateful am I to be proven so. It was a grand thing thee did. Songs will commemorate thy deed. And this one's, whose service is unprecedented." He indicated Yulour, standing in front of the crowd.

"I don't understand, Teacher," Yulour said.

"Dear, sweet, brave Yulour," Lyra murmured. "I know thy customs and why thy kinfolk did not come, but why did thee?"

"It seemed a good thing to do, so I did it." He looked embarrassed.

"I'll make it up to you," she told him.

"Make . . . up to me? I do not understand."

"I know you don't. Do you understand what I mean when I say that Etienne and I thank thee very deep?"

"Thee are welcome," the porter replied gravely. "Now I must go and find my friends."

Tyl watched him go. "A peculiar soul, but many-times blessed, I think."

"He certainly has our blessings," said Lyra. She looked toward the wall. The shouting had ceased and the Tsla were leaving the top of the palisade, chatting easily among themselves.

"It seems the Na have given up and gone away. Do you think they might attack again?"

"They vented evil gestures and many shouts," Tyl informed them, "but I think they will not come back for some time. They are not animals and know they cannot break into

Jakaie without first surprising its people. This time there was no surprise, so they have gone."

"So we're safe?" Etienne mumbled.

"Yes, all are safe now. Jakaie owes thee a debt for the dead thee have restored to them alive."

Etienne's back improved slowly under Lyra's ministering hands. The worst of it was the body wrap she made him wear. It enveloped him from beneath the armpits to below his waist and he walked like a recently resurrected mummy.

Among the prosaic Tsla the novelty of the rescue quickly wore off and they returned to their daily chores. But there were frequent, shy visits from those he'd saved and from their relatives and friends to thank him.

The debt they owed, they insisted, could never be repaid. Until Tyl came aboard the hydrofoil one morning to see the patient.

"There was a meeting." The temperature in the main cabin was seventy-five and Homat sat shivering off in a corner.

"What kind of meeting?" Lyra asked.

"A community meditation. I am sorry thee were not invited, but there was no time. I have made the people aware of thy problem. Thy wooden undercarriage is still serviceable, is it not?"

"The wheels haven't fallen off, if that's what you mean," Etienne replied.

"There are not here the large draft animals like the Mai have. No vroqupii. There are *lekkas*, but they are for riding, not for pulling. Unlike Turput, here the land is cultivated mostly by hand. But we are Tsla. The Tsla are strong." He flexed both arms and they saw the muscles ripple beneath short fur.

"All Jakaie will assist. Will it not be easier to lower thy boat back to the bottom of the Barshajagad than it was to bring it up?"

Etienne considered their guide's words, trying hard to restrain any excitement. Excitement hurt his back.

"Sure it would be easier, but still a difficult descent."

"I have talked long with Ruu-an and the other elders. There is a way north of here that descends to the Skar and bypasses the Topapasirut. They say also that the way is longer and gentler than that which climbs the side canyon we used. They say, Etienne and Lyra, that it can be done."

"Who am I to dispute Ruu-an?" said Etienne. He felt like shouting but restrained himself lest he strain something.

"When can we start down?"

"Soon. The families of those thee saved demand the honor of taking up the ropes nearest the spirit boat, where the work will be the hardest."

"Our thanks go out to them," Etienne said.

"Thee can thank them thyself." Tyl readied himself to leave. "It will take some time to organize provisions and find the rope sufficient to secure thy craft. Thee will have ample time to thank thy new friends and repair thy back."

"Wait a minute," said Lyra, frowning. "What about the Na? What if they come back when the town is nearly deserted, or catch everyone out in the open?"

"This too was discussed during meditation. They will not come near Jakaie for a long time, so embarrassing to them was their defeat. And after a few days of descent the temperature will grow much too hot for them to follow us."

"We won't argue with that, will we, dear?" He stared meaningfully at Lyra.

As usual, she wasn't intimidated. "If the townsfolk feel confident of their security, I don't see why we shouldn't permit them to bounce you all the way down to the river."

In contrast to the agonizingly difficult haul up from the bottom of the Barshajagad, the descent to a rocky beach northwest of Jakaie and the bulk of Aracunga mountain was almost relaxing. There were a few rough places, easily surmounted by the hydrofoil's repellers, but as the Tsla promised the slope was far gentler than the steep side canyon route on the southern side.

Chanting in unison as they leaned into the heavy ropes, the Tsla were able to lower the boat on its wheeled cradle faster than the Redowls expected. It was hard to imagine the vroqupii and their Brul doing the job any more efficiently than the citizens of Jakaie. It helped that there was none of the sense of competition among the townsfolk that there had been among the Mai. Homat grudgingly conceded that sometimes cooperation was worth more than skill and strength.

When at last the wooden cradle was removed from the hull and the boat bobbed once more in the waters of the Skar, Etienne passed among the villagers trying to thank personally each and every Tsla for their help.

Ruu-an chided him. "Too many thanks. If thee would truly thank us, thee may share thy knowledge with us when thee return this way. We will be waiting to take you up and past the Topapasirut a second time."

No obstacles ahead to hold us back now, Etienne thought excitedly. No more blank spaces on the topographics, no second Topapasirut. According to the Mai, the Barshajagad began to widen once more north of that place. For the moment they still floated between immense sheer walls, but now that the birthplace of river devils lay behind them the stark cliffs no longer seemed quite so forbidding.

The seven of them reboarded and the Redowls settled into their boat with a sense of relief. It had become their home and refuge, and it was good to be surrounded once more by familiar objects and the comforts of an advanced technology.

As Etienne let the boat float free in the current, the townsfolk assembled on the shoreline set up a plaintive, haunting chant of farewell, as different a music from the whirling frenzy of the Mai as Ligeti is from Gregorian chant. The swift current pushed the hydrofoil out into the center of the river.

Lyra stood on the foredeck alongside Tyl, executing with him the Tsla posture of good-bye. The song of farewell was beginning to fade with distance when Lyra turned and called to her husband. "Don't you think that's enough? Let's move." He made a face up at her. Suddenly she was concerned.

"What do you think I'm trying to do?"

She pressed her face to the plexalloy. "What do you mean you're trying?" They were accelerating steadily, but in the wrong direction. Only the boat's internal stabilizers kept them from spinning in helpless circles like a leaf caught in a flash flood.

"Everything's functioning except the intake feed."

"Dammit!" She rushed for the nearest gangway.

As she looked aft she saw the canyon narrowing further behind them, forming the immense granitic funnel which

Etienne had theorized constituted the upper limits of the To-papasirut. In the distance and coming rapidly closer she could make out thickening mist and the first faint, threatening rumble of water attacking rock. She dropped through the gangway and in seconds stood alongside her husband.

"Everything checks out, everything. Except the intake feed. Every time I try to open her wide she locks shut on me."

"Emergency override?"

"Forget it. I'm still trying, though."

"Repellers?"

"No way. We used our stored power during the descent from Jakaie. We need time to recharge or else we can recharge by moving Upriver. Of course, if we could move Upriver we wouldn't need to recharge." He worked rapidly at the diagnostic computer, canceling unhelpful replies to his queries. Unfortunately, those were the only type of reply he could extract.

The rumbling astern was becoming thunder. Dense mist enveloped the narrow cleft of the canyon. He switched the stern scanner to sonic and tridee black-and-white graphics appeared on the screen as ultrasound penetrated the obscuring mist. In a very few minutes the current would slam the helpless boat into the unyielding sheer cliff that was the upside-down waterfall, the Topapasirut. Fragments of the hydrofoil would boil out of the water Downriver, to be wondered at by any Mai who encountered them on nameless beaches. Of the crew there would be only a memory. Nothing so fragile as flesh and blood would survive the coming concussion.

The boat was enveloped in a storm as the river rained toward the sky.

"Do something!" Lyra shouted above the crash of the water.

"Do something yourself!"

She eyed him a moment before turning to disappear below. Her voice reached him via the engine room intercom.

"Everything looks okay. The fuel cells are produc—"

"I can see that on the readout!"

"Just letting you know what I see down here. The engine's quiet, and—wait a minute."

"That's about what we've got left." The boat vibrated anxiously beneath his feet. Would they know when they hit the cliff? He couldn't begin to calculate their velocity.

"Try it now!" Lyra ordered him.

He ran numbly through the restart procedure, was startled when the *Function* light turned green. He stabbed the accelerator, bringing thrust up to maximum.

For an eternity they hung motionless in the vortex, suspended in fog between open water and oblivion. Then very slowly the hydrofoil began to creep Upriver. To Etienne their progress seemed infinitesimal. His anxiety was heightened by the knowledge that whatever had shut down the flow of water to the jet once could do so again at any moment. Gradually their velocity increased to the point where the boat could rise up on its hydrofoils. As the river fell away beneath the hull, relinquishing its grasp, they started to make some real speed. Thunder faded behind them.

As they left the mist Lyra emerged from belowdecks. Her hair was strung like paint across her face, alternating with rivulets of sweat. She stank of Skar.

"What did you do down there?" He spoke without looking at her, refusing to take his eyes off the controls lest something else fail before they were out of danger.

"Emergency surgery." She slumped into a seat. "Very complicated." She held up something in her right hand. As he turned to look he saw that she was wearing heavy-duty insulated work gloves.

A half dozen glistening worms twisted in her grip. They had dark heads.

"These were glued to the conduit just above the main feed to the jet. Watch this." She held up a small diagnostic probe with her left hand, touched it to the tail of one worm. A loud buzzing filled the cockpit and the readout on the front of the tool went berserk.

"Local relative of the terran gymnotids. Generates quite a current for its size. They must have thought they'd found themselves a nice new home when they slipped in through the mesh intake strainers on the foils. Every time you ordered the boat to open the intake feed they responded with a corresponding jolt. No wonder the computer couldn't locate the source of the short-out in the system. It was external. You'd order the feed opened and these little cuties would short it shut, countermanding the directive."

She rose and turned to open one of the ports in the cockpit. With great deliberation she flung her slimy acquisitions as far out into the river as possible. Then she closed the port and spoke toward the stern.

"You can come out now, Homat."

Hesitantly their Mai guide emerged from the heated storage locker in which he had secreted himself. "We're not going to die, de-Lyra?"

"No, we're not going to die. Not today, anyway. The spirit boat is functioning normally again."

He crept out to join them, still encased in his cold-weather gear to combat the cabin's air conditioning. Soon that air conditioning would no longer be required. That would be no comfort to Homat, who would continue to pile on clothing the nearer they drew to Tslamaina's arctic circle.

The population of Jakaie was still assembled along the riverbank. As the spirit boat reemerged from the mouth of destruction, alien voices expressed relief. The villagers lined up quickly and once more the occupants of the hydrofoil were treated to the chant of farewell as Tyl and his companions performed the gestures of good-bye.

"Calm acceptance," Lyra murmured, "no matter what our fate." She was standing on the foredeck alongside their Tsla friends. "Tell me, Tyl, what would the reaction have been if we hadn't come back out?"

"There would have been no reaction that thee could have seen, save that after a suitable time they would have begun a funeral chant instead of one of farewell."

"There didn't seem to be any panic as we slipped downstream."

"Why should there be? There was nothing they could do to help us," he explained patiently. "Thee should know, Lyra, that we are not given to violent displays of emotion in public."

"I recall. Would any of them have grieved for us in private?"

"I imagine so. But they could do nothing to help us."

"Just as nothing could be done to help those who'd been taken by the Na." Etienne spoke from inside the cockpit, addressing his wife in terranglo. "I don't care what the level of mental serenity is among these people, they're not going to make much progress until they dump this fatalism. If they don't watch out, the Mai are going to push forward to develop a complete, advanced technological civilization. The Tsla will end up becoming wards of the Mai, just as it will be the Mai who will push out to tame the Na and the Guntali."

"Specious argument for radical change," Lyra shot back. "The Tsla are content as they are, much happier than the Mai."

"Sure, and the ancient Polynesians were happier and more content than the caucasoids who ministered among them, and we remember what happened to *their* culture."

"Etienne, the analogy doesn't apply here. The Tsla are a different race, occupying a radically different ecological niche. It's not the same thing at all." And she launched wholeheartedly into a lengthy dissertation on history and anthropology that both Homat and Tyl desperately wished they could understand.

Upriver, according to the best information available to Ruu-an and the elders of Jakaie, two last immense tributaries fed into the Skar: the Madauk and the Rahaeng. Beyond that lay the far narrower but still impressive Upper Skar, and unknown lands.

Several hundred kilometers above the Topapasirut the geology of the land altered radically. The gorge of the Barshagajad widened and the river rose in frequent steps, reducing the depth of the canyon. The Redowls were constantly being wakened from sleep by the insistent beeping of the computer. Since the boat could not negotiate rapids on autopilot, Etienne or Lyra would stagger sleepily forward to run the whitewater or lift the hydrofoil past it on repellers.

The steady rumble of the rapids was in stark contrast to the silent river south of Aib. At night Tslamaina's four moons transformed the streaks of white water into thousands of pale crystalline tentacles. Not all was difficult, however. There were quiet stretches of relatively calm water of great beauty.

They began to relax for the first time since leaving the Skatandah. As the temperature grew chillier and the river climbed its ancient bed they encountered fewer signs of settlement, as the land was fit only for Mai hunters and gatherers. Occasionally they saw a few ramshackle houses clustered around poorly irrigated plots. No elaborate terraces had been built there.

Shaped by a harsh land, the local Mai were a hardier breed than their southern cousins. They were also open and much more honest. Or perhaps they were just so startled by the appearance of the hydrofoil and its strange inhabitants that the urge to thieve never crossed their minds.

"I'm not sure that's it at all," Lyra theorized one day. "The truism seems to hold among nonhuman primitives as well as among our own kind that the poorer the people and the more isolated their homes, the more trustworthy and helpful they are. Hardship seems to breed a need for companionship which extends to lending assistance to any who come your way."

Etienne did not argue with her because he was more interested in the locals' openness and lack of fear. They were startled but there was none of the fearful paranoia or jealous awe the Redowls had encountered farther south. He surmised it was because everything was new to these pioneers. For all they knew the Redowls came not from another world but from some unknown distant city-state bordering the Groalamasan. When one shares a world with two other intelligent races it's not difficult to accept the existence of a third.

They expected to encounter a few Tsla villages, but Ruuan told them to expect none, and the information supplied by the elders of Jakaie turned out to be accurate. Whether the abandonment of the northern latitudes by the Tsla was a decision of choice or due to some unknown circumstances, Lyra could not determine. Homat and Tyl argued about it long into the nights, with the Mai staking a claim for greater adaptability among his kind and Tyl retreating into calm conviction that a perfectly good reason existed for shunning such a barren land.

A considerable surprise awaited everyone aboard the boat, however, when they reached the confluence of the three great rivers. Where the Madauk and Rahaeng joined their volume to that of the Skar, several small villages had grown, trading posts, no more.

It was not their existence or location that shocked the travelers, but rather the population—Mai and Tsla traders and hunters mingled freely, working side by side with a lack of self-consciousness that was stunning when compared to the uneasy peace maintained by their southern relatives. The need to work together to survive in a harsh land had overwhelmed ancient suspicions and inhibitions. Homat and Tyl were startled as much by the implications as by the reality.

"It bodes well for the future," Lyra commented. "Maybe when the Mai gain the technology that will enable them to live and work in colder climates and the Tsla the ability to move more freely through the humid river valleys, they'll discover this living example of racial cooperation waiting up here to show them the way."

"They cooperate here in order to survive," Etienne argued. "Without that external pressure, technological advancement may only heighten ancient conflicts, not solve them."

"You're such a damn pessimist!" she said angrily.

He shrugged. "I look at things the way they are, not the way I want them to be."

"And so do I, or are you making one of your frequent criticisms of my objectivity?"

"It's just that it's so much easier to be objective about this." He hefted a sample of dark schist chipped from the riverbank where they had anchored inshore the day before. "On Earth this would be called precambrian or Vishnu schist. It's much older than its terran equivalent, however. There's nothing subjective about it."

"Lucky you."

"Nobody forced you into xenology. You chose it."

"I sure did, because it's a damn sight more exciting and interesting when the subjects of your studies can talk back to you and help you with your research. Better that than a life of drudgery and dirt. My work provides me with new revelations every day."

"All well and good, so long as you don't get personally involved with your revelations." Too late to retract, he thought furiously. Once more his mouth had moved faster than his brain.

She eyed him strangely. "Now what's that supposed to mean?"

He tried to escape into silence, stared at the rock walls about them. The cliffs on either side of the river were barely a thousand meters above the water now.

"When we first arrived in Turput," he mumbled, concentrating on his instruments instead of looking at her, "you spent an awful lot of time," he hesitated over the right word, "meditating with Tyl."

"It was very instructive," she replied. "I'm still not following you, Etienne."

"I thought maybe you were diving a little too deeply into your work."

"I don't—" she broke off, gaping at him. Then her expression twisted into a smile. "Well I'll be damned. You're jealous of Tyl, aren't you? Jealous of a primitive mammalian alien."

"I didn't say that," he snapped quickly. "There you are, jumping to conclusions again, seeing things the way you want to see them."

"Well you can relax, Etienne." The smile grew wider. "Among the Tsla the length and shape of oversized probosces are important sexual characteristics, but a flexible shnoz holds no attraction for me whatsoever."

His head jerked round and he stared at her. "I just said you were spending a lot of time with him, I didn't mean to imply that—you've got a dirty mind, Lyra."

"You mean a dirty husband. Etienne, I can't believe you. I don't know whether to be flattered or insulted."

"Oh hell," he muttered, embarrassed to the soles of his feet, "be busy." Footfalls sounded behind them. "Anyway, our passengers are coming in."

"So what? They can't understand terranglo."

"Don't be so sure. I'll give the Tsla this; they're quick on the uptake. Don't be too surprised if we learn that they can draw a few inferences from our private conversations, especially when their names are mentioned."

"Not just a dirty mind, a dirty paranoid mind," she murmured, but she broke off when Tyl and his companions trundled in.

Homat was sandwiched between two of the porters, a ball of thick cloth and fur among which only eyes and mouth were visible. "I can't go outside anymore, de-Etienne," he whimpered. "No more."

[XV]

Days passed and the temperature fell slowly, but outside the hydrofoil the climate was working dramatic changes on the landscape. Though sheets of frozen water hung from the much reduced cliffs, hundreds of fast streams flowed into the Skar.

Homat was squatting in the main cabin behind the cockpit, heavily bundled and warm but far from comfortable.

Etienne had been mulling the problem for several days. Now he spoke to their Mai guide. "Maybe we can fix something up for you, Homat."

"No matter, de-Etienne. I will not go outside any more."

"Lyra, what about trying to fit him with one of your spare thermal suits? You've got two backups. You two are about the same height, though you're much more—"

"Watch it," she said warningly from her seat.

"—Rubensesque. Homat would swim in a suit, but couldn't you concoct some kind of strap so that the sensors would stay close enough to his skin to function, and adjust the thermostat for Mai comfort?"

"I'll see what I can do." She escorted the nervous Homat down to the lower deck.

Several hours later they reemerged. The thermal suit ballooned around Homat's arms and legs but she'd managed to secure the fabric around his torso.

"It's still a little loose. I had a hard time convincing him he couldn't wear his furs inside because the thermal sensors had to have some skin contact. He finally gave in, but I thought he was going to turn blue before he finally got out of his old attire and into the suit. It wasn't hard to adjust the circuitry." She put a hand inside one sleeve, pushing back the elastic material. She drew her fingers back hastily.

"Are you sure you're okay like this, Homat? It's hot enough in there to burn."

Their guide was jubilant. "For the first time in many many days I am truly comfortable," he replied. "So delighted I am! Thank you, de-Lyra, thank you all much!"

"What about you, Tyl?" Etienne asked the Tsla who rested on the floor behind him. "Will you and the others be able to handle the weather here if it's necessary to go outside?"

"We have our double capes and hoods, Etienne, and we can tolerate colder climes than thee. We will be all right, as long as it does not prove necessary to remain outside for too long."

Etienne unexpectedly leaned forward and the hydrofoil lurched sharply to port. "Sorry. Instinctive reaction." He pointed. "What's that?"

A small mountain stood in the shallow water by the riverbank. The mountain had a half dozen legs, two of which were busy in the water. As they watched in fascination the multi-ton beast brought up a twisting hundred-kilo fish in hooked claws, transferred the catch to a long snout lined with sharp triangular teeth. For so massive a creature it moved with blinding speed. Long black hair covered the entire body and dragged in the water.

Eyes with narrow pupils peered out at them from beneath bony ridges. Etienne edged the hydrofoil toward shore for a closer look. As he did the beast turned with a deep grunt then galloped away on all six legs, its catch clutched firmly between extended jaws.

"I have never seen anything like that before, de-Etienne."

As he spoke Homat made rapid protective signs across his chest and stomach.

"I have," Tyl said softly. "A Hyral. I have seen only two such before and both were dead, having fallen over the edge of the Guntali."

As they stared the hirsute fisher crested a slight slope, where it dropped its catch between its mate and two massive roly-poly cubs before turning to throw a penetrating, high-pitched roar toward the boat.

Lyra was staring through her recorder as she committed the new discovery to their records. "Family group. I wondered what else the Na ate."

"Speaking of the Na," Etienne said as he steered the hydrofoil back into the middle of the river again, "it's cold enough here for them to come right down to the water, but we haven't seen any."

"Perhaps they stay away from the river out of superstition, some kind of taboo."

"I wouldn't think that. Not with all the fish to be had in these waters."

"Maybe the air's too thick here. We're not nearly as high as the Guntali near Turput. It wouldn't matter. The river's still wide and deep enough to protect us." She looked thoughtful.

"Something will have to be done about the Na, Etienne. We've seen proof that Mai and Tsla can work together, but the Na appear too primitive and combative to be brought into any worldwide interracial process without extensive education and a great deal of care. Just because I'm not fond of them doesn't mean I want to see the other two dominant races exterminate them.

"They're not animals. They're intelligent and have developed a rudimentary society. If you consider the amount of territory they control then a case could be made that they and not the Mai or Tsla are Tslamaina's dominant life form."

"I'm glad we don't have to make the ultimate decisions," he replied. "Someone else will have to decide whether it's right to intervene in local affairs to protect the future of the Na, and that's a long way down the road."

* * *

Though the Skar's course twisted in a steady curve farther eastward, they continued to travel north toward the planet's sole ice cap. The occasional appearance of the sun through the uneasy clouds did little to warm them. Despite this Homat spent an inordinate amount of time out on deck, luxuriating in his thermal suit and the freedom it provided, a freedom to laugh at temperatures that would have frozen an unprotected Mai in minutes.

They saw evidence of the ice cap before they set eyes upon it. It announced itself as a brightening ahead, where the ice reflected the sun back against the undersides of scudding clouds. The next morning they lifted on repellers to clear still another rapid, turned a bend in the river, and saw the southernmost edge of the frozen rampart.

The once awesome canyon of the Barshajagad had been reduced to a meandering river valley. Numerous waterfalls tumbled down the melting edge of the cap. They would freeze solid again during the night.

They did not have to trace dozens of the streams to locate the source of the river Skar. The much shrunken but still navigable stream emerged from a huge hole in the wall of ice, having eroded a tunnel a hundred meters high at the entrance. Etienne guided the hydrofoil in until it floated beneath the lip of the vast cavern. Then he carefully nudged the boat ashore, scraping bottom several times before beaching on the gravel.

Overhead the ice had thinned and sunlight poured through the translucent, frozen ceiling, tinting the ice a pale blue and illuminating the river for a distance of several dozen meters from the entrance. Then it was swallowed by cold night. Cold water dripped from smooth icy stalactites, stinging the upturned faces of the crew as it stood on the deck to examine the surroundings.

"What a beautiful place," Lyra murmured. Somewhere a faint echo concurred with her opinion.

The four Tsla kneeled in a circle, chanting and making signs. The Redowls waited respectfully until the ceremony had concluded before Lyra inquired as to its purpose.

"We give thanks," Tyl explained. "We feel in our souls a great warmth, as must thee, for thy journey has been far longer than ours."

"We couldn't have made it without your help," Etienne told him, "and without the aid of your people."

"All given freely in the pursuit of knowledge. We were glad we could help." Swd and Yij likewise expressed their feelings, while Yulour stood nearby and looked on with bemused contentment.

"What do we do now?" Homat inquired, peering out through the eyeslits in the cloth that covered his face. "Do we begin our return tomorrow? A long journey."

"I know you're anxious to go home, Homat, but we've come all this way to see the source of the Skar and we're not leaving until we do so."

Homat sounded puzzled. "But have done so, de-Etienne." He gestured at the spacious cavern and the distant darkness. "What other source can there be?"

Etienne smiled as he turned to point into the blackness beneath the ice. "This isn't the river's source. Somewhere back there it emerges from the mass of the ice cap, probably in the form of a hot spring. I can't think of another mechanism which could have bored so deep a cave in the body of the ice. I need to record it."

Homat's eyes grew wide. "You can't mean to go back in there, de-Etienne! This is the top of the world. Who knows what devils and monsters lie in wait for us in the night which lives throughout the day?"

"Why should any lie in wait," Lyra asked gently, "since no one ever comes here? If any did live back in there they'd long since have given up hope of any meals coming to visit them."

"You argue very plausibly, de-Lyra. My mind wishes to believe you, but my insides are not convinced."

"If you'd feel safer you can camp on the shore here and wait for us to return. I doubt the river runs very far back, hot springs or not."

"No, no, I will come with you," the Mai insisted bravely. "I would rather do that than stay here alone. You are certain there is not far to go?"

"I can't be sure, but I'd be willing to bet we'll have less than an hour's journey in the boat. If the water becomes too shallow, we'll travel the rest of the way in on repellers."

"Why do your words not make me feel confident, de-Etienne?"

"Relax, Homat." He turned to Lyra. "When we reach the source I want to take some core samples. This must be very old ice and the geologic history of the planet is stored here, conveniently waiting to be thawed out for study."

Lyra offered no objection. Their goal was within reach. Soon they would begin the long journey back to warmer climes. Let Etienne enjoy his fieldwork for a day or two. There was no reason to rush now that they'd arrived at their intended and eventual destination.

He looked to his right, deeper into the cavern. "There's a nice wide spot. I'm tired of rocking. The water there is gentle and shallow. I'll move us over and set the foils down on the gravel. Be nice to sleep without rocking for a change."

"Second the motion," Lyra said. "It should be safe enough. There's no sign of carnivores about, no bones or dung on the beach, and the water should keep any small vermin clear of the boat, assuming this enviroment is benign enough to permit their existence."

"I'll run a good charge through the hull. That ought to keep off any late-night visitors."

"It would be delighted to sleep so quietly," Tyl agreed.

"Then it's settled. We owe ourselves the rest," Etienne declared. "First thing tomorrow morning we'll go Upriver to the source so I can get my samples. With luck this ice may predate the collision that created the Groalamasan. That will give me plenty to do on the way back Downriver."

"You did enough griping about the heat down south to fill a book, and now you can't wait to get back to it," Lyra chided.

"I've always been cold-natured, Lyra, you know that. It doesn't mean I enjoy sweating down to skin and bones, though." For a change the argument was friendly. In its own way that was as great an accomplishment for the two of them as was reaching the head of the Skar.

Lyra was sound asleep when the muffled scream woke her. She blinked as her head lifted from the pillow and she stared across the cabin. Soft green lights from ship's instrumentation lit the darkness. A soft wheeze alongside indicated that her husband still slept.

The scream had barely faded and she was beginning to wonder if she'd dreamed it when suddenly a cluster of the green lights changed to red and a warning horn started to blare. Etienne woke instantly, slid off the bed and struggled with his pants.

"False alarm?"

"I don't know," she told him, still straining to hear. "I thought I heard something yell." The horn continued its racket as a soft knocking sounded at the door. Lyra opened it as she fought with the seals of her blouse.

"What is happening?" Tyl asked sleepily. The remaining Tsla clustered in the corridor behind him. "There are strange noises outside and Swd thinks he smells something even though we know we are protected from the air outside."

"Noises and smells and you think you heard something," Etienne muttered as he sealed his coat. "That settles it." He pushed past Tyl on his way to the cockpit.

The light of three of Tslamaina's four moons poured through the transparent plexalloy. The horn continued to shout as Etienne strained to check the instruments. "Don't see anything outside. No abnormal readings. We haven't moved from where I parked us yesterday evening and the hull's still electrified."

"I'll check astern," Lyra told him. She removed her pistol from its charging slot.

"Watch yourself," Etienne admonished her.

With the Tsla following curiously she worked her way aft. There was no sign of Homat, but that didn't worry her. Anything less than a complete upset of the boat would not be enough to pry him from the comfort of his overheated cubicle.

Cautiously she cracked the stern doorway. Freezing air brought her all the way awake. The rumble and gurgle of the shallow river was the only sound as she stepped out onto the rear deck.

A glance forward showed only darkness. There was no movement in the upper reaches of the cavern. Outside only the moons moved in patient procession against the sky. Something shorted out, she thought, wondering if some other strange local critter was somehow playing havoc with their instrumentation.

A heavy weight landed on her right shoulder. She went down hard. The asynapt went flying across the deck. A big chunk of dead log lay next to her.

The Na who had thrown it now peered over the gunwale, eyes glittering in the moonlight. Several similar hairy faces joined the first. One huge, muscular arm reached over the top of the railing and Yij disappeared over the side.

Tyl and Yulour took Lyra under the arms and hauled her toward the doorway. A second club flew toward them. It landed short, booming across the metal deck.

Through the wash of pain that radiated from her shoulder Lyra gasped, "The gun...get my gun!" The source of the scream must have been a Na who'd made contact with the electrified hull as it tried to board the hydrofoil.

Careful not to touch the metal another Na took aim with an axe. The bone blade was a meter across. At the last instant Swd lunged into its path, to fall gushing blood and life back against Lyra, the weapon's intended target. Yulour had to kick the nearly split body aside as they fell inside.

Etienne was there to help, his eyes on Lyra's shoulder where the club had struck. She moaned when he touched her.

He closed the hatch, then ordered her to move her right arm.

"Hurts like hell, but it works," she told him.

"Rotate," he said curtly. She did so, turning the arm palm up, then palm down. "Lucky you."

"Not so lucky," she told him painfully. "My pistol's outside. That's twice I've lost it when I needed it most. Going to have to work on my grip." She glanced at Tyl. "Did you see where it landed?"

"The lightning thrower flew through the air. I saw not where it landed."

"The little metal tool," Yulour mumbled frantically, trying to keep abreast of what was happening, "I saw where it is."

"Why didn't you go after it?" Lyra asked him. "I told you to go after it."

Yulour looked away, hurt. "We were more concerned with saving thee, Lyra," Tyl told her. He looked at the porter and said gently. "It's all right, Yulour. Tell us where the lightning thrower landed."

"In the water," he said brightly.

"Oh hell!" Lyra looked up at her husband. "I'm sorry, Etienne, I'm sorry. I never saw them. We went out on deck, everything seemed normal, and then something landed on me like back taxes."

"Never mind that now. Just take it easy with that shoulder."

Something went *whang* atop the cabin and everyone looked upward, but the metal held. Thin as it was, the alloy was far too tough to yield to mere bone and stone.

"What will we fight them with?" Tyl wondered. "It is dark and they are very close."

"We don't have to fight them with anything, Tyl. Help Lyra forward."

Outside the cockpit was a choice scene from Dante. The hydrofoil was surrounded by at least thirty of the towering aborigines, who were jumping up and down, howling and spitting and gesturing angrily at the boat. The Na carefully avoided all contact with the hull and when one of them attempted to express his feelings by urinating on it, they no longer tried that either. They did use long spears and the ubiquitous clubs to hammer on the sides. The wood and stone were poor conductors and the Na had discovered they could flail away at the hull without risk to themselves.

As the Redowls watched, one especially massive warrior tried to vault over the railing. He didn't quite make it and grabbed a hold with his hands. His lower body slammed into the hull and he lit up in a shower of blue sparks. When the thick fingers finally let loose the huge body splashed into the river.

Etienne assumed the pilot's chair, his fingers flying over the controls. A muffled roar sounded aft as the engine came to life. The hydrofoil lifted half a meter on its repellers and shot forward, scattering Na. One didn't dodge quickly enough, and a sickening *thud* sounded from the bow as the aborigine was knocked aside.

Nightscope screens came alive, revealing the rest of the war party falling astern. Several bodies bobbed in the shallow water together with pieces of the individual run over by the boat and a smaller silhouette: Yij. Angrily Etienne spun the hydrofoil on its axis and sent it roaring down on their attackers, plowing through the now panicky Na and sending several additional bodies flying. The sound of metal meeting flesh momentarily filled him with an unholy delight and he damned himself even as he pivoted for another run.

As the Na threw their weapons aside and scrambled onto the beach he bashed through the survivors two more times. By then they were in full retreat outside the cavern, not even turning to hurl an occasional insult back at their intended prey. Etienne slowed as he beached the boat on the far side of the Skar.

"The middle of the river's still deep enough here to prevent them from crossing after us," he muttered. "Stay here." He took his pistol as Lyra assumed the pilot's seat, favoring her injured shoulder.

"One nighttime stroll on deck's enough for this little lady." He smiled thinly at her by way of reply.

Tyl and Yulour followed him aft. The doorway opened easily, readmitting the night. He had a sudden thought, closed the door immediately and directed the Tsla to wait for him as he disappeared belowdecks.

He reappeared carrying a pair of long metal rods, showed one to Tyl. "These are for making seismic soundings in spots inaccessible from the boat. Never mind what I mean, just take them." The Tsla did so.

"Those are explosive charges on the tips. Small lightnings. There are five charges on each pole. You press this here," and he showed the fire buttons to his companions, "after you've touched the end of the pole to your target. They're difficult to use, but they were not designed as weapons. They'll be effective if you have to use them, though."

"I understand, Etienne," Tyl told him, lightly fingering the fire button. Etienne turned to the other Tsla.

"How about you, Yulour? Do you understand? See, you press there after you touch whatever you want to stop with the other end of the pole."

The porter eyed him blankly, his expression a bovine mixture of sadness and confusion. Sighing, Etienne carefully set the second pole to one side.

"Never mind. Stay close as we go outside."

He cracked the doorway to the deck for the second time. Outside it was silent as the departed, an unfortunate simile.

Holding the asynapt out in front of his body he edged out, keeping low and nearly stumbling over the cleaved corpse of Swd. The porter had been a faithful worker, obedient and always ready to lend a hand. Now he was only a lesson in Tsla anatomy. Etienne found he was too mad to be sickened by the sight.

Tyl and Yulour stayed tight on his heels. Three Na bodies lay draped over the stern rail where they'd perished in a last-ditch attempt to board the boat. They looked even bigger up close than they did from a distance. Etienne inspected the shore. Nothing moved on the gravel. The river itself and the mouth of the ice cavern were equally devoid of life.

"Shouldn't have let them surprise us like that. Always underestimating. You'd think we'd have learned our lesson by now."

"I am sorrowed," Tyl said solemnly.

"Nothing for you to be sorry about, Tyl. The responsibility's ours. We're the 'masters of superior technology.'" He let out a rueful laugh. "Some joke. It's just that we haven't seen Na or signs of Na since that day back in Turput and I didn't expect to encounter them this far north. Shows how adaptable they are. I didn't think. I'm the one who should be sorrowed." He gestured at Swd's body.

"Now two more of your people have died."

"Death comes to all of us eventually," Tyl replied. "You ask that I not sorrow for thee. Now I ask that thee sorrow not for us. Swd and Yij achieved what they could not have in a dozen lifetimes, because of thee and thy mate. Their souls are grateful to thee, not angry."

"Well I'm angry! Damned angry. Angry at myself, angry at . . ." the wind went out of him with a rush as Yulour struck him in the midsection and drove him backwards. As a result the small spear passed beneath his arm and pierced his side instead of his spine.

Tyl whirled and leaped to jab the end of the seismic probe against the neck of the Na who had thrown the spear. He pressed the fire button. With a sharp report, the Na's head blew off its wide shoulders, arching into the darkness in a spray of blood and bone fragments. It landed in the water with a splash.

Yulour was rolling away from Etienne, who lay on his

back, staring up at the roof of the ice cave. With great care the porter extracted the spear. Blood quickly rushed from the wound. Tyl rose to alert Lyra but she'd heard the explosion and now joined them on deck.

Her eyes widened as she saw the extent and depth of the wound. She vanished belowdecks again and reemerged moments later carrying the boat's first-aid kit.

Etienne was breathing raggedly as she worked to halt the flow of blood. His pulse was racing and uneven.

"What happened?" she asked the Tsla as she worked.

Tyl explained while Yulour looked on helplessly. "That one," and he indicated the decapitated body of the Na who had thrown the spear, "was not dead but only pretending."

Lyra saw that the headless corpse was spraddled across the two other bodies. "It was shielded from the full charge. It lay still, waiting for its chance. They have that much intelligence, anyway. Too damn much intelligence by half, the hairy bastards." She glanced up at Yulour. "Throw them over the side, and be careful not to touch the metal outside. It's still holding a charge, a spirit death."

"Yes, Teacher."

Yulour showed his considerable strength by disengaging each corpse in turn and shoving the dead weight into the water. Then he returned to carry Etienne into the Redowls' cabin.

Both Tsla looked on respectfully as Lyra ministered to her husband. A third figure joined them later.

"I didn't know what to do, or how to help." Homat looked very small alongside the two Tsla.

"Be quiet, Homat." To his credit the Mai said nothing more, remaining silent alongside his taller companions.

They watched as Lyra slowly passed a small plastic device over Etienne's side and chest. When she finished and put it aside her expression was grim. Etienne tried to reassure her by smiling, but the pain made it difficult.

"Well . . . doctor?"

"You're bleeding internally. I can stop it temporarily. I'm afraid it may be an arterial lesion. I have to stop it, Etienne, or you'll bleed to death. I wish I knew more surgery."

"Thank God you don't," he whispered. "You've spent

twenty years messing up my mind. I don't need you fouling up my insides as well."

"We've got to get you back to Steamer Station where they can fix you properly. You know how good the thranx physicians are."

"I know. It's funny when you think that they're better than human surgeons, them not having any bones and all. How long can you 'temporarily' stop the bleeding?"

She didn't look at him. "I don't know. The spear went a long way in, Etienne. I can seal the break and stop the bleeding and close you up, but there's no guarantee it won't break open again anytime. If it does, I don't know if your circulatory system will accept another heat patch.

"The computer says you should rest as much as possible. Some medication will help. But you can forget about jumping around boulders and cliff sides or you'll tear your guts open again."

"I'll be a good little boy." Despite the mild sarcasm his ready acquiescence confirmed the seriousness of the damage. Normally she had to strap him down to get him to take a vitamin pill.

She tried to take his mind off the injury by explaining how the surviving Na had lived long enough to fling the spear.

"We won't be that careless again," she finished. "Not that I think we've anything more to fear from this particular band. First thing in the morning we'll start back Downriver. As soon as we get within reception range of the Station we . . ."

"No," he said sharply.

"No? No what?"

"No we can't start home first thing in the morning. We're not finished."

"Maybe we aren't, but you are. We've come all the way."

"Not quite, Lyra. We go on to the end of the river first, then we can turn back. Not before then. I'm not leaving until we reach our last goal. If you try to stop me I'll throw a tantrum and kill myself."

"Listen to me closely, Etienne, because I may only be able to say this once," she said softly. "You are an utterly impossible man. You have no more sense in you than a sponge. You would try the patience of Job, let alone a tired little woman like myself."

He squeezed her hand tightly. "I love you, too."

"That's what I said. Who would I shout at if you weren't around?"

"I know. A good target is hard to find."

"I agree." Angrily she rubbed at the moisture welling up in her eyes. "Which is why I'd like to keep you around for another couple of days or so. My shoulder still hurts. That we can keep joking about. There's nothing funny about the hole in your ribs."

"You're telling me?" He let loose of her hand. "Lyra, you have to do this for me. I'll be very careful. No climbing, no quarrying. If I can help it I won't even bend over. Yulour can help me get around, can't you, Yulour?"

"Yes. Yulour is strong, Teacher. I can carry thee wherever thee wishes to go."

"Too risky, Etienne. You *must* let that side heal as best it can."

"On the way back I promise I'll stay in the cabin for months. It can heal then. But it would be insane to turn around and head back when we're only a few hours from the end of our journey. I want those ice samples! We don't have anything else to compare to them and taking them from the edge of the ice cap won't mean nearly as much. If you insist, you and Tyl can take the corings and I'll just watch." He paused, added quietly, "Besides, if this turns out to be my last expedition I'm damned if I want anything left undone."

"Don't talk like that," she said quietly. "I'll kill you if you talk like that."

Somehow he manufactured another smile. "Then we'll go on?"

"All right. No more than half a day. I don't want to spend a night in glacial darkness. Whether we come to the hot springs or whatever, we go on for half a day and then we turn around."

"Fair enough. I wouldn't want the repellers to fail in here, anyway. And I promise to let you do all the heavy work."

"You're so good to me." Twenty years, she mused. Twenty

years of performing in the same play together and they each had their lines down pat.

She prayed she would be allowed to keep acting opposite the same male lead.

[XVI]

He slept soundly the remainder of the night. Lyra knew because she stayed awake at his bedside monitoring his condition. The computer's diagnostic program indicated that the internal bleeding had been halted. Getting the arterial wall and surrounding flesh to heal would be a much slower and more difficult process.

The machine assured her of an eighty-five percent probability of survival for her husband, provided that he adhered to all instructions, took his medication and ultrasound treatments regularly, and received proper surgery within six months. There would be no permanent damage except possibly to some torn lemnisci in the area. That would keep him out of any gymnastic competitions. She greeted the evaluation with relief.

They would have to be exceedingly cautious during the return journey. No chances could be taken, no more violent encounters with belligerent life forms, intelligent or otherwise. Her studies among the elders of Turput would have to wait.

One half of a component whole was useless, and it took at least two to make a team.

Exhaustion and darkness finally conspired during the early hours of the morning to send her into a deep sleep. When she awoke it was to discover that most of the morning was gone. He was upset when she woke him for his breakfast but didn't argue very strenuously. Instead he sought refuge from his discomfort and fear by making delicious wisecracks about her cooking and waiting on him. She enjoyed every criticism.

At Etienne's insistence Yulour carried him forward and they installed him on a raised pallet so he could see out through the cockpit bubble. Lyra settled herself behind the controls.

The hydrofoil hummed as it lifted above the water. She turned inward and sent the boat toward the black maw that was the rear of the cavern. There was no sign of the night's attack. The current had mercifully carried off the three bodies Yulour had shoved over the side.

Lyra would have been gratified to learn that her husband's opinion of the Tsla had risen several notches. Not because of their calm acceptance of their fates or their precocious knowledge of the intricate workings of the mind, but because of the way in which they handled themselves through one crisis after another.

Ice swallowed distance and daylight until the mouth of the cavern had been reduced to a distant dab of white ink. Lyra switched on the hydrofoil's running lights and fore and aft search beams, bringing gasps of surprise and admiration from Tyl and Homat. From the pilot's chair she used the two beams to scan the opposite shore. The river continued to narrow beneath them. Fish fled from the intruding illumination.

Surprisingly, the ceiling of the cavern remained far overhead, testament to the length of time the Skar had been flowing. They flew slowly along the winding tunnel beneath millions of tons of permanent, ancient ice.

"Spirits live here," Homat murmured nervously. "This is the top of the world. Spirits live here." Beneath the roof of the planet even the thermal suit was hard pressed to keep him warm.

"We should be taking periodic samples from the shore gravel," Etienne told Lyra.

She eyed him uncertainly. "Think you can handle the controls?"

He grinned. "They're no heavier than the breakfast you fed me. Yulour, give me a hand up, will you?"

After making sure Etienne wasn't working in pain, she donned her own thermal suit and a long-handled scoop and went out on deck. She gathered samples for another thirty minutes before she was obliged to scream at him.

"Stop the boat, stop the boat!" Her tone was urgent, not alarmed. He nudged the requisite controls and the whine of the hydrofoil's repellers died as it settled into a meter of frigid water.

"What is it?" he called toward the speaker membrane in the bubble wall. His first concern was that she had spotted signs of Na, but that didn't jibe with her attitude. She was standing by the railing, staring off to port.

At the shout, Tyl had bundled up and rushed out to join her, with Yulour close behind. Homat crowded close to Etienne.

"Come out on deck, if you think you can make it without hurting yourself." Now she sounded funny, he thought.

"What is it, what's wrong?"

"Everything's wrong. You'll see." That was all he could get out of her as he painfully worked his body into his own cold gear.

As he started for the gangway Homat reached out with a delicate hand. "Don't go, de-Etienne. Spirits live here."

Gently he disengaged himself from the Mai. "Lyra's not confronting any spirits, Homat. We don't believe in spirits."

"No one does, until the spirits come for them."

"A good point, but I'm willing to bet they're not coming for us here."

Yet when he stood on deck and stared at the cause of his wife's excitement he found himself seriously considering Homat's warning. For while the spirits did not present themselves for inspection, they had left ample evidence of their presence.

The Redowls gazed quietly at the shore until Tyl broke the silence. "What is it, Learned Etienne?"

"I'm not sure, Tyl. I think they're machines of some kind. At least, they look like machines."

Using the tiny remote control he'd brought from the cockpit he aimed both searchlights. The powerful beams swept into the side cavern Lyra had discovered, illuminating unpredictable metallic blue forms and piles of twisting, curving gray shininess. Yellowish-white coils of tubing connected separate structures and smaller adjuncts of green and deeper yellow protruded from the larger shapes.

"You don't know what this place could be?" he asked the Tsla.

"I have never heard of it, Etienne. No Tsla has ever visited here, to my knowledge."

Lyra's breath congealed in the cold still air of the cave. "We've got to have a closer look." She glanced over at her husband, her companion in discovery. "If the Tsla didn't build them it's almost certain the Mai didn't."

"Then who? Surely not the Na?"

"You ask the simplest questions. Get back to the controls and move us over before you fall down."

He nodded, returned to the cockpit. As those on deck steadied themselves the hydrofoil lifted out of the water once more. Etienne pivoted the craft and moved inshore, setting down halfway between river and revelation.

Lyra broke out hand beams from the ship's stores and distributed one to each of their three companions so that even Homat, who had to be half-dragged from the cabin, had his own source of light. In addition they could control the spotlights mounted atop the boat by means of two remotes. Thus armed against the dark they climbed the polished gravel toward the alien construct.

It was clear that the facility had not escaped the ice intact. Bits and pieces of metaloceramic matrix littered the ground. But the damage seemed minor.

"Wonder how old this place is?" Lyra whispered.

"No telling 'til I can run some analyses." He bent carefully at the knees and picked up a section of some tubular material. Tiny strands of opaque metal were embedded in the core and protruded slightly from the ragged end. He ran a finger along one of the flexible filaments.

"Not glass."

"Poured quartz?"

"Silica-based, anyway. That's not all." He handed it over.

Her arm dropped a centimeter before she could recover from the initial surprise. "My god, that's heavy. Any ideas?" She turned it slowly in her hands, examining the metal.

"Alloy of iridium; something in the platinum group, anyhow. Hard to say for certain just looking at it."

Homat could not understand the strange alien words, nor was he sufficiently versed in metallurgy to comprehend even if the Redowls had spoken in his own language. It did not matter, because regardless of what the humans decided, he *knew* what this spirit home was constructed of.

Solid sunit.

More sunit than *jreal* addicts saw while lying dazed and doped on their dream-couches. More sunit than the most avaricious philosophers could conjure up in their imaginations. More sunit than even Moyts possessed.

The old merchant's story was true, his dying admonition to the Zanur of Po Rabi founded on fact. He had been to this place of spirits and had returned with the proof of his tale. Homat swelled with pride. No Tsla had visited the spot before, but an old Mai had done so. His travels had killed him, but not before he had made truth his tombstone. And of all the Mai only he, Homat, had duplicated that epic journey.

Not all the strange shapes and terrifying forms were pure sunit, but there was more than enough laying about to shock the members of the Zanur who had sent him on the journey in the guise of a scout. Here was wealth enough to buy more than businesses and trading vessels, storehouses of grain or gems or the services of others. Here were riches sufficient to buy a city-state entire, to purchase all of Suphum or Ko Phisi—or both.

Enough wealth to purchase the world.

Stunned by the visions before him, he wandered among the spirit buildings, hardly daring to touch the solid gray masses of the precious metal. Lyra warned him not to stray too far. She was concerned by the obvious effect the discovery was having on their Mai guide, though she did not realize its source.

Some of the constructions towered two hundred meters

toward the ceiling of the cavern, where the ice cap had drawn away from the metal. The reason for such spaciousness was self-evident, revealed by mere touch. Much of the metal surrounding them was comfortably warm.

"Not a great deal of heat," Etienne commented, "but a lot of energy is involved. Some kind of mechanism is still functioning here, protecting this place from encroachment by the ice."

"No sound," she replied.

"Insulation. Makes sense in a cold place."

"It's more than that," she said, running her fingers over the smooth frostfree flank of a contorted metal ellipse. "There's nothing moving anywhere, no vibration from within. I think the heat may be a characteristic of the alloy." Removing one of her gloves, she searched the ground until she found a short thick chunk of the yellowish material.

"This has broken away. See the ragged edge?" She leaned back. "Probably fell from somewhere higher up. There's no telling how long it's lain here, but it's just as warm as the intact stuff. Generation of heat's a property of the metal. The damn stuff's exothermic."

"All right, I'm convinced. And not only is it exothermic, I think the property's variable. The temperature of the metal is just high enough to hold back the ice without melting a big hole in the ice cap."

"Maybe," she said quietly, "this installation was built before the ice cap moved so far south. Maybe the glaciers moved over and around it, burying it here."

"That would make this place a minimum of ten thousand years old, given what little we know of Tslamaina's geological history." She said nothing.

They continued their examination, but they found nothing to suggest the nature of the builders. Everything was a solid mass, seemingly formed whole from molds. They found no doorways and no windows, nothing to hint at the builders' size or shape. Only smooth-sided featureless geometric forms. Equally striking was the absence of visible controls.

"If this is a fully automated installation," Lyra pointed out, "designed to function for a long period of time without supervision, there would be no reason to expose sensitive controls to the cold."

"Possible. We'd have a better idea if we could tell whether it's operating now, or dormant, or kaput."

"Instruments," she murmured. "Sit down and rest, Etienne. I'll be back in a minute." She turned and jogged toward the hydrofoil, gathering up the two Tsla as she ran.

With their help she set up several sensitive probes next to the hull, aimed them at their discovery, and began to take readings. Some of the instruments operated efficiently from a distance while others required her to pass among the structures with remote sensors.

Except for the heat emanating directly from the metal, from the standpoint of radiant energy the enigmatic erections were dormant. The residual readings that appeared on the instrumentation matched the output of their flashlights and the hydrofoil's batteries. Though the examination could hardly be considered exhaustive, considering the limitations of their equipment, the Redowls agreed that regardless of what the constructs had been designed to do, they weren't doing anything now.

A library search informed them that self-exciting exothermic metal alloys had existed only in theory—until then. As for the machines themselves, their design did not match the technological architecture of any known civilization.

However old it was, most of the alien technology seemed to be in excellent condition. Though fragments littered the ground, there was no evidence of extensive degeneration within the metal or ceramics themselves.

While they couldn't give a date to the installation or a name to its builders, they could determine the composition of the materials used. In addition to iridium, Etienne noted the presence of two dozen alloys that defied chemical and spectroscopic analysis, including one thin metallic whip that the computer insisted was an alloy of metallic sodium, despite the fact that in the damp air of the cavern there wasn't the slightest evidence of oxidation on its shiny surface. When they dipped it in the river and nothing happened, the Redowls thought they could hear Homat's beloved spirits move a little closer.

Much of the spirit boat was still strange to Tyl, and he was having trouble finding the fresh lightning pack that Lyra called a battery cell. He rummaged carefully through the storage bay, trying to disturb as little as possible. A noise overhead caused him to pause.

Curious, the Tsla climbed the walkway. His snout was extended, the tip probing the air. The sounds drew him up from the hull, through the second deck and onto the upper. He walked past the humans' sleeping quarters, past the place of food they called the galley, until he was standing in the passage that opened into the open bubble of the cockpit. He stared for a long moment before speaking.

"What do thee here, Mai?"

Startled, Homat spun around. When he saw who confronted him he relaxed. "I am simply curious. We Mai are always curious about new things."

Tyl gestured with his snout, a mildly insulting display. "Thee should be outside helping our friends."

"I know, I know. I'll be there again soon. But it's so cold out there, so cold." He shivered.

"I am cold outside also, but the coldness is settling now inside me."

"I don't understand you, meditator."

"Thee linger too long and too frequently over the important places of this craft. For several days now I have noticed this. Thee have always stared as our friends worked here, but never more so since the attack by the Na. I think that this interest has escaped the attention of our friends, who though sophisticated in many ways are childishly naive in others. They are preoccupied with their study of our world and ways. But I am not so occupied, nor so naive. This unnatural interest of thee must be remarked upon." He turned to leave.

"Stop there, meditator!" The chill had suddenly slipped from Homat's body into his voice.

Slowly Tyl turned. His gaze fell to the device the Mai clutched firmly in his left hand. It was heavy for the six-fingered grip and Homat had to support part of it with his other hand. But the correct end was pointed at Tyl. He had seen the device in operation often enough to know that much.

"Mai," he whispered, managing to combine a whole paragraph of insults into the inflection he wrapped around that single noun.

Homat was neither impressed nor intimidated. The Tsla

usually overawed the Mai, but not him, not Homat. The hairy ones were bigger and stronger, but not necessarily smarter. No, size was no indication of intelligence, as he fully planned to prove.

"Do you know what this is?" he said, enjoying himself thoroughly as he gestured with the device he held. "This is the humans' lightning thrower. I have seen it operate many times. It may be difficult to build, but it is very simple to use." He pointed toward the clip holsters attached to the lower part of the control console.

"They sit there in their little homes, drawing strength from the spirit world until they are ready to serve the humans. These spirits are stupid. They do not respond to sacrifices or prayers or offerings, but will serve any who learn the rituals of operation. I have made an extensive study of such rituals these past many months."

"To what end?" Tyl inquired softly even as he estimated the distance between them.

"You have seen the sunit that sleeps here, and the other metals. Enough wealth to buy half the world."

"I am sure," Tyl said carefully, "that the humans would not object to thee returning with enough of the gray metal to make thee wealthy until thy passing."

"I'm sure they would allow me to bring a small amount, but not any more than would interfere with the plain rocks de-Etienne has already collected, for example. Why should I bow and scrape for a beggar's pouchful when I can have all that the spirit boat can carry?" He produced a thin Mai smile. "I can have the spirit boat itself. The sunit will make me master of Mai. This vessel can make me master of the Groalamasan."

Tyl's initial anger dissolved into sadness and pity. "Poor Mai. Thy dreams are so much larger than thy body."

"Are they?" said Homat hoarsely. "I planned to wait, but you push me toward delightenment. The Tsla have always pushed the Mai. In the end we will overwhelm you. See, how simple the humans' spirit devices are to work? You just touch this little round thing here..."

Etienne looked up from the base of the metallic mass he was studying, using the crutch Lyra had fashioned for him from a scoop net, and glanced back toward the boat. The glare from the two powerful spotlights made him squint.

"Did you hear something, hon?"

Lyra lifted her eyes from her work. She was trying to decide if some scratches they'd discovered on one wall might be writing. "Hear what?"

"The boat. I thought I heard something arc."

She shrugged. "Missed my ears."

He thought a moment, glanced to his right. "Yulour. Did thee hear anything from the spirit boat?"

The patient Tsla was sitting on the ground, playing with some colored stones. "I heard nothing, Teacher."

Just then Etienne saw a shape approaching them. "Here's Homat. Maybe he heard something."

Lyra returned to her studies and Etienne waited until their guide emerged from the glare. "Homat, you were near the boat. Did you hear something?"

"Yes, Etienne." He sounded odd, Etienne thought, though he couldn't define the difference. "I heard. It was your lightning thrower dealing spirits."

Lyra heard that, slowly rose from where she'd been sitting.

Etienne spoke precisely. "The lightning thrower? You mean it went off? How did that happen?"

"The way it always happens." The Mai was careful to keep his distance from Etienne, despite the severity of the man's injury. He removed the pistol from the pocket of his thermal suit. Etienne stiffened and Lyra backed toward the metal wall behind her.

"It happened," Homat continued, his confidence starting to build, "when I touched this place you call the trigger. I touched it and called upon the lightning spirits. I, Homat, did this."

Etienne struggled to choose the right words. "That's a very dangerous thing to do, Homat. You don't know what you're doing. The lightning spirits can be very unpredictable. You could hurt yourself."

Homat laughed softly. "You clever humans. You come here from another world, with your wonderful magical devices, and you try to make us think none but you can make them work." He shook the asynapt at them. "Well, *I* can make them work!"

"Where is Teacher Tyl?" Yulour asked uncertainly, looking past the Mai toward the hydrofoil.

"Be quiet, simpleton. The meditator is dead. I killed him, with this." He shook the pistol again.

"But *why*?" Lyra cried as she looked toward the boat.

Homat's voice was as icy as the air around them. "To make certain that I did know how to call upon the lightning spirits. Truly it is very easy. You just touch this trigger place here." One finger eased toward the firing button.

Etienne negotiated a couple of awkward steps backward, leaning on the crutch.

"Don't be frightened," Homat told him. "I don't think I have to kill you. Besides, I need your arms and your backs."

"What for?"

Homat looked past him, his eyes afire. "To load the spirit boat with the gray metal, the sunit."

"The iridium alloy? Your people value it too?"

"More than any other thing of this world. It will make me master over much of it."

"We don't care if you take some sunit back with you," Lyra said. "Enough to make you rich, if you wish. We promised you a reward for helping us."

"The meditator said much the same thing. I take my own reward, Lyra. I want to take back as much sunit as the spirit boat will hold. We will make room by throwing out the useless things you have gathered during this journey, bits of plants and rocks and clothing and cheap trinkets."

"Homat, you can't! We need to take samples of your world back for study."

"You don't listen, Lyra. What is important to you does not matter now. It doesn't matter that your civilization is smarter than that of the Mai. It doesn't matter that you are smarter than me, though I am not so sure of that anymore. It does not matter that you are larger and stronger. This is all that matters now." He gestured with the asynaptic pistol. "I have not touched it since we fought the Na. It slew the meditator. I am certain it can slay you. This is something even we simple Mai can understand."

"Irquit wasn't the Zanur's representative," Etienne said accusingly. "It was you all the time."

"Oh, no, Etienne, she was a representative of the Zanur. We both were. But she was in charge over me, and I couldn't have that. I did not need her around, watching as I made careful study of your magic. I knew we would fail at Changrit."

"So you're a traitor then. To your city-state of Po Rabi, to your Zanur, to your Najoke de-me-Halmur."

Homat dug his toes into the ground, a sign of disrespectful disgust. "From this moment on Najoke de-me-Halmur is nothing. He is become less than the grains of gravel that roll from the mouth of this cave, less than the droppings of the *prewq* upon the fields. The Zanur is become nothing. Po Rabi itself is as nothing beside the wealth that lies here. If I choose I will buy Po Rabi for a winter home. I will be Moyt over all."

Lyra fought to restrain her temper. "Now listen, Homat. Maybe you can operate that pistol without burning your foot off, but running the spirit boat is another matter entirely."

"Is it so? I have watched for a long time now while you thought me shivering and cowering behind you for protection. Already I have steered the spirit boat once. I think truly it is not so complicated to use. A very few controls run it mostly, and one allows the spirits within to run by themselves."

"Even an autopilot needs occasional instructions."

"Does it? I think you try to deceive me. We will see."

"And what happens," Etienne pressed him, "if we don't return and our friends come looking for us? They'll find the boat and they'll find you."

"Perhaps. If they do I will shiver and cower some delighted more and explain that you were slain by the Na and that I, Homat, not knowing what else to do, was returning the spirit boat to its rightful owners. I think they will let me keep the sunit and award me honors for my bravery and dedication."

"Even assuming you could run the boat," Lyra said, "how can you get it past the Topapasirut without the help of the Tsla of Jakaie?"

"I think they will believe my story also. If they are reluctant to believe, there are other ways." He gestured past them toward the mountain of metal. "The Tsla are also traders. They are not immune to the promise of great wealth. Not all the hairy ones sit and meditate their lives away. They work hard in their shops and fields and when they come down to the Skar, wealth changes hands. And there is another reason why I know this can be done."

"Another reason?"

"An elderly merchant of Po Rabi preceded us to this place. Without lightning throwers, without this wondrous delighted clothing you have given me, without a spirit boat, he came to this place, stood perhaps on this same spot, and returned to Po Rabi with proof that he had done so. With all your wonders at my command, I cannot fail to do as well.

"But why this talk of your not returning? I bear you no malice, and I need your strength to load the sunit into the spirit boat. Then we will see. It would be easier if you agreed to help me return to the Skatandah. Perhaps I will even let you keep your boat. You will not have the useless rocks and weeds that you have gathered, but you will still have the magic images you make of them.

"One thing is certain: you have no other choice but to help me. If you do not, it will take longer to load the sunit with the help of only this simple one," he gestured toward Yulour, "but it will be done nonetheless. And I will surely kill you."

"Yulour and I will help load your precious sunit," Lyra said bitterly, "but Etienne cannot. If he does much lifting he stands a good chance of reopening the wound inside him."

"If he does that you can fix it again."

"I don't think it can be fixed again, at least not in the same way with the tools we have on the boat."

"He works like you and the Tsla or he dies now. I cannot spare the attention to let him sit and watch for a chance to surprise me."

Etienne limped forward. "I'll watch myself, Lyra, don't worry. I can rig a sling and work with my left arm."

"Our specimens," she muttered disconsolately. "Everything we've worked so hard to assemble, the first pieces of the puzzle that would enable us to start bulding a picture of this world's ecology, all thrown away."

"They won't do us any good if we don't live to deliver them."

"Not so stupid," Homat said approvingly. "I didn't think you were that stupid." He gestured again with the muzzle of the asynapt. "I do not like this place. Let us hurry."

Though he worked very carefully, the pain in Etienne's side never let him alone. The internal bleeding didn't start again, but Lyra ached in her own heart as she watched him struggle to load the heavy alloy.

Homat supervised the loading silently and displayed not a twinge of remorse. The lower hold was filled and they began stacking piles of broken metal on the second deck. Yulour carried twice his share of the load as he toiled quietly next to his human friends.

Several days later an exhausted Lyra, sweating inside her absorptive thermal suit, slumped to the ground and spoke sullenly to Homat.

"That's all she'll carry."

"No, there is yet room," Homat insisted. "Much more room. You must continue."

"Listen to me, Homat. The sunit, the metal, is very heavy. If you stack any more on the upper decks you'll ruin the boat's stability. All the sunit in the world won't do you any good if you turn over in the middle of the Skar." She held her breath as she dropped her gaze to the ground. Actually the hydrofoil could carry another ton or so in comparative safety, but she doubted Etienne would last another day.

Homat looked uncertain. "Very well. That is enough. Enough to buy two cities, and I can always come back for more."

"Fine," Etienne commented. "Now let us help you deliver your damned fortune so we can go our separate ways, which won't happen soon enough for me."

"Or if you insist on trying to take the hydrofoil back by yourself," Lyra added, "at least let us go with you as far as Turput. We can find transportation back to Steamer Station from there, and by the time we reached our outpost you could be halfway around the Groalamasan."

"And then what?" Homat inquired suspiciously, his inherent Mai paranoia surging to the fore. "Then you'll organize your friends and come looking for poor Homat with more of your strange weapons, to punish him and steal his glory." His grip on the asynapt tightened.

Slowly Lyra got to her feet. "Homat, don't be a fool."

"Truly that is not my intention."

Etienne was backing toward the silent mass of alien metal. He stumbled and Lyra rushed to help him, her eyes never leaving the pistol.

"There's no need for you to do this, Homat. We won't come after you. It's not worth it to us. It's not worth the spirit boat. We can always get another."

"Can you?" She knew enough of Mai psychology to see that he was working himself up good and proper, trying to excite himself to the point of pushing the trigger. Killing Tyl was one thing. Mai and Tsla disliked one another and sometimes fought. But the thought of slaying them was something new. There were powerful spirits involved, strange alien spirits, and he was still unsure of himself.

He was going to do it, though. She could see it in his eyes, read it in the way he stood, hear it in his voice. The scrawny bald little humanoid primitive was going to kill the two of them in cold blood there at the top of his world, beneath a ceiling of ancient ice, their backs to an enigma that would now never be properly studied.

"I will keep the slave," Homat said solemnly. He gestured toward Yulour, who stood nearby looking worried and confused. "I will make use of his strength on the homeward journey. Him I do not fear, but I do not trust you. I cannot stay awake all the time to watch you. As soon as I slept you would forget all your promises, set aside your assurances, and toss poor Homat into the Skar to take his chances with the fish.

"It is not I who is destined to be food for fishes. Not Homat the brave, Homat the great." He took aim with the heavy pistol.

"When he settles on me," Etienne whispered as he took a step forward, "run for it. I'll take the shot and if you can get beyond the ship's lights you'll have a chance."

"No, I won't..."

"Don't be an idiot!" he said huskily, taking another step forward. "Now of all times." The muzzle was shifting to

[229]

cover him, Homat's finger moving toward the trigger. "Use your legs, Lyra. For both of us."

The tears were coming again, blinding her worse than the glare from the spotlights. She didn't know what to do and there was no time to make careful decisions. If only Etienne wouldn't be so damn logical! But he was right. If she could hide in the darkness of the cavern there was an outside chance she could slip aboard the hydrofoil without Homat seeing her. She was bigger and stronger than the Mai.

Homat saw her start to back away and moved the muzzle back to cover her instead of Etienne. It was impossible to outrun the charge, but the heavy weapon was awkward in Homat's grasp. Etienne saw that he was anticipating Lyra's flight and steadied himself to leap between them to take the shot.

He didn't have to. The same thought had occurred to someone else. Certainly no one, least of all Homat, expected Yulour to interpose himself between the pistol and its intended targets.

Etienne didn't have time to wonder at the Tsla's unaccustomed assertion. He was shoving at Lyra with his left hand.

"Now, run now."

Lyra was gaping at the Tsla. "I don't understand. Yulour doesn't act on his own."

"Don't worry about it now, shut up and run!"

She left him leaning on his crutch as she whirled and bolted for the blackness to their left. Homat turned to aim at her, but once more Yulour made certain his body was between hers and the gun.

"Get out of the way, moron!" Homat shouted. Yulour stood quietly, holding his ground. "I said get out of the way! I need you for the journey Downriver."

He could hear the gravel flying from beneath the human female's boots. Of course, he could abandon both of them, leave them to die slowly, but he was furious that his carefully rehearsed triumph might be spoiled by a simpleminded Tsla. He stared over the barrel of the lightning thrower.

"You brought this on yourself, idiot. I'll just have to get along without you. Downriver I'll find plenty of willing backs with sensible heads atop them." He touched the trigger.

[230]

There was a bright, crisp flash of light as the asynapt fired, accompanied by a familiar faint crackling sound. Etienne shouted, "No!" and tried to throw himself at Homat. Given the distance that still separated him from the Mai, it was a futile gesture. A sharp pain ran from his side down his left leg and he crumpled despite the support provided by his crutch.

Dust stung his eyes as he lay staring dumbly across the gravel. Yulour had not fallen under the impact of the charge. He hadn't fallen because he was no longer there.

But something else was.

〖 XVII 〗

For an instant Etienne was positive that the charge had
struck him instead. That would explain the illusion. Or perhaps the silent Yulour possessed the power of old. He blinked,
and the illusion remained. His side still flamed. His nose was
running. It was real.

Where Yulour had been, what Yulour had been rose four
meters toward the roof of the cavern. It was slim and silvery.
The coldly viscous sides twisted and flowed like the ripples
that spread out from a pebble dropped in a pond. Indeed,
what had been Yulour looked a lot like a tower of opaque
water. Where an internal ripple reached its apex the silvery
hue became suffused with other colors: gray and white, blue
and purple. They spread in irregular chromatic blotches across
portions of the unstable tower, fading gradually back into
the silver.

Homat stood motionless, the asynapt still clutched con-
vulsively in both hands. Probably he could not have dropped
it had he wanted to. Suddenly all the terrors, all the childhood
fears, all the old Mai stories of demons and devils and evil
spirits that he had automatically absorbed as he had matured

had solidified before his bulging eyes. He started to tremble and lost control of his bowels. He was trying to scream but only a thin whispery whine passed between his parted lips.

Through his pain Etienne thought he heard Lyra shout from her hiding place back in the artifacts. She wasn't trying to maneuver behind Homat now. All she could do was stare in wonder at the tower of pulsating quicksilver that had been Yulour. Of the three who saw, it might have been that she was the most stupefied of all, for only Lyra Redowl was familiar with the folklore and mythologies of half a hundred worlds, and thus only she knew that what stood before them in the cavern had a basis in hypothesized reality.

It had been seen before—or had it? No one was certain because no reputable evidence was ever presented to conclusively prove the existence of such a creature. Rumors gave it different names, of which the one that stuck was more hopefully descriptive than verifiable.

"I'll be damned," she murmured in awe, "a Mutable."

Etienne heard and the word sifted through his numbed brain. A Mutable. Folktales spoke of them not only on commonwealth worlds but on the worlds of the AAnn empire and the inhabited globes that turned in emptiness outside the boundaries of the principal political entities. Every space-traversing civilization had legends of encounters with true shape-changers, silhouette shifters, metamorphs.

Mutables.

But myths and fraud dissolved in the dank cavern before the glittering reality that had been Yulour the slow-witted Tsla. Legend or folktale or hallucination made real, whatever it was it had saved Lyra's life. Its intentions beyond that were shrouded in speculation.

As Etienne lay there staring at the rippling silvery shape, it occurred to him that he and Lyra were likely the first human beings ever to see a Mutable in its natural state.

It had protected Lyra. That was all that really mattered.

He wondered if the body's constant movement might be an indication of some permanent instability. As he wondered, the tower turned slightly, showing a suggestion of what might be an eye near the top. The deep gray oval swam in a sea of silver. A second might drift alongside the first, beyond his sight. It might have a half dozen hidden duplicates.

Traveling like a tree on greased treads, the Mutable moved toward the hydrofoil. The motion was silent. A single pseudopod emerged from the center of the tower, formed tentacles that reached for the asynapt in Homat's shaking fingers. As he watched, Etienne wondered how the creature had shaken off the effects of the burst from the pistol.

He wasn't given the opportunity to observe the result of a second shot, because the Mai let out a single final massive shudder, then fell sideways onto the gravel. The gun fell from limp fingers.

At this the tentacles withdrew. It mattered not to Homat, whose crumpled form lay motionless now near one of the boat's hydrofoils, knees drawn tight against the thin chest, all hint of aggression fled along with the life force. The cause of death was clear and no autopsy could have made it any clearer: Homat had died of fright, murdered where he'd stood by his own guilt and thousands of years of accumulated racial fears.

The Mutable inclined forward over the Mai's body. Then it straightened, pivoted slowly, and moved away. Rocks and gravel were depressed where it had passed, as if a large, heavy ball had rolled across the ground where the Mutable moved.

Despite its size the creature traveled with ease and a graceful fluidity. Lyra kept her eyes on it as she helped Etienne back to his feet and handed him his crutch. She could recall no legend of a Mutable's harming anything, but that was small comfort as she stood in that cold, dark place supporting her badly injured husband.

Though no pupils were visible, Lyra thought the pair of large gray spots atop the silvery mass were focused on her.

"Please do not be afraid," the Mutable said. It spoke clearly, in Yulour's familiar voice, though without that Tsla's slowness. "Yes, I am what you call a Mutable. I am the native you knew as Yulour. Please do not be alarmed." The upper portion of the tower inclined toward the hydrofoil. "I did not mean for that one to expire, but as are all his people he was a prisoner of his own private terrors. You, however, are more mature and not subject to such."

"Don't give us too much credit just yet," Etienne found himself mumbling. "I'm scared as hell."

"You must not be frightened." The Mutable's voice was almost painfully gentle.

"Mutables don't exist except as rumors," Lyra murmured.

"That is how we prefer to exist. It simplifies much."

Lyra left Etienne to stand on his own and stepped forward, extending a hesitant hand. "I don't want to offend, but—could I touch you?"

"If it is required to establish my existence in your mind."

"It's not. I know you're here. It's just something I'd like to do."

"Then please do so."

She lightly pressed against the silvery flank, discovered that it felt like warm vinyl. It took an effort of will not to jerk her fingers away, not because it was too hot but because the surface was in constant motion. She stepped back, her palm tingling.

"If you two don't mind," Etienne said, "I'm a little tired. I think I'd better sit down." It was a measure of his exhaustion that he allowed Lyra to help without his uttering a single wisecrack.

"You said, 'it simplifies much,'" Lyra repeated. "What does it simplify?"

"Our work. We are caretakers, we Mutables."

"Caretakers? For whom?"

"For the Xunca."

Lyra frowned. "Never heard of 'em."

"But you know of the Tar-Aiym and of the Hur'rikku, who dominated this grouping of stars, this galaxy, until they destroyed each other in a great war."

"Yes, I know the histories," Lyra replied. "Both races have been gone, from this portion of the galaxy, anyway, for at least a hundred millennia."

"The Xunca predate both. They are so ancient little more than their memory remains. We are their caretakers. Whether we are an independently evolved race or machines fashioned by them, we ourselves do not know. We know only our work."

[235]

"These Xunca lived and ruled before both the Tar-Aiym and the Hur'rikku?"

"They did not rule. They simply were. Their probings reached regions that can be expressed only by pure mathematics. Reached beyond this galaxy, beyond the satellite clusters of stars you call the Magellanic Clouds. They went such places."

"You imply a technology capable of traversing an intergalactic gap," Etienne observed. "Such technology is not possible."

The Mutable admonished him gently. "Did not your own kind once say the same of faster-than-light travel, before they learned of space-plus and null-space? I say to you that they the Xunca did this thing.

"This world you call Horseye and that the dominants call Tslamaina is itself a product of Xunca technology."

"This planet is a construct?"

"No." Thoughtfully the Mutable moved to its right so they could observe it free of the glare from the hydrofoil's lights. It was a gesture of courtesy and Etienne let himself relax further.

"The Xunca did not build this world, they modified it to suit their needs. The asteroidal collision which produced the oceanic basin now filled by the Groalamasan's waters was not an astronomical accident."

"Why do that?"

"The Xunca required a large body of water which would circulate only in one direction, whose currents would never change. The positioning of the four small moons assures this. Here the oceanic currents flow eternally in the direction you call clockwise.

"This perpetual motion, driven by lunar gravity, never needs refueling or maintenance. It exists and was designed to drive great engines buried in the ocean floor. Since Tslamaina is tectonically stable and has been for eons save for one regrettable massive earth tremor, there is no danger of the machinery's being destroyed by subduction. It sits and waits, ready to be driven by the mechanism of the ocean currents. The currents that scour the bottom of the Groalamasan are very powerful by the standards of most worlds. This construction was necessary because there are no other

[236]

stable oceanic worlds in this area. The machinery is shielded against detection by space-going peoples. It has lain dormant for tens of thousands of your years."

"How many tens of thousands?" Lyra wondered aloud.

"Enough to total several hundred millions."

"And you've been 'caretaking' the facilities all that time?"

"We are long-lived or well-designed," the Mutable explained matter-of-factly.

"I don't care," Lyra argued. "*Nothing* lives for a hundred million years!"

"The rocks beneath your feet do. Our internal structure resembles them more than it does yours. You may be interested to know that a smaller installation, similar to that which sleeps beneath the ocean of this world, exists on yours."

Lyra started. "On Earth? Nothing like what you describe has ever been found. Is the shielding against detection that effective?"

"Yes, but that installation was destroyed by your world's continental drift. It was emplaced when your continents were one large land mass and there was a single, much larger, world ocean like that on Tslamaina. The Xunca were not omnipotent. They could not plan for every eventuality.

"But that was only a small relay and its loss not vital to the system. The main transmitter was constructed on this world. The three local intelligent life forms evolved independently long after its emplacement. They do not suspect its existence. None do." He gestured past them.

"This is a tiny portion of the transmitter's antenna system. Most of it lies beneath your feet. It is our task to see that it remains in operating condition, together with the extensive relay network to which it can be linked."

"Can it operate through the ice cap?"

"No. In the event that the transmitter system becomes active, a portion if not all of this ice will be melted."

Etienne's thoughts moved rapidly. "That would raise the level of the Groalamasan enough to flood every major city on Tslamaina."

The Mutable sounded apologetic. "As I have said, all this was designed a very long time ago, and the Xunca could not foresee everything. However, it is possible this will never occur. The system has not become active in all the hundreds of millions of years since it was fashioned. Who knows how many millions more will pass before anything happens? Nothing may ever happen."

"Nobody builds something like this," Etienne muttered, "thinking it will never be used."

"Why not, Etienne?" Lyra said with disarming calmness. "What about the security alarms people put in their homes?" She looked startled. "Is that what this is?"

"We do not know what the system is for," the Mutable replied sadly. "Not one of us knows. We are only caretakers, not operators or builders. We do what we were instructed to do eons ago. Watch over the system and insure that it remains intact.

"Do not think that we merely sit and wonder. We discuss and debate. We have our own culture. Now and then we assume one of the shapes of the space-going races and visit each other, for only one of us is assigned to each world. We assist one another in diagnosing and solving problems, but generally there is little to do. The Xunca built for the ages. But as to the purpose of the system, only the Xunca themselves know that."

"What happened to them?" Etienne asked. "If they were such masters of science, why did they let the Tar-Aiym and the Hur'rikku usurp their place?"

"The Tar-Aiym and the Hur'rikku usurped nothing. Both races rose to power in the vacuum left by the departure of the Xunca. They did not force the Xunca to leave. The Xunca were never forced to do anything. They departed because they found something their technology could not cope with."

"Then why leave this elaborate system behind? To let them know when it was safe for them to return? You must know something about it?"

"Only that it will become active if whatever it was intended to react to manifests itself." The Mutable hesitated. "We do know that it involves one particular section of space."

"Can you be any more specific?"

"It lies in the direction of the constellation you call Bootes, as seen from your Earth, but farther out. It is an area of modest size, some three hundred million light-years across, encompassing a volume of approximately one million cubic megaparsecs."

Etienne frowned for a moment until the figures quoted by the Mutable linked up with something in his memory.

"The Great Emptiness. We've known of it for hundreds of years. It's a 'modest' region, all right. It ought to be as filled with galaxies and nebulae as any other section of space, but it's not. There's nothing there, astronomically speaking. Some free hydrogen and a few isolated stellar masses of uncertain composition."

"This we know," the Mutable admitted. "What we do not know is *how* the Xunca transmitter is involved."

"I'd rather it were connected to something simpler to explain," Etienne muttered. "We humans are a gregarious bunch. We like crowds, not big emptinesses."

"You are concerned."

"It seems the Xunca were. Don't you sense some kind of threat?"

"We do not worry, nor should you. Too much time has passed without anything happening."

"Then you *do* think a threat of some sort is involved."

"We have had much time in which to evaluate possibilities. When one's entire existence is devoted to a single task, there is a fair amount of time to devote to idle speculation. I must admit that some of us believe the Xunca system to be a warning device."

"Strange, but your words don't give me much comfort," Lyra muttered.

"I wish that I could allay all concerns. We wish no less for ourselves. You should know that. We have had to content ourselves with a saying: 'the Xunca moved in mysterious ways.'"

Etienne forced himself to think of more immediate matters. All the talk of vast empty sections of space, of alien devices lying dormant for incalculable eons waiting for some unknown problem to manifest itself, of caretakers who could change their shape moving unobserved among different civilizations, was making him dizzy.

He needed to talk about something he could relate to. "Your task, then, is to ensure the inviolability of the Xunca system."

"That is so."

Etienne drew Lyra close to him. "Then that means you must have decided by now what you're going to do with us."

"It has been a very long time since this transmitter was checked," the Mutable said quietly. "In that time this river has enlarged the cavern considerably around it and opened a wide entrance. That must be sealed with ice."

"You're avoiding my question. What about us?"

"I have enjoyed the opportunity to study you for many days, Etienne Redowl man. It would have been simple to let the native dispose of you or to do so myself." Lyra's arm tightened against her husband's back. "But after hundreds of millions of years of dedication to a single task, one develops a high respect for indigenous life forms that have succeeded in developing intelligence without destroying themselves in the process. When one is governed by insights that may be more than a billion years old, one develops laws and insights of one's own. And there is one thing more."

Etienne allowed himself to hope, wondering what ancient philosophical conclusion might stay the executioner. "What's that?"

"I like you. You are simple, uncomplicated, primitive. But you are likeable. Many peoples do not place likeability high on the list of survival traits. We do. I do. I like you for yourselves and for what you are, what you represent. We are not merely components of a carefully constructed machine. We are also individuals. As such we can admire individuality in others. Your persistence and dedication, your"—was that a *smile* atop the silvery column?—"immutable devotion to your chosen professions reminds me of our own."

"I'm glad you like us," Lyra said. "I think we like you. But how do you plan to insure that we don't bring others of our kind back to this place, to tell them the story and show them the tip of the transmitter?"

"I will see to it not only that this cavern is sealed, but that the transmitter is moved—and shielded so that your most sensitive instruments cannot relocate it no matter if they spend years scanning the northern hemisphere of this world.

"As for relating what I have told you to your colleagues, we have observed enough of humankind for me to believe that you would not be taken seriously. And there is a third protection. You will give me your word."

Lyra glanced at her husband, then back at the Mutable. "I hope to live a while longer yet, but I never expect to be flattered like this again. For what it's worth you have our word."

"Thank you, woman. It is done, and I am much relieved."

"I only wish," she added, "that Tyl could be here to give his word also."

"I am sorry. Revealing my true nature is not something done lightly. I held back in the hope that the Mai would spare you and I could then help you return safely without exposing myself. I could do nothing for the Tsla."

As they stared the Mutable's exoderm began to flow and ripple violently. They stepped back as the silvery skin started to cloud over with patches of dark gray. These changed to white, pale yellow, and then became a rich hazel color. Simultaneously the sentient tower began to collapse, the internal structure shrinking and compacting. The transformation was accomplished in utter silence. Once more Yulour the Tsla stood before them.

"I thought you would find my company during the return journey less unsettling in this guise. I hope my company will not upset you. I have already set in motion the machinery necessary to conceal the transmitter from potential prying minds." Indeed, as she stood there listening Lyra was certain she could detect a rising hum from behind them, and a slight vibration beneath her feet.

"I enjoy your company," the Mutable went on, "and have not had the opportunity to spend much time among your kind since I have never been assigned to a human-occupied world. You are an interesting adolescent race."

"You're certainly welcome to our interesting adolescent company," Etienne replied dryly. As if they could prevent the creature from accompanying them if it so desired. "Whatever your motives, you did save our lives, even if you did compel us to share a mystery that we know won't be solved in our lifetime, let alone *your* lifetime."

"Myself," Lyra said dreamily, "I prefer to think the Xunca went away for personal reasons and that they left this relay system behind to help whatever intelligences might arise in their absence. That's a nice thought, anyway. I'd rather think of any people that brilliant as altruistic rather than indifferent."

They started down the slight slope toward the hydrofoil. Yulour moved to help Etienne, who flinched, but only for a moment; the fur against his arm was real, the smell pure Tsla.

They gave Tyl a formal farewell, and Lyra restored some lightness to a situation weighty with solemnity by suggesting Etienne carry out the standard Tsla funeral ritual. That sparked an affectionate exchange of insults to which Yulour listened with interest.

Etienne finished it by doing something he hadn't done in quite a while. He took Lyra in his arms and kissed her long and hard. They stood enfolded in each other for a long time, and Yulour watched that with equal interest. Such mayfly relationships were not for his kind, but there was a decided poignancy to them that forever escaped those condemned to near immortality. The Mutable sighed an ancient, silent sigh, no louder than the winds that move the hydrogen between the stars. Existence for these people was a brief explosive flash of consciousness, then limbo. A breath of life blown by in a rush of emotion and a few hasty thoughts.

The Mutable could only empathize. For it life was an infinite march toward an unknown end. Besides, there was work to do.

Etienne assumed the pilot's chair, nudged several touchplates, looked uneasy. Lyra moved next to him.

"Trouble?"

"Looks like it. We've had these spotlights on for a lot longer than we planned. The batteries are drawn down too low to power the engine, much less the repellers. We're going to have to drift out until the current and the sun can recharge us."

Yulour studied the control console for an instant. "I think I can help. No reason not to, now."

The un-Tsla's right arm began to change. Fur and muscle became a single thin strand of faintly radiant metallic silver. The tendril slipped through the small opening of a power socket. A tremor ran through the boat as a half dozen readouts suddenly flared brightly.

[242]

"Sorry. The resistance was less than I thought," Yulour explained as the silver tendril was withdrawn and became an arm again. "It is not only that a Mutable is powerful. A Mutable *is* power."

"Also handy to have around for a difficult trip. Nothing like a couple of hundred million years of specialized evolution to give you an effective jump-start, though it does seem a bit disrespectful somehow." Lyra seemed bemused.

Etienne tried again and the engine whined to life. The hydrofoil rose two meters above the gravel and pivoted toward the river. Spotlights illuminating their way, they commenced the long journey down the Skar toward Turput, Steamer Station, and eventually, home.

There they would take a long sabbatical to write their official report, one which would be haunted by memories. Somehow that report no longer seemed as important as it had when they'd started their expedition up the Barshajagad. Very little seemed important anymore, beyond the way Lyra clung tightly to Etienne and how he played with strands of her hair.

Behind them the visible tip of the Xunca transmitter was engulfed by arctic dark. It brooded motionless now but soon it would move. Within the seemingly solid mass pimesons and guons and bits of matter and bits of stuff that wasn't matter traveled their assigned pathways at speeds approaching that of light—as they had for uncounted centuries.

Unnoticed by uncomprehending humans or caretaking Mutables, one tiny section suddenly showed signs of activity where for ages there had been none. The unusual movement at the subatomic level within might intensify or it might shut down again.

But something was happening. Something had triggered a minute portion of the machinery beyond that which was responsible for normal maintenance. How soon the something might require attention, not even a watching Mutable might have said. "Soon" was a relevant term, an abstract, a precession through infinity. For a more specific explanation of what it meant in this instance the Xunca would have to be consulted.

Wherever they were.

ALAN DEAN FOSTER

THE END OF THE MATTER

Three entire planets are about to vanish and the Commonwealth's scientists can do nothing to save them.

The disappearance of several small spaceships has proven the existence of a vast collapsar, an all-devouring black hole that is carving its way across the Galaxy. To evacuate the three planets in its course would be impossible. To stop such an incomprehensible astronomical force is not even worth contemplating.

There is a slim chance, a remote possibility that the key to survival lies with a strange and seemingly insane creature named Ab that Flinx adopts as his pet. No one knows or understands what Ab is or what powers he has. All Flinx knows is that he is suddenly very important – and with a death sentence on his head, he could soon be very dead.

A Royal Mail service in association with the Book Marketing Council & The Booksellers Association.

Post-A-Book is a Post Office trademark.

ALAN DEAN FOSTER

MISSION TO MOULOKIN

For Ethan Frome Fortune and his musclebound side-kick Skua September, the frozen planet of Tran-ky-ky had become too much of a cold thing.

Aboard their giant icerigger *Slanderscree*, they headed for the trading post of Brass Monkey to book a passage home.

Then fate intervened with the news that their Tran friends were being exploited by ruthless off-world profiteers.

To help, Ethan and Skua – interplanetary sales team extraordinaire – must make a desperate mission to Moulokin, the fabled fortified city across the frozen seas and ringed with chilling peril . . .

NEW ENGLISH LIBRARY

ALAN DEAN FOSTER

THE TAR-AIYM KRANG

The Tar-Aiym had been dead for perhaps a million years. Once they had fought against and then ruled the galaxy. But now they had vanished, leaving only the legend of their final artifact – the lost Krang.

Nobody knew what the Krang might be, but everyone wanted it. Until it was found . . .

For the Krang had a purpose. The Krang had power and a will of its own.

NEW ENGLISH LIBRARY